Compliments of
Topsail Township
Friends of the Library

PLEASE JOIN

DANCING

BACKWARDS

DANCING

BACKWARDS

SALLEY VICKERS

FARRAR, STRAUS AND GIROUX · NEW YORK

Farrar, Straus and Giroux
18 West 18th Street, New York 10011

Copyright © 2009, 2010 by Salley Vickers
All rights reserved
Distributed in Canada by D&M Publishers, Inc.
Printed in the United States of America
Originally published in 2009 by Fourth Estate, an imprint of
HarperCollins Publishers, Great Britain
Published in the United States by Farrar, Straus and Giroux
First American edition, 2010

Library of Congress Cataloging-in-Publication Data
Vickers, Salley.
    Dancing backwards / Salley Vickers.— 1st American ed.
      p.   cm.
    ISBN 978-0-374-22316-8 (alk. paper)
    1. Women poets—Fiction.   2. Transatlantic voyages—Fiction.
I. Title.

PR6072.I333 D36 2010
823'.914—dc22

                                                          2010014579

www.fsgbooks.com

1   3   5   7   9   10   8   6   4   2

for Rosie & Co.
a birthday book

For whatever we lose(like a you or a me)
it's always ourselves we find in the sea

e e cummings

FIRST DAY

Chock-a-Block: Full to capacity or overloaded. If two blocks of a ship's rigging are so tight together that they cannot be tightened further they are said to be chock-a-block.

1

'What on earth have I done?' Violet Hetherington asked herself.

She was standing in one of several queues in the dock at Southampton. The queues, by now spilling out of the cattle shed marked 'Departures', to board the *Queen Caroline* were long and none was moving. 'It's best to get to the docks late,' her friend Annie had advised. 'If you get there too early you can grow roots hanging about.' Annie, married to a diplomat and full of advice, was a seasoned traveller. But on this occasion her advice was mistaken.

After a while an announcement came through the loud-speakers: there had been a 'breakdown in the computer system'. In the face of this setback the atmosphere among the waiting passengers darkened. Some attempted patience, some brave souls even tried to rise to jollity but for the most part the mood became rebellious. The world was going to the dogs and they had paid good money – through the nose, many were inclined to feel – for this voyage. It might be their last chance for a bit of luxury. That they could not even be got aboard efficiently did not promise well.

Vi's own instinct was to turn tail. She felt in her bag for her phone and discovered that it was missing. This was a good deal more annoying than the length of the queues. It confirmed an uneasy sense that the whole idea of a cruise was one of her mistakes. She hated any form of group activity and here she was, thrown to the lions and entirely of her own doing. And now there was the nuisance of the phone. Either she had left the wretched thing behind or she had lost it at some point on the journey to the port. She couldn't ring the minicab company to check because the number – along with all her other numbers – was stored in her phone. The very error that her elder son Harry was always counselling her to avoid.

Behind her in the queue stood an approachable-looking couple. 'I'm sorry but, stupidly, I seem to have left my mobile behind. I couldn't borrow yours to make one call, could I?'

Vi rang Harry on the obliging couple's phone and left a message asking him to ask Kristina, her Polish cleaner, if she would check to see whether the phone had been left behind. If it was not in her flat then she was going to be in trouble, since she had no other means of finding the numbers she needed in New York. A large part of her thought, Good riddance! But this she did not confide to Harry. Harry had come to the view early in life that if not older than his mother he was a good deal more worldly wise. Daniel, her younger son, was more sympathetic to her foibles but that was because he shared them. Dan might easily forget to give Kristina the message at all.

The couple whose phone she had borrowed remarked that they had also arrived late expecting to avoid the crowds. 'It was a breeze last time,' the woman, a tall blonde with a ponytail and cowboy boots, recalled. 'We walked straight on. I'm Jen, by the way. He's Ken.'

She nodded towards her companion, a broad-shouldered man with a lot of reddish chest hair. 'Ken and Jen Morrison,' the man said. 'We're a double singing act.'

'Really?' Vi was impressed. 'I'm Violet Hetherington. Vi.'

'He's just kidding. Don't be daft.' Jen whacked her husband's chest with a copy of *Elle*.

'We did think of doing a singing act when we first met, because of Van Morrison,' Ken explained. A gold Star of David was visible beneath his shirt. 'But her over there sings like a neutered cat.'

'Charming,' Jen said equably. 'Look out, we're on the move.'

The press of people moved urgently forward, although, as Ken remarked, the boat could hardly leave without them. Reaching the head of their queue at last, Vi parted from the helpful Morrisons and was ushered towards a window where she handed over her travel documents, credit card and submitted to a photograph for the security pass that acted on the cruise in place of money. As she prepared to go aboard, a man stepped forward with another camera.

'Is this necessary?' She detested having her photo taken.

'Smile nicely,' a young woman in uniform suggested.

'But is it a requirement?'

'Excuse me?'

'I do not want another photograph of myself unless it is a requirement for boarding the ship.'

'Not a problem,' said the girl. 'It just makes a nice souvenir of your trip.' She made the hint of an eyebrow gesture towards the photographer, who was not bad-looking and was booked for the whole of the world cruise. 'Go right ahead, madam.'

A couple already wearing *Queen Caroline* sweatshirts had squeezed past and were now blocking the way as they posed, arm round each other's waist. Vi waited while they pronounced 'Sex' for the photographer and everyone had laughed heartily and then, thank goodness, she was walking up what she supposed would once have been a gangplank but was now an arcade adorned with ugly pots of artificial plants.

The ship's foyer resembled one of the not-so-grand hotels that have set their sights too high. There were panels of shining fake walnut, extravagant cascades of chandeliers, polished brass plating and carpets patterned in the style commonly found at airports. Vi followed the signs to the 'Elevators' which were lined floor to ceiling with mirrors and crammed with passengers who, bedraggled from early morning starts, luggage disposal and the incurable anxiety induced by travel arrangements, might have preferred to be spared the sight of their multiple reflections.

Squashed against the side of the lift by a party of voluble Germans, Vi felt claustrophobia mount along with the lift, which moved upward, stopping at each floor to release a tide of thankful prisoners. But, at last, at the twelfth floor, she stepped out to freedom.

And, thank heaven, her room had the balcony she had requested. She had been anxiously rehearsing what to say if it had not. Ignoring Annie's suggestion that she wait for a last-minute deal, she had thrown caution to the winds and paid the highest price she could afford in order to be sure of the sea.

The cabin was fitted out in the same would-be-luxury hotel style. The bathroom taps were in the shape of gilded swans, the beaks acting, disconcertingly, as spouts. The bedroom was plain enough, with a double bed covered by a heavy gold counterpane, a desk and chair, a brown velour sofa and, on the wall, three pictures: a field of poppies, a still life of some seashells and a solemn-looking couple in what appeared to be Dutch national dress.

Vi examined this to see if it could be removed; but it was screwed to the wall, presumably against the Atlantic swell.

She made a mental resolution to pack a screwdriver in future and was unpacking her books when there was a tap at the door and a small man, whose smile revealed excellent teeth, entered and introduced himself as Renato, her steward. He enquired after the state of her health, pledged himself to her service and instructed her about the changing time zones.

'Each day, madam, the clock is set back one hour.'

This was the first piece of good news. It had not occurred to her that rather than wasting time she might actually be acquiring it. Renato also informed her of an impending safety drill.

'Guests must assemble for drill in main salon, Deck Three, to practise drill in case of emergency.'

'You mean like the *Titanic*?'

Renato laughed heartily. 'Yes. The *Titanic*. Very famous. You see the show?'

Vi said she had seen the film.

'The show is better. I see it on Broadway. Very good dance.'

Renato, it emerged, was a ballroom dance devotee. He explained that before their marriage he had won numerous medals with his wife.

'Where is your wife, Renato?'

'She is in the Philippines. She and the kiddies.'

'That seems a shame. You must miss her.'

'Oh no.' He smiled brilliantly. 'Much better she stay home with the kiddies.'

When Vi returned from the drill (conducted amid general, and to her alienating, hilarity) she stepped outside, on to her balcony, to watch the ship get under way. The ship slid out of harbour so gradually that it barely registered that they were on the move. Impossible not to feel a thrill at the sheer enterprise of the thing. A little way off, a fishing trawler was making a white wake. A piece of foam detached itself and became a solitary bird, which flew up into the unblemished sky. A memory of walking along a pebbled seashore on the Suffolk coast, with the gulls crying their cold hearts out in the sky above, assailed her. Well, she had embarked on a voyage of recovery: she must expect these stabs from the past.

She squinted her eyes trying to make out the bird performing a graceful arc above her now. An arctic or a common tern? It was too far off to distinguish. It would have to be a comic tern.

A summary of the dining regime had been included in the information sent in advance of the voyage. Vi was in the Alexandria Grill, one of the upper echelons of the ship's hierarchical dining system. The 'dress code for tonight in the Alexandria', she read, was 'casual elegant', whatever that meant. She put on a sleeveless linen shift and a plain black jacket. Too bad if it was not sufficiently elegant, or casual.

There was the question of what to do with her jewellery, Ted's jewellery: the diamond, sapphire and emerald hoops he had given her as milestones of their marriage; and all the earrings, the brooches and pearls. Vi, who on the whole was carefree about her possessions, had not liked to leave Ted's jewels unprotected. Harry would be sure to disapprove. Eventually, she had packed the lot so now there was the problem of where to keep them. There was a safe in the cabin. But she might easily forget them altogether there and leave them behind.

In the end, she put on all the rings and bundled the other jewellery into a shoe bag in her suitcase, which she stowed in one of the wardrobes. She had continued to wear the large solitaire diamond, so worryingly valuable she had forgotten precisely what it was worth, with which Ted had proposed marriage. But she no longer wore the wedding band by which he had sealed the contract. Ted would not have liked this.

But poor Ted was dead. Oh, but why always say 'poor' of the dead? Isn't it the living who are in need of sympathy? Violet Hetherington thought, avoiding the cruelly reflecting lifts and running impatiently down the red-carpeted stairs to the restaurant.

A questionnaire had been included in the pre-voyage material, requesting that passengers select the numbers with whom they wished to dine. Annie had recommended a table for twelve. 'It makes it easier to get away from bores,' she advised. 'There's safety in numbers.' Quite why Vi had followed Annie's advice in this she couldn't now remember. Maybe it was simply easier: Annie was so full of advice, it was not always possible to be discriminating.

Only one fellow traveller was there before her when Vi found her table in the Alexandria, an elderly man with a weathered face and a pepper-and-salt beard, rather more salt than pepper. He looked so like a retired sea captain that she couldn't help feeling smug when it turned out that she had hit the mark.

'Captain Ryle, ma'am. I used to be master of one of the line's ships. They can't keep me away.'

Vi allowed her hand to be gripped, somewhat painfully on account of the massed rings.

'Violet Hetherington.' The captain's large sun-spotted hand was unexpectedly soft. Noticing him glance at her left hand, where the solitary diamond glinted, she added, for his sake rather than from any need to confide, 'My husband died last year. This is my first holiday alone.'

Captain Ryle's leathery face crumpled into comprehension. 'My wife left me five years ago. Still not got over it.'

'I'm sorry.' She understood that it was death and not any domestic fracture that had removed his wife's company.

'I miss her every hour of the day.' The captain blew his nose unselfconsciously into his table napkin. 'Still, mustn't complain. Kathleen wouldn't approve. She was always one for life, Kath.'

'Yes?'

'She wouldn't have wanted me moaning on. Here.' He thrust at Vi a basket of breads – really, more of a miniature bakery so exotic was the choice. Vi took a roll, changed her mind and then, not liking to put it back, took another.

'Good grub,' the captain said, nodding approvingly at her two rolls. 'Always get good grub on this line.'

A couple of Americans were being shown to the table: a long-limbed black man with heavy-rimmed glasses and a small, older-looking woman who might have been taken for his mother had she not been white. The man, in a grey suit and a cream shirt, gave an impression of easy elegance. The woman's hair was done up in an untidy loose bun and her evening suit was a shade of pink which did not suit her pinkish complexion. Side by side, they made a somewhat ill-matched couple.

The woman introduced herself as Martha Cleever and her husband as Dr Balthazar Lincoln.

'Balthazar as in the Three Magi?' Vi asked, and was rewarded with a smile so winning that she at once fell a little in love with him.

'I am generally known as Baz. No one manages the other, except my mother.' Leaning across Vi, he helped himself to a roll and she detected in his aftershave a pleasing scent of limes. 'My mother belongs to a mad sect which holds that the "wise men" were angels from Babylon. May I trouble you to pass the butter? She likes to claim she saw an angelic presence hovering over my father's head when I was conceived.' Baz, buttering his roll, afforded Vi again the smile that suggested the conspiracy of long friendship.

Encouraged by this, Vi asked, 'Didn't your father mind?'

'If that is who he was. It might easily have been some other chancer. But the man I knew as my father was a patient man (he has passed away now) and he was devoted to my mother. She would not be swayed in any conviction. She is a very stubborn woman, my mother. I am stubborn too, so I know.'

'Baz is one of seven and his mother's favourite.' Martha's tone was mostly indulgent. She explained that she was an attorney in general litigation and her husband had been on a six-month sabbatical at the London School of Economics. They were returning home by boat as he had acquired so many books that it was cheaper for them to accompany the books home by sea. 'Baz just adores books. He wouldn't care what in the world we lost provided his library was saved.'

'Better hope the ship doesn't go down, then!'

Two newcomers had joined the table. The man who had spoken introduced himself and his wife as Les and Valerie Garson. Until last year, they had run a garage with a Toyota franchise in Hampshire. They had been promising themselves this trip as a retirement present for he didn't know how long.

'It's ever so exciting, isn't it?' Valerie asked. She looked, Vi thought, a little depressed.

Her husband had several complaints. 'No room to swing a cat in our cabin, never mind the wife! Daylight robbery when you think what we're paying for this. Have you seen the price of the booze?'

'Baz doesn't drink,' Martha said, 'so I tend not to much either.' She turned to Vi. 'How about you?'

'I drink like a fish,' Vi said and was rewarded by another dazzling grin from Baz. 'Did you never drink?' she asked.

'My mother's religion forbade it but, you know, when I

got to college and it seemed that at long last I could defy her I found I didn't like the taste after all.'

'Did you tell your mother?'

'He did and she said "The Lord works in mysterious ways",' Martha said.

Captain Ryle was confiding to no one in particular that until he met his wife his mother had been his rock and stay, when another couple, Greg and Heather, who had left their four-year-old, Patrick, asleep in the cabin, joined the table.

'There's a baby alarm,' Greg explained. He was still under the delusion that everyone was as captivated by his child as he was. 'It goes through to a central minding station and if there's any crying they come and let you know. At least we hope they do.' He laughed nervously.

'He's usually very good.' In the absence of any interest from the other diners, Heather took up the baton of parental concern. 'Only we were worried that the movement of the ship might wake him, you know, in a different environment . . .'

Vi said that she felt that the rocking of the ship might induce rather than hamper sleep. Patrick's mother looked grateful. The other diners ignored this exchange, supposing, perhaps correctly, that if a stand was not taken from the start the topic of childrearing could take over.

The table was set for eleven but only eight guests appeared.

'D'you think they cancelled?' Valerie Garson asked, over her seared yellowfin tuna.

'They won't have got a refund,' Les assured the rest of table. 'I looked into it when it looked as if Val's mother might fall off the branch.'

Captain Ryle was tucking into a lamb chop. Years of being at sea had given him an understandable aversion to fish. 'They'll be at one of the other restaurants.'

'Can you eat just anywhere, then?' Valerie Garson pursued. Les had been advising their friends in Liss that the Alexandria was the most superior of the several dining possibilities.

The captain explained that if she fancied a change, then there were several other first-rate venues. He also explained, to anyone who cared to listen, what 'first-rate' meant while Vi, who knew already, alone affected interest.

'Still, it's nice to dress up once in a while,' Valerie Garson said, looking doubtful.

'She's packed for Bloody Britain. Different fancy dress for every night. Nearly broke the bank!' Les had ordered a bottle of one of the cheaper champagnes.

Martha said, 'Oh dear, I've only brought one long dress. Do you think it matters?'

'Of course not,' said Vi, becoming impatient with all this fuss. 'If I have to dress up each night I shall certainly not bother to dine here.'

After dinner, Les became expansive and invited everyone who cared for a postprandial nip to join him at the bar. The captain asked Vi if he could show her round the ship.

'There's a champion little show on at the theatre tonight. *Kiss Me Kate*. It's a company from Exeter. Kath had a cousin, a second cousin, to be precise, in Exeter.'

Vi excused herself with a fictitious headache and went out on deck. A lopsided luminous moon had risen and was laying out across the black water long ribbons of fragile fraying silver. Waves slapped arhythmically against the steel flanks of the ship as she powered purposefully on into the heart of the Atlantic. The air, infused with the moon's chill silver, wrapped itself freshly and sweetly around her face.

She stood, absorbing the subtle shades and distinctive smells of the sea. What a peculiar thing she had done. And for what would very likely turn out to be a wild-goose chase. Crossing over to the kingdom of night, time seemed suddenly to gather with new possibility. Out of the darkness a strange sense of well-being descended on her. A feeling that things might turn out all right after all.

SECOND DAY

To know the ropes: *On a square-rigged ship there were many miles of rigging. It took an experienced seaman to know the ropes.*

2

Before going to bed, Vi pushed open the heavy glass door which divided the cabin from the balcony. It took an effort, she wasn't strong and a wind was getting up and the door was designed to spring back against any influx of weather. Finally she managed to wedge it open with one of the metal balcony chairs, so that her night could be spent as close as possible to the sea, being rocked in its strong grip like the baby in the old nursery rhyme.

When she was a child, her mother had told her that long ago there had been a pirate in the family, whose career had ended dramatically when he was hanged for treason on the high seas. Her mother had died when Vi was not quite ten. As with many of the best storytellers, the boundaries of her mother's reality were, Vi now suspected, blurred. But whether or not it was the legacy of piratical blood in her veins, the sea was comforting to her.

When she woke next morning, the ocean which had beaten all night in her mind had dissolved into the sound of the steady irregular thrashing of water on the ship's sides. She slid from under the heavy counterpane, which she'd kept over her against the cold, and went barefoot out on to the wooden deck of the balcony.

The sky was not quite fully alight. Splashes of crimson and orange shivered on the shot-satin water. A solitary white bird made a graceful arc above her head against the olive- and rose-dragged sky. She stood in her nightdress, flexing her bare toes on the cold wood, the breeze wrapping the thin cotton close round her body, looking out to the faint line where the deceiving eye suggests that sea meets sky. Before her the ocean stretched, calmly offering nothing but its own vast, limitless, unapologetic being.

You see, said a voice. You were right to come.

She was not so sure when, a little later, washed and dressed, she went down to breakfast. A kind of frenzy had set in. Cereals of all kinds were available: corn flakes, bran flakes, Rice Krispies, Shredded Wheat, Weetabix, Coco Pops, Fru-grains, muesli, together with stewed prunes, apricots, green figs, sliced cheeses, ham, salami, smoked salmon, as well as bacon, sausage, black pudding, kippers, haddock, eggs cooked to order, mushrooms, tomatoes, pancakes, porridge, waffles and every conceivable variety of bread, muffins and toast. Besides these were jams, honey, marmalade, Marmite and peanut butter (with a prominent health and safety warning about possible allergies). Lest this were not enough, there were plates of fresh pineapple, cantaloupe, watermelon, grapefruit and piles of apples, pears, oranges, grapes, strawberries, blueberries, mango, kiwi fruit, guava, passion fruit and bunches of bananas.

Although the food was continually being replenished by teams of attentive waiting staff (and no passenger was left from 5 a.m., 'Dawn snack', till midnight, 'Bedtime cookies and cocoa', for more than fifteen minutes without ready supplies), a fever of impatience had overtaken the line of passengers as Vi queued for a bowl of muesli.

Even more consternation was being stirred up over the

question of the tables. Those with sea views were sought after hotly. A bagging system was in operation: books and cardigans had been left to establish possession. This strategy, however, was not proof against the more experienced voyagers, who were willing to brazen it out and remove these colonising tokens in order to stake out their own claims. Those who had been on past cruises, and knew the score, took the precaution of leaving one party on guard while others foraged for food.

The single were at a disadvantage here. Vi, hesitating with her tray, was hailed by Ken on his way to the hot food counter.

'We were wondering where you'd got to. Come and join us. Jen's over there by the window.'

Vi found Jen sitting at one of the prime locations which commanded an unobstructed view of the sea. To Vi's surprise, Jen was leafing through a book about the Russian Revolution but it turned out the book belonged to Ken. 'He only reads non-fiction,' she explained. 'Loves his history. I like novels myself. Where are you sitting?'

'Ken said to join you here.' Vi was ready to beat a retreat.

'No, I mean where are you in the evening? We're way down in the Beatrix. It's not bad, though I didn't much like what they did with my sea bream.'

'I'm in the Alexandria,' said Vi, concerned that it might seem like showing off.

But Jen was only impressed. 'That must have cost an arm and a leg. Still, you can't take it with you. That's what we said. What are the others on the table like?'

'There's a retired sea captain. He used to work on this line.'

Jen divulged that some people at their table had had a death in the family. 'It cast a bit of a pall on things, to be honest. You have to feel for them, of course, but Ken's going to try to get us moved.'

Ken returned with two plates on which he had piled, as if against a coming famine, bacon, black pudding, sausages, mushrooms, tomato and fried potatoes. 'You not having any?' he asked Vi. 'Go on, we'll keep your place.'

'Really. I never eat cooked breakfast.'

'That's why you're so slim,' said Jen, amicably. 'I'm a greedy pig, me. Can't resist food. I had a twenty-two-inch waist when I met Ken.'

'Too skinny by half,' said Ken. He speared a sausage and examined it as if to ensure it had no plans to acquire a waist. 'Not you, though,' he added quickly to Vi. 'Suits you. She,' he nodded at Jen, 'was a bag of bones before I took her in hand.'

Jen pulled a face at her husband and asked Vi what her plans were. Having no 'plans', Vi, who didn't want to appear standoffish, said she thought she might explore the ship. Then, unequal to spinning out any longer a bowl of muesli and a cup of coffee, she said goodbye to the Morrisons. As she walked away, she heard Ken urging Jen to another helping of bacon. 'Go on,' he was saying, 'you know you'll regret it later if you don't.'

Vi went out on deck, which had been colonised by those pursuing health programmes. Elderly joggers, in shorts or tracksuits, sporting baseball caps and bedecked with iPods, pounding the boards to the throbbing engines, swerved perilously around troops of speed walkers who, in turn, were being frustrated by strolling passengers whose only aim was to enjoy the traditional health-giving properties of the sea air. Others had given themselves up to indolence and were sitting reading or lying, well-oiled against the sun, on the wooden loungers which lined the perimeter of the deck.

Vi shaded her eyes against the sun spangling the water with dancing points of silver and wondered how the silver of sunlight differed from the silver of the moon, and then if it really differed at all. Probably not, she decided. She strolled on round to where a small group of smokers, defiantly outfacing the disciples of health, had gathered. Above the mint green foaming train of the ship, gulls cruised the breeze, as if released by some airy conjurer's legerdemain.

Enjoying aimlessness, she wandered round towards the ship's bow and ran into Captain Ryle.

'Look,' said the captain, seizing her arm. 'Over there. Look, look, porpoises.'

He passed her a pair of heavy binoculars and, adjusting the focus, her eyes caught up with the line of lithe, gun-metal hoops, leaping through the water which rocked slightly under her gaze. She followed the school until it was lost to the eye, and then, tilting up the binoculars, explored the horizon.

'Did you see them? They're lucky, porpoises,' said Captain Ryle. 'Sailors say so, anyhow.' Too well-mannered to betray this openly, he was impatient for the return of his binoculars.

'Thank you,' said Vi, handing the glasses back. She had rather wanted to continue examining the self-renewing horizon.

'These were a present from Kath on our Ruby Wedding,' the captain said, restoring the binoculars to the safety of his own neck. 'I never go to sea without them. Care for a coffee?'

Vi, who didn't at all want coffee, said she would love one and wondered how she was going to manage Captain Ryle. It was apparent he had taken a shine to her.

They sat in the Queen Bess Bar, on seats designed to resemble lifebuoys, while the captain recounted how he had begun his seafaring career on the ferry to the Isle of Wight and had graduated from this to channel crossings before getting his real break, a berth as second mate on the *Queen Eliz-*

abeth. 'Now she's a ship and a half, the *Queen Liz.* Ever been on her?'

Vi regretted that she hadn't.

'Too late now. They let her go. Turned her into some flipping hotel. Makes you want to weep.'

'Oh dear.' She could see that sympathy was called for. But sympathy, that comes so readily to some, can be hard work. Vi decided it was time for Bunbury.

Vi had learned about Bunbury from Edwin. The original Bunbury, the fictional fiction, employed as an alibi in Wilde's most famous play, was, Edwin had taught her, a concept capable of being usefully recruited.

'I'm so sorry,' she said after they had drunk one cup of coffee and she sensed that the offer of a second was imminent, 'but I have some work I must do.'

'Work?' The captain's good-hearted face betrayed puzzlement. 'But you are here to enjoy yourself.'

'Oh, but one can enjoy one's work, don't you think?'

'It is true, I enjoyed being a skipper.' The captain sounded wistful and his pale sea-burned eyes began to fill.

Vi, not quite able to bear this, said, 'You see, I'm a poet,' hoping that would put the lid on any further questioning and instantly wished she had said nothing.

'A poet?' said the captain. Had she confided that she was a belly dancer he could hardly have looked more ill at ease.

'I don't generally mention it, because people can be nervous of poets.' Guessing she could rely on his chivalry, she went on, 'So if you wouldn't mind keeping it to yourself?'

As she had hoped, flattery – not a bad strategy if it is only employed for self-preservation – did the trick.

'Of course, dear lady. Our little secret. Kath liked poetry. She was the clever one. Over my head, I'm afraid, except for the one about the tall ship and the star to steer her by. Kath read that to me sometimes.'

'Yes,' said Vi, 'people do seem to like it. But on the whole, poetry is not most people's cup of tea.'

It was yours, the voice said. It was yours once.

Back at her cabin, she found Renato energetically shaking out the gold counterpane. 'Mrs Hetherington, please, I can go away now and come back later.'

'No, Renato, it's OK, you go on.' He had switched off the TV but she had caught the picture. 'You were watching dancing?'

'It is our own dancers on the ship. The TV programme which is relayed to your room, you see. They give demonstrations. Every day in the King Edward Lounge is a tea dance. You go?'

'I'm afraid I can't dance, Renato.'

'You dance well. Nice figure. Not like some ladies.' Renato made an obscenely fulsome gesture with his hands and giggled. 'Forgive me I speak like this to you, Mrs Hetherington.'

'Nobody minds a compliment, Renato.'

'Excuse me?'

'I am delighted you think I might be able to dance. But I'm afraid you're wrong.'

'Oh yes. You dance well.' Renato began to spray the desk with a vile-smelling cleanser.

'Renato, would you mind, only my eyes . . .'

'Excuse me?'

'The cleaner you're using. I'm sorry, but it is making my eyes sting.'

'Excuse me, Mrs Hetherington, but I must clean the cabin.'

'Couldn't you just dust it or wipe it over with a damp cloth?'

Renato looked opaque. He left the room stinking to high

heaven and to escape the fumes Vi went outside on to the balcony.

And there was the sea, reminding her that nothing that happens matters much in the great sum of things. And yet, she thought, how can we help minding?

She walked back into the cabin. On the zealously cleansed desk, Renato had stacked her books in neat piles. Beside them he had placed, in a parallel pile, her notebooks. She had not opened the notebooks in years. Who knew what had induced her to bring them.

But you do know, said the voice.

What would it be like seeing Edwin again after all these years? She had set out on something stronger than a whim. It was an impulse, but with an attendant caution that had led to her making the crossing by sea. But for what? Time, she supposed. Time to consider. Time for reflection.

You've had all the time in the world for that, said the voice. You're scared. Scared to meet him again.

She tried to recall when she and Edwin had last met – but the years had evaporated to a mist in which her memory floundered. Had they even said goodbye? She wasn't sure of that either.

3

The first time Des saw Mrs Hetherington she was sitting a little way off so that he couldn't see her hands. Des liked to see the hands because this gave him valuable information. Nail polish or no nail polish, rocks or no rocks. You could gather quite a lot from such clues. She attracted notice because she had that air of being a little apart, with her attention not on the room and the other passengers, as was the case with most of the single women who came for tea, but directed only at the sea.

'Any idea who she is?' he asked Boris. 'The skinny one in the corner over there.'

Boris was one of the many Eastern Europeans who had been joining the staff of the shipping lines in droves. They were unpopular among their colleagues. Having acquired stamina under regimes founded by Stalin, they were willing to work longer hours than those raised on more easygoing political systems. There was a general feeling that if the redundancies which were threatened struck, they would take advantage.

Boris adjusted one of the immaculate white gloves worn by the waiters serving tea. 'Mrs Hetherington, Deck Twelve, single occupancy. I think she is not with anyone. But your guess is as good as mine.'

The Eastern Europeans' command of English idiom, which

they appeared to pick up with demonic cleverness, was another ground for complaint, particularly with the British staff who were naturally suspicious of any ability with other languages.

Des, however, was Italian, at least on his father's side.

'She dance?'

Boris raised bored aristocratic eyebrows. Long ago, his family had owned serfs, and vast tracts of woodland where wolves had loped. In the family annals it was alleged that on nights when the moon was full an ancestor of Boris's had loped alongside the wolves.

Des made his way over to the thin woman's table and noted that she already had a pot of tea. 'Can I ask the waiter to get you anything to eat, Mrs Hetherington? A pastry maybe? Some sandwiches?'

'You know my name!' She had flushed.

'It is our business to get to know our guests, madam.'

'Of course.' She looked bothered. 'I don't think I want to eat anything, thanks. I seem to have done nothing but eat since I came on board.'

'You can afford to. You are so slim.' Plenty of rocks and no wedding band but a big diamond on the ring finger of the left hand.

'I came to watch the dancing.'

'But you are looking at the sea.'

She seemed to like this approach better. 'Until there is dancing I would rather look at the sea than at cake.'

'You dance?' No nail polish either.

'No.'

'But you like to watch it?'

'My steward wanted me to.'

'Your steward?' The guy must be a smooth worker if she had formed a crush on him already.

'I offended him so I'm being polite and following his suggestion, you see.'

'I see,' Des said, not seeing at all. Maybe the woman was a little touched. 'Well, enjoy yourself with the sea, Mrs Hetherington. There's plenty of it.'

Five days a week the ship's band played for the tea dance in the King Edward Lounge, hosted by a pair of professional dancers, Marie and George, whose photographs (George in tails, Marie in glittering-bodiced costumes) winning prizes in competitions as far apart as Eastbourne and Barcelona were available for sale at the rostrum. The pair had been hired by the *Caroline* to give presentation dances at the regular evening balls and to run the five-times-a-week dance lessons ('11 to 12 noon in the Tudor Room, bring suitable shoes'). The tea dances allowed a further opportunity for passengers to try out the steps they had learned at the classes. In order to accommodate the large numbers of single female passengers additional male dance hosts were employed.

Des had begun to learn to dance at the age of six at Miss Butler's Dance School. His mother, at the age of not quite fifteen, had visited southern Italy with a school coach party. One of the tyres had burst, near a trattoria run by the driver's cousin. While the driver had been hard at it changing the burst tyre, the party had enjoyed a long lunch. They were having their fortunes told in the coffee grounds by the driver's cousin's wife when young Trisha Claybourne took a glass of wine out to the toiling driver who had just completed his task. He had expressed gratitude for the wine in the discreet interior of his coach.

Trisha, who was slightly built, had not recognised the consequence of this encounter, and for a while had assumed that she was annoyingly putting on weight. By the time the penny dropped, there was no remedying the situation. Nor was it possible to track down the coach driver. Trisha didn't even know his name. When pressed she thought it might have been Dino but she wasn't sure.

Des grew up calling his mother 'Aunty', her brother 'Uncle Steve', and his grandparents 'Mum and Dad'. His grandmother loved him with a passion. Her first child, Melanie, had committed suicide. It was not something she ever discussed with her husband, and for Trisha and Steve, who came later, her anxiety was so great that it paralysed the full expression of her feeling for her own offspring. It was she who, noticing that her little 'son' had a natural sense of rhythm and an ear for music, decided that he should learn to dance.

Children have a way of feeling the reality of any situation, and long before the truth of his parentage was made known to him Des felt out of place among the Claybournes. Only at Miss Butler's school did he not seem to feel a fish out of water. He began to win medals at competitions and passed all his dance exams as expertly as he failed his school ones.

He was seventeen when he decided to leave home and, perhaps because she was the person he was least close to, it was to his Aunty Trish that he confided his plan. 'I'm going to work in a night club in Rome – don't tell Mum yet!'

Trisha had given a yelp of laughter and said, 'That's all right. Anyway, I'm your mum. What you think's your "Mum" is really your grandma. Did you never guess?'

He hadn't guessed. And now there was no one to whom he could confess that the news made him cry.

Aunty Trish, who had so confusingly turned out to be Des's mother, went on to tell him the little she knew about his father. What she couldn't recall she fabricated. Des had taken this as a chance to change his name. On the basis of his mother's supposed recollection of the coach driver, Des became 'Dino' and with the change of name went, as is often the way, a change in character.

He picked up Italian easily and became quite extroverted, even a bit of a flirt. In Rome, he found a dance partner, Sam, a determined brunette from Bradford, and for a while they performed a dance double act round the clubs. But Sam nursed ambitions to settle down. She finally ran off with a Roman priest who had left the Catholic Church over the loss of the Latin Mass.

Without Sam's purposeful character to drive him, Des drifted, making a living with seasonal hotel work, where his easygoing manner made him popular. One slack evening, chatting to a customer, he learned about crewing on the ships.

'It's a great deal,' his confidante told him, 'everything found, food, accommodation, the lot. And the best thing is if you're out of the country for a year you pay no tax. I've saved up the deposit for a flat.'

Des wrote to several shipping lines' offices asking about bar work. His handwriting was neat and his bar references correct if not enthusiastic. In the end, it was his dancing accomplishments which landed him a job.

'There are rules, mind.' The well-groomed woman who interviewed him spoke with tired authority. 'The passengers – we call them "guests" – will want you to sleep with them. If you do, and we find out, you are put off the ship at the next port.'

'What age are the "guests" then mainly?'

The woman looked at Des as if there were no depths of behaviour to which she did not expect him to sink.

'Mostly old with no men. There are younger ones too, but they more easily find other people to sleep with. It's the old ones who cause trouble.'

'Don't worry. I won't have any trouble.'

'Are you gay? We have trouble with men too.' His interlocutor turned an appraising, skilfully made-up eye on Des.

'I don't sleep with people I don't like.'

Disbelief registered in the perfect scimitar eyebrows. 'Like them or not, we throw you off.'

'I understand.'

'And tips. They will offer you tips. You take tips only if they add it to their account so it goes through our books officially. No cash tips or you are off the ship before yesterday. Understand?'

'I understand.'

'Good. Report on Monday week, please. Here is the list of things you must get for yourself. Underwear is not provided.'

Des, no longer sure how he should address his family, wrote a postcard: *Dear All, Glad to say have got a berth on a round the world cruise liner, Queen Caroline, as a dance host. Should be fun! Will keep you posted. Cheers, Des.*

By now, Trisha had been married and divorced and was back living at home. She read the card and tossed it across the kitchen table to her mother.

'Looks like our Des's fallen on his feet.' Her frankness, the day Des shared his plans for leaving home, had been her sole effort towards maternity.

Her mother read the postcard and then turned it over to inspect the picture of the liner, like a child's white toy on an improbably blue sea.

'D'you think he'll be safe?' She was frightened he might

30

drown but dared not let her only daughter see how badly she missed the boy she had raised as her own.

'Oh, Des'll be all right. I don't expect we'll hear much of him from now on.'

Trisha, who for years had pursued a strategy of incremental revenge on her mother for her preoccupation with her lost daughter, had given nothing to her own son other than her knack of sensing what mattered to people, and thus where they were most vulnerable.

4

Vi would never have set foot in the King Edward Lounge if it hadn't been for Renato. She had wandered back to her room before lunch and found him busily spraying the TV screen. When she wiped her eyes and blew her nose he had turned sulky.

It is foolhardy to quarrel with someone in a position to make one's daily life uncomfortable. Vi, taking stock, asked, 'Where was it you said there was dancing, Renato? I might take a look after lunch.'

Renato brightened and made a token wipe over the TV screen with a damp cloth. 'Deck Seven, same one as the spa. You come back doing the cha-cha-cha. You see, the cha-cha-cha not difficult for a lady like you.'

Of the many tyrannies which constrain us, Vi thought, it is extraordinary how pervasive are those that persuade us to follow other people's notions of what we want rather than our own desires. It was easier to give in to Renato than to resist. But that had been her life's strategy.

And whose fault is that? asked the voice. No one's but your own.

She settled herself in an out-of-the-way table by a window in the King Edward Lounge. A waiter with unnaturally blue eyes came over and rapidly recited the repertoire of available teas. She ordered a pot of Darjeeling and rejected the offer of sandwiches and pastries.

At the other end of the room, the band was assembling and she watched as a man with thinning hair extracted a trumpet from its case. Stooped over, his back straining the seams of his jacket, he looked a discouraged figure. Once, she thought, he had probably had musical ambitions and now he was reduced to playing in a third-rate band.

The waiter, whose badge disclosed that he was called Boris, brought her tea and asked her name.

'Do you need it for the bill?' His eyes were such an extraordinary blue that she wondered if they could be contact lenses.

'I ask to be polite, madam. There is no charge, of course.'

Vi decided they were not lenses and, rather unwillingly, gave her name. Not that it was hers anyway. When all was said and done it belonged to Ted.

Ted. How he would have enjoyed drinking tea in the King Edward Lounge. All the years they were married she had been aware, even when she pushed it to the back of her mind, that he longed for her to say something like 'Let's go on a cruise together' – or 'Let's sell up and go and live in Corfu'. Anything to show that she saw their life together as that of a couple.

But you cannot make yourself a couple, or anything real, by willing it.

Other members of the band had arrived and were unpacking their instruments. The sax player, a young man with a shaved head and a wealth of necklaces, was joshing the trumpeter and she could hear from his tone that the trumpeter was answering back with good-tempered banter. Maybe she was quite wrong and he was perfectly content with his lot. How could you ever know what it was to be another person? We are all such solipsists, she thought, trapped in the mesh of our own desires.

A slight, dark-skinned man, who she saw from his badge was called Dino, now came across the floor and addressed her by name. He must have learned it from the waiter with the dangerous eyes. She didn't like this much but she supposed they were only doing their job. This man's eyes were a gentle brown. And there was something in his face, a trace of what . . . ? A melancholy quality, not cruel anyway.

'*One* two three, one two three, it's the all-time favourite's all-time favourite, you've got it, ye-es, the waltz! *One* two three, nice an' easy now . . .'

George's voice, furred with an adult lifetime of unfiltered cigarettes, propelled the would-be dancers round the floor. 'Gentlemen, steer those lovely legs before you, don't trip over them for thinking what you'd like her to do with them! *One* two three, *one* two three, ladies, don't forget what Ginger Rogers said, now, you have to do it backwards and on high heels! *One* two three, *one* two three, nice an' easy, that's the way . . .'

'You're called Dino, then? Is that Italian?' The woman Des was dancing with had an angrily curious face.

'Nice an' easy there, gentlemen, there we go.'

Des produced his amiable smile. 'That's me, Mrs Rotherhyde.'

'And *one* two three, ladies, you're doing swell, knocking those gentlemen into a cocked hat, if Marie will forgive me expressing my prejudice in favour of the fairer sex . . .'

'Arsehole!' Marie breathed into George's ear as he danced by with a woman in red patent heels.

Seeing they were reaching the edge of the area that passed for a dance-floor, Des whirled his partner expertly round and executed a neat double chasse.

'Nice and easy does it, Mrs Rotherhyde. There you are, not

many ladies could've followed me so well. There we go now.'
He couldn't wait to get rid of her.

'And bringing it on now to an end, ladies and gentlemen,
thank your partners, please, as we get ready for the next number, the all-time favourite, ye-es, it's the foxtrot.'

'So you're Italian?' Mrs Rotherhyde, catching her breath,
suggested again. She was trying to delay his passage to a new
partner. Usually he felt sorry for them when they tried this on,
but not this one. This one, he could tell, was dangerous.

'You do look kind of dark.'

Thanks, Mrs Rotherhyde. Slightly desperate now, Des
looked about for another partner. A woman came across the
floor towards them.

'Excuse me, were you wanting to dance . . . ?'

'I'm afraid I'm just leaving.' It was the thin woman by the
window, apparently on her way out.

'And taking your partners now for the foxtrot,' George's
voice commanded.

'Can I tempt you to a foxtrot, Mrs Hetherington?'

'Oh he's foxy, he is, that one!' Mrs Rotherhyde's mulberry
lips glistened ravenously.

The thin woman looked at him. Expecting her to turn him
down, Des was taken aback when she said, 'All right, if you like
I'll have a go.'

He could tell she had never danced a foxtrot in her life. But
she moved well. Her body followed his easily and when the
dance was over she smiled at him nicely and he felt able to
go across to the little woman with the bad perm, whom he
privately called 'Miss Muffet' on account of her height and
her baby-doll clothes, and Miss Muffet had been surprisingly
gracious, and did not try to hang on to him when the dance
ended. Instead, she said quite cheerfully, 'There's others look-

ing for a partner. I'll sit here, my dear, and rest my old feet and watch you twinkle your toes.'

The band had started up again but Des paused for a moment to look out through the tall plate glass windows at the sea.

It had been something of a surprise to him how fascinated he had become with the constantly shifting colours and patterns made in the water. It soothed something in him to which he could not have put a name. As he stood, absorbed, two white birds wheeled down out of the sky. Mrs Hetherington, the woman he had danced with earlier, must have stayed on to watch, because at that moment he saw her leaving the room and wondered if she had also seen the birds.

Vi, who had found dancing the foxtrot surprisingly agreeable, had lingered to watch the rumba. Perhaps worn out by the unaccustomed exercise, she went back to her cabin and fell asleep on the gold counterpane.

She dreamed that she was helping Harry climb to a high platform in a children's playground. Harry's feet, in his Clarks sandals, kept slipping and she was trying to place them securely on the rungs. She could feel his slender ankles and see the pale crepe of the sole which, dream-like, was visible on the palm of her hand. The rungs were wet and slimy and Harry began to slip and slide down through them. And suddenly the ladder was frighteningly high off the ground and swaying. And where had she left Daniel? He was a baby still and, wrapped in a jacket but nothing more, was sleeping, oh help, was it under the pile of rubbish they had made for a bonfire? She cried out and woke not knowing where in the world she was.

There was knocking at the door. Someone outside had been calling her. 'Mrs Hetherington. Coo-ee. Coo-ee, Mrs Hetherington. Are you there?'

It was Renato wanting to know did she need anything.

'No, thank you, Renato, I am dressing for dinner.'

'How was the dancing, Mrs Hetherington?'

'Very nice, thank you, Renato.'

'I said you enjoy it, Mrs Hetherington. Have a nice dinner now.'

She drifted off again but Harry and Dan had walked on without her, through the valley of sleep – where those we have been close to, for good or ill, mingle – and had gone out into the adult world where things are done differently and her children no longer needed her.

5

Vi woke to the chugging engines and saw it was time to go down for dinner. The information in her cruise folder warned that it was 'formal' tonight. Oh, what a bother it all was. She would so much rather stay here in her cabin and drift in and out of sleep. Ted's voice said, 'You've paid good money for this, Violet.' Well, that was true. Ted's money. Very well, she had her black evening dress. That looked OK with Ted's pearls.

She pulled the dress over her head, caught a thread in an earring, took it off again to untangle the earring, decided to take off her knickers which were spoiling the line, brushed her hair into shape, extracted Ted's grey pearls from the suitcase and added a silver belt and the silver slippers that Annie had given her for the voyage. Good old Annie. She still had that eye.

For all her hurry, Vi was late for dinner and when she arrived there were ten already at the table. One of the newcomers, an elderly woman in a long beaded navy suit, had collared Captain Ryle, who looked across regretfully at Vi. The woman introduced herself as Miss Foot and apologised for not joining them the evening before but explained that she had felt the need to acclimatise.

The other pair missing from the previous evening turned

out to be part of the programme of entertainment laid on for the passengers: a New York theatre critic and a writer of popular historical fiction called Kimberley Crane. Minor celebrities were invited to travel on the ship, all expenses paid, in return for a session of book signing in the ship's bookshop.

Vi had heard of the theatre critic who was known by his pen name 'The Critic at the Hearth' and was famed for his savage reviews which could close down Broadway shows overnight. He was a little, bird-like man with round tortoiseshell glasses and mild hazel eyes. Kimberley Crane, the novelist, was a statuesque woman wearing a white fishtail dress which showed off impressive breasts. She was explaining, when Vi arrived, how the evening before she and the critic had been summoned to the captain's bridge for cocktails and had subsequently been unable to find their way to the Alexandria.

'You should have seen us. We were like babes lost in the wood.'

'What did you do for food?' Valerie Garson asked.

'We made do,' said the critic, with a benign-seeming smile. (There was a widespread fear among his New York acquaintances that he might one day publish his reminiscences.) 'We amused ourselves with some crumbs of pizza dropped by the woodland birds.'

'He did,' said Kimberley. 'I can't touch gluten.'

Martha asked Vi how her day had been, and the captain gave her a conspiratorial look and passed her the basket of bread rolls.

Les said, 'I spotted you dancing with that Eyetie fellow. Don't you worry, Val here'll tell you not much gets past me.'

Vi looked at him levelly and said, 'He was a very nice young man,' and then, seeing that the captain looked crestfallen, to spare his feelings explained, 'My steward is a ballroom dance fan. He was keen for me to try it out so I went to the tea dance to please him.'

'My wife was a wonderful ballroom dancer.' The captain spoke wistfully.

Vi, seeing where this was heading, said hastily, 'I'm really no good at dancing. I only went to please Renato.'

'Extraordinary,' said the critic. 'I do hope my steward won't insist.'

The sommelier, who introduced himself as Pedro, came to take her order and recommended the Rioja. Vi ordered a large glass. 'My steward's very keen on the *Titanic*,' she said to the critic. 'The show, I mean, not the ship.' She remembered that this had been the target of one of his most scathing pieces.

Conversation drifted generally to other topics. The critic and Martha began to debate the recent changes of domestic policy in the U.S., Kimberley and Valerie begin to compare the pros and cons of breast reduction and Les said that he preferred his women natural and what was wrong with a bit of tit? Greg and Heather, in the absence of any outside interest, spoke between themselves of their son's latest accomplishments and Miss Foot asked the captain if he was acquainted with the work of Rudolf Steiner, of whose philosophy, she confided, she had been a life-long disciple. The captain was patently out of his depth but he was too far away for Vi to rescue him. She turned, rather thankfully, to Baz.

'What was it you were doing at the LSE, if that isn't too nosy?'

'I'm an anthropologist.'

'Not economics, then?'

'Not at all. African religion is my field. My speciality is traditional healers, "witch doctors" to you. The LSE happens to be rather good on witch doctors.'

'How funny,' she said. 'Someone I knew is, or was, interested in witch doctors, sorry, traditional healers, I should say.'

'No?'

'Yes. He was at the LSE too.'

'I admit to being surprised. Rather big-headedly, I get to thinking I am the only witch-doctor doctor. We tend to be kind of thin on the ground.'

'I should imagine. What is it you study especially?'

'My healers are the Sangomas, the traditional healers of southern Africa. I guess you could say they work as psychiatrists. But they practise as physicians too. Herbs, mostly, but also, for example, they prescribe lion's fat to give courage.'

'The person I knew was interested in Voodoo, sorry, I mean Vodun, but I was never quite sure whether he was telling tall stories,' Vi said, thinking she wouldn't mind some lion's fat.

'These esoteric religions generate tall stories. After all, who can check them? The Catholic missionaries of course exploited this like crazy. But I'm intrigued. Who was your friend?'

'No one you would know,' Vi said swiftly. 'It was ages ago.'

After dinner, Greg and Heather hurried away to monitor the peacefully slumbering Patrick. Kimberley Crane remarked that if that was what having kids did to you she was glad she hadn't any and announced that she didn't know about anyone else but she for one was heading for the bar.

Vi went up on deck but it was chilly and the boards were wet with sea spray and slippery. Not quite knowing what to do with herself, she looked in at the Golden Hinde, where she found Ken and Jen.

Jen grabbed her arm. 'Did you know Kimberley Crane was on board?'

'As a matter of fact she's at my dinner table.'

'Oh my God, she's my hero!'

'Heroine,' Ken corrected. He was holding a pint of lager and, swaying slightly with the motion of the ship, looked a little tipsy.

'No, Ken. Hero. Vi, can you get me to talk to her? I'll be your best friend if you do.'

Vi said, 'I can try. But I only met her myself this evening.'

Kimberley Crane was standing by the bar in the thick of admirers. She clearly had no idea who Vi was when she made her way through the throng to introduce Jen, who looked quite bashful and said, 'I simply *adore* your books, Miss Crane.'

Vi left Jen to fight her corner with the other fans and tried in vain to attract the barman's attention. She was rescued by Ken, who bought her a brandy and steered her through the crush.

'Thank you, Ken. At my age, you tend to become invisible.'

'I reckon you're visible enough, Vi.'

'Thank you, again.'

'Old as you feel.'

Vi, who frequently felt as old as the hills, agreed. The ship lurched a little and he held the crook of her arm while she steadied herself.

'Easy does it. Do you mind the swell, Vi?'

'Actually, Ken, I quite like it.'

'Jen doesn't,' Ken said. 'Lucky I brought her seasickness tablets. She's a terrible sailor.' He looked admiringly over at his wife, who was at the bar talking excitedly to the other Kimberley Crane fans. 'She'd forget her head, Jen, if I weren't there to remind her.'

Kimberley Crane was still at the bar when the critic wandered by later that evening. 'You know,' she swayed a little on her heels, steadying herself on his narrow shoulder, 'my agent thinks I've got a play in me.'

'Extraordinary how many seem to have,' said the critic, stepping aside adroitly to help himself from a bowl of crisps on the bar.

'I'd adore to run something past you. I have this idea about a play about rape victims.'

'How fascinating,' said the critic. He nibbled at a crisp.

'You know, the trauma of rape is quite indescribable.'

'But nevertheless you propose to describe it?'

'What I thought – my God this ship is moving, I need something in my stomach, can you pass the potato chips?'

'Certainly,' said the critic, handing her an almost empty bowl.

'I thought maybe of getting some real rape victims to participate – Jesus, I hope to God it's not going to be like this all the way. I mean, a kind of therapy session but dramatised on stage. Do you know what I mean?'

'Surprisingly well.'

'It would go down big in New York.'

'You believe so?'

The ship lunged, and deprived of the critic's support Kimberley clutched the bar with both hands. 'You see, people like you and me, we're creative.'

'How kind,' said the critic, finishing off the second bowl of crisps. 'Did you catch the Welsh harpist playing in the Rose of York today? I believe she is called Vivian. Not a name one naturally associates with Wales.'

6

Vi returned from the Golden Hinde to her cabin, where she found two small squares of chocolate, positioned at a scrupulously judged diagonal on the turned-down bed. Beside them was a reminder to put her clock back by one hour. Too tired to undress, she lay down fully clothed and ate the chocolates. Her mind had returned to Edwin.

Their correspondence had been punctiliously polite. She had initiated it, nervous of how a letter from her might be received. And for a long time there had been nothing from him and she had supposed that he had moved or didn't want to hear from her – either, or both, being possible. Or perhaps he had died? People did die. Not only her mother, and Ted, but quite a few of those she had known well had gone into the dark. (Her mind flashed, as it always did when thoughts of death arose, to her sons.) Months after she had stopped scrutinising the post, an airmail letter arrived and the neat italic handwriting told her, before she looked inside, whom it was from. Who else, other than old-fashioned doctors, would still be using a fountain pen?

Edwin's letter was friendly if guarded. It contained news, of a public kind, about his work, which he reported as going 'quite well'. She had heard that his latest collection, *The Dust Gatherers*, had been short-listed for the Galliner Prize, one of the top awards for poetry in the U.S. She alluded to this in her reply, offering congratulations. In the same letter she had enclosed her email address. His reply to hers made no mention of the Galliner but explained that he didn't use email or even possess a computer.

'I continue, as you can tell, as an unreformed Luddite,' he wrote. 'To everyone's irritation, and the alarm of some, I don't even own a cell phone. These things possess us, I feel, rather than the other way about.'

The last gave a glint of the old Edwin, and she had written back swiftly (perhaps, she judged afterwards, too swiftly, since he took noticeably longer to reply to this one) to say she wished she had his moral courage but, coached by her two sons, she had succumbed to technology. When his next letter arrived, it contained no reference to the sons but he did make an oblique enquiry about her work. 'What are you doing these days? (I hate that question so please feel free to ignore it.)'

And what *are* you doing? the voice asked.

'I wish I knew,' she said aloud, getting up from the bed to take off the pearls and the black frock, put on her nightdress and wedge open the doors to the sound of the ancient and blessedly unjudging sea.

Down in the crew bar Des bumped into Boris. 'How did you get on with Mrs Hetherington? I saw you schmoozing her.'

'Fine.'

'You going to pull her?'

'Fuck off,' Des said.

Boris levelled at him an insolent blue gaze and laughing

knowingly moved off to conclude a deal he had going with one of the waiters in Beatrix, who claimed to have access to a supply of Rolexes.

Des stayed at the bar drinking a couple of beers. He moved off to see what was showing at the lower-deck cinema. A romantic comedy, of the kind favoured by the female crew. Sandy, one of the bartenders in the Golden Hinde, was in there watching the film. He had had a brief fling with her but she had begun to be pushy and demanding and he wanted to get some distance between them to give the affair time to die down. To avoid meeting her, he decided to go back to his cabin.

Crew members of the same sex and in similar posts were generally berthed together as cabin mates. But there was always some wheeling and dealing going on. Des had worked things so that he shared with one of the male hairdressers, who was having an affair with a masseuse who worked in the spa, who in turn shared with a yoga instructor, who was having an affair with the purser, who, happily for everyone, had his own private quarters.

This meant that, by a knock-on effect, except on the evenings when the yoga teacher was in a bad mood, or had her period, Des had the cabin to himself.

He reached up and felt for a shortbread tin with a picture of two Scottie dogs on it, one white, one black. Leila Claybourne, in the days when he thought she was his mum, had used it to store the biscuits she had liked to make for him, and he had smuggled it into his luggage, along with his comic albums, when he left home. She must have noticed it had gone and wondered if he had taken it. The tin now held a gold watch, a pair of jade cufflinks, a lighter, a couple of photos of himself as a child winning dance medals, a building society book and a notebook. When he had enough capital, his plan was to set up his own dance school, perhaps in the U.S., where you had more of a chance to get ahead. The tax-free earnings from the four years at sea helped, but the extra input from his 'private clients' was a real boost.

Opening the notebook, he wrote in a shorthand he had devised for the purpose, 'H 12', and then stopped and thought about the slight pale woman with the long legs he had danced with. She looked not unlike his own mother, whom he still preferred to think of as Aunty Trish. Like her, but most unlike her too. The eyes were quite different. But she was like Trish in being a loner, which had its dangers. Loners were lonely. He'd had a narrow escape the cruise before last, with a woman he'd had to prise off him as she knelt naked at his feet, clasping him round the knees. It had been a hell of a worry that he'd not got out of her cabin undetected. She'd given him two hundred dollars, with a plea to visit her in her Manhattan apartment. It was possible that she would repent of this later and report the gift as a theft. They did this, once they had come to their senses, to get the insurance, and it was important to work out in advance those who wouldn't go on to report you as well. If you chose carefully, and followed your instincts, you'd know who was unlikely to follow this pattern since it would expose them too much. Still, it was a gamble. H 12 was a risk. On the other hand, there was that funny business about her steward. And she had after all danced with him.

There was a tap at the door and he opened it, to his dismay, to Sandy. 'Oh, hi there.'

'You avoiding me, then?'

'Why would I be doing that?'

'Boris said he saw you go into the movies. You must've seen me there.'

'Boris is a cunt.'

'Good-looking, though.'

'You're welcome.'

'So d'you fancy a beer or something?'

Sandy tried to peer round him where, conscious of the open biscuit tin lying on the floor by his bunk, he was blocking the doorway.

'Not tonight, thanks.'

'Got a headache, have you?'

'No, I'm busy.'

'Oh, what you got to be busy about?' Sandy moved across to get a better look into the room.

'This and that.'

'Oh, right. So see you around, then?'

'Yeah, see you, Sandy.'

THIRD DAY

Footloose: The bottom portion of the sail is called 'the foot'. If it is not secured, it is known as 'footloose' and dances in the wind.

7

When Vi woke next morning bands of mist had settled round the ship. Standing in her white nightdress on the balcony, she could see nothing before her but an all-obscuring white.

She had dreamed about her mother. She tried to let her mind open up again. But it was almost always hopeless if you didn't catch hold of a dream at once, before it evaporated. Brushing her teeth, she wondered, as she had wondered before, if dreams too closely grasped were dangerous. Maybe, like those people in legend who wandered into fairyland and never properly returned, dreams took you too far from what was called 'the real world' to continue to survive in it.

The guardians of oblivion relented a little and allowed a fragment of the dream to escape. Her mother was explaining something. She tried again to let her mind go free. Something about a family her mother had had, another set of children before she had Vi. And this other family, who appeared out of the blue, wanted to meet Vi. But try as she might she couldn't recover any more.

Around the time of her mother's death, Vi had often dreamed of her. Then the dreams petered out and she hardly dreamed about her mother at all until the marriage to Ted. How unfathomable it was, the trade between the daylight and the night mind. Was there something about Ted that allowed her mother to return from wherever she had settled? Would she have liked Ted? Or was it one of those coincidences which make up more of life than we want to admit because it is so tempting to endow them with a profounder meaning?

Thoughts of her dead parent led inevitably to the living one: her father in his dreadful 'Home', which wasn't a home at all. They had never really got on. For all her best intentions, she had never been able to break through that impenetrable-seeming barrier which he had thrown up against his wife's death. They had never found a way to know each other better. Perhaps after her mother died neither of them wanted to be close.

Deciding she had had enough of queues, and with no desire for conversation, she rang room service and ordered toast and coffee. She was sitting on the balcony in the early morning sun when there was a knock at the cabin door and Renato came through and out on to the balcony carrying a breakfast tray.

'Mrs Hetherington, you take some repose on your balcony. It is good.'

'Thank you, Renato.'

'I pour your coffee?'

'Thank you, Renato. I can manage.'

Renato's expression took on its sulky cast. Vi wondered again quite why it was so difficult to prevent people taking trouble for you when the only trouble you wanted from them was to be left uninterrupted in peace.

'I bring you hot milk as well as cold, Mrs Hetherington. And fresh orange juice.'

'Thank you, Renato, that's very kind of you.'

'You like orange?'

'Yes, thank you.'

'I bring you some tomorrow.'

'Thank you,' she said again. And more to please him than from any formed desire, 'Or maybe grapefruit?'

Renato left the room, his back and shoulders registering disappointment that for the time being there were no opportunities for further gallantry.

This was something she could never explain to Ted. Ted had thrived on attentive service and she could never convince him that it was not principle, or perverseness, that made her shrink from it. Ted, who liked what he called his 'creature comforts', was glad to spend his money on hers. And all she wanted from him, and from his money, was freedom to be left to her thoughts. It had hurt him. *She* had hurt him. And she couldn't even justify this by saying she was unaware of the fact that she was hurting him. She had been aware of it.

She heard Edwin saying, 'Opposites may attract but they rarely bond.' But Ted wasn't even an opposite. He was other. Not your kind, the voice said. 'But he *was* kind,' she objected. She had puzzled and bewildered Ted and now he was dead. And she was alive. And crossing the Atlantic to see Edwin whom Ted had never met.

Vi had never felt the desire to keep a journal but she had, for a time, kept notebooks where she wrote down observations, quotations and jottings of odd information, and kept letters and cards. Drinking coffee now, she opened the oldest of these notebooks, a school exercise book with stiff green covers.

Meeting a past self was bound to be a jolt. Some of the entries were in ink, in a handwriting that she barely recognised. On one of the first pages there was a quotation: *They say miracles are past* . . . and then a blurred smudge of what looked like coffee. It was Shakespeare but, for the life of her, she couldn't recall where it came from. A few pages on she encountered Edwin.

*   *   *

53

Vi had gone to Cambridge in the days when the entrance candidates sat a special examination. She attended a comprehensive school in Bromley where, to an ugly box-like house, she and her father had moved after her mother's death. The school had an indifferent record in sending students to university but Vi had been lucky in her English teacher, Miss Arnold, who, just down from university herself, was still ambitious for her pupils. It was Miss Arnold who had been responsible for Vi sitting the Cambridge entrance exam.

For all her teacher's confidence, Vi was astonished when she was awarded a place at Newnham, then one of only three colleges where women could study for a Cambridge degree. It was Vi's private conviction that her papers had been muddled with someone else's. This suspicion was confirmed when, at their first meeting, Mrs Viney, the Director of Studies, who was Anglo-Irish and claimed a distant connection to Goldsmith, asked Vi a question about *Tristram Shandy*, a book greatly disliked by Miss Arnold and which, as a result, Vi had never read.

When Vi looked scared, Mrs Viney said, 'You wrote so well on the Shandean influence on European thought in your entrance exam, Victoria.'

Vi's spirit never quite recovered from this, even when she learned that Mrs Viney was generally disappointed in her current students and frequently confused them with past students, with whom she had been just as disappointed once but who shone in memory with retrospective glory.

The discouragement with Mrs Viney was only one of several. Cambridge is notoriously cold since wind blows more or less unimpeded across from the bleak Ural Mountains. The poorer women's colleges were stingy with their heating and students were obliged to post shillings into their gas meters to light their hopelessly inadequate gas fires. Vi's grant covered only part of her fees and living expenses and the money was not made up by her father. Rather than ask for what she suspected would not be forthcoming, Vi scrimped and did without extra food and heat in her room and consequently was always catching cold.

But the physical chill was not the worst of it. She missed her school friends, who, if they had gone to university, had gone to jollier-sounding places like Sussex or Newcastle. Her best friend, Annie Packer, had not gone to university at all. To Vi's admiration, and some envy, Annie had been taken on as a trainee buyer at Marshall and Snelgrove. The job suited Annie, who had aspirations to become a model. She was also unusually informed about Marshall and Snelgrove's stock since she had been in the way of supplementing her school wardrobe by regular shoplifting from their dress department.

As a new undergraduate Vi did what she believed was expected of her: she bought a bike at the police auction, though she never got round to collecting it from the bike shop to which she took it for repairs; she joined societies and made a few, not very congenial, friends. In the first term, she went out with a boy from Selwyn called Derek, who was a member of the English History Society. They hadn't much to say to each other and Vi found Derek's sexual advances, at a late-night showing of *La Dolce Vita*, annoying rather than enticing. She auditioned for a production of *Topol*, where she was cast in a minor role, which was subsequently cut when the show ran overtime. After that, she joined a dull Sunday choir and drank dutifully with the others at the pub. But she found the whole experience of being away from home confusing and missed Annie, who was sharing a flat in Earls Court with three high-spirited Australians from Adelaide.

* * *

There was a tap at the door and a militantly beaming Renato came through to the balcony. 'Mrs Hetheringon, I bring . . .' He proudly presented on a salver half a grapefruit, cut into efficient segments.

'Thank you, Renato.'

'You finish the rest of your breakfast? I take away this tray?'

'Please.'

Deftly shouldering the tray with one hand, Renato produced from his pocket a token.

'Free offer to use the spa. It is meant only for Decks Thirteen and Fourteen but my friend there he give me some and so I say, This for Mrs Hetherington.'

'Thank you, Renato. That is very kind.'

'You like the spa, Mrs Hetherington. Very good for ladies.'

'I am sure I shall like it.'

'Very peaceful. Let me know when to do your room, Mrs Hetherington.'

'Thank you, Renato, I shall.'

'Remember, put the notice on the door.'

'I will try to remember.'

A postcard from Annie, a hand-tinted sepia print of the Eiffel Tower, coloured like marzipan, was stuck into a page of the notebook. The aged brown Sellotape peeled away easily. *Having a ball*, the card read. *Fab frocks this year. Skirts knickers-high.*

Vi had followed Annie's advice and chopped her own skirts so short that she was unable to go home for fear of her father's retorts. There was a blurred photograph of her wearing one, with Annie looking like Mary Quant with bobbed hair and black tights (probably nicked).

There was another tap at the door. 'Mrs Hetherington, it's me.' Renato, with a brand new idea. 'I forget to say. If you have any laundry or dry cleaning it must go before twelve o'clock.'

'Thank you, Renato.'

'You know where the laundry bag is?'

'Yes, thank you.'

'In the bottom drawer. Two bags: one, blue, for laundry, the white one for dry cleaning.'

'Thank you.'

'You like I take it now?'

Vi threw in the towel. 'I do have some cleaning. I'll sort it out. And why not do the room now, Renato?'

8

Vi, reaching the stairs, found that she had picked up the free token to the spa. Well, why not? It was free. She returned to her room and interrupted Renato happily hoovering with the TV on.

'Madam, look, the quickstep. You do this easy.'

'I'm just getting my swimming things, Renato. I'm going to follow your advice and try the spa.'

She was being issued with a gown, a locker key and a towel by a glamorous Indian girl in a white overall when Jen showed up.

'Hi there, Vi. Have you got a free token?'

'Yes.'

'Me too.'

'Oh.'

'Our steward told us that no one is joining, too pricey, so they're giving out these to tempt us in.'

So much for Renato's special favours. Vi undressed and got into her bathing costume, which no longer seemed to fit in any of the right places.

'God, I wish I had your figure, Vi.'

'I think you look a treat,' Vi said, meaning it. Jen in a bikini patterned with vivid sunflowers was a tall, bronzed Amazon.

'"She wore an itsy bitsy, teeny weeny, yellow polka dot

bikini" I don't think,' Jen said. 'Come on, let's take the plunge.'

The 'spa' was a small swimming bath filled with warm saline water and fitted with a variety of pumping devices set at various levels to massage different parts of the body. Vi tried all the massages in turn, swam twice round the pool and then discovered, at the far end, an underwater couch, made out of metal bars through which the water surged.

Lying with the warm water gently thrashing her back, Vi's feelings towards Renato relented. This was the second adventure he had sent her on and, like the dancing, it had turned out to be fun. She lay back, with the water kneading her shoulder blades, thinking about Edwin.

Edwin's seminars on poetry, attended by first- and second-year students in preparation for Part I of the University Tripos exams, were held in his rooms at Corpus Christi, above the sundial in Old Court, where the young firebrand Christopher Marlowe once lodged. Seminars were often taught by postgraduates such as Edwin, engaged in writing doctoral theses and usually woefully behind in their schedules and thus short of funds. Vi had gone to Edwin's seminars, as she did to every university class, in a state of debilitating anxiety of which she was hardly aware, since any condition suffered long enough becomes normal. Squashed up against other students, on a sofa shiny with use, in aged rooms whose walls, where visible between crammed bookcases, were yellowed with years of coal fires and nicotine, she made no attempt to contribute to the discussions. Convinced as she was of the meagreness of her understanding and her own insignificance, the whole business of being there at all had become a condition of chronic dread. She had nothing to say that would not sound, she knew, ridiculously unsophisticated.

Each week, Edwin handed round copies of xeroxed poems for the class to analyse. At the very last seminar of the spring term, to her astonishment she recognised one. It had been a favourite of Miss Arnold's, who, still alight with the zeal of the novice, had given the poem to her sixth form to read over a half term.

Vi was the only one in the class who had read the poem closely, if at all – and really more for what it might reveal about her teacher than for any improving mental exercise. One verse in particular had caught her attention.

> *When love with one another so*
> *Interinanimates two souls,*
> *That abler soul which thence doth flow,*
> *Defects of loneliness controls.*

The word 'interinanimates' intrigued her and stuck in her mind, and while she didn't quite understand the poet's meaning she was taken by the sound of the words.

'You have a good ear, Violet,' Miss Arnold had said, when Vi, a little nervously, mentioned this. 'You will get along well with Donne. He had one of the best ears of all time. Do you know what "ecstasy" means?'

Vi, who supposed it was what happened when you took LSD, thought it prudent to say that she didn't.

'Good,' said Miss Arnold, who approved of ignorance in her pupils. 'Ecstasy is a mystical state in which the soul escapes the body to seek union with the divine. Donne, you see, has made a conceit (that's also a form of pun, by the way) in suggesting that the entities which flow from his soul and his lover's unite to create a third entity, a perfect whole or divinity. The divinity

60

is sexual love, not God. It is a characteristic piece of his sublime profanity.'

People generally feel well-disposed to those they have helped and it was this exchange that had led to Miss Arnold's suggesting that Vi try for Cambridge. Thereafter Vi thought of the turbulent seventeenth-century poet and preacher as an ally.

Donne came to her aid again in Edwin's class.

'So,' Edwin had said after a more than usually empty few minutes, 'does anyone have any thoughts at all about this poem? What is, or what was, ecstasy?' He glared at the class. His eyes, one blue and one a greenish hazel, were like those of a white cat Vi had had as a child, before her mother died and pets were banished for good from the household.

There was a further silence. Motes of dust danced crazily in the sunlight over the drowsy heads of the students, who shifted uneasily on their bottoms and looked bored or sheepish according to their temperament. It was the last week of term and most of the room had spent it in serious late-night partying, enjoying less ethereal forms of ecstasy.

'Forgive my interrupting your repose.' Edwin's hair, sticking up at the back where he had not combed it, made him look like a ruffled bird.

Vi, who had been to no parties and was sensitive to embarrassment, said, very rapidly in case she lost the impetus, 'Ecstasy is a mystical state in which the soul escapes the body to find union with the divine' and blushed horribly.

Edwin habitually taught the class perilously balanced on the arm of his desk chair and with his own legs twisted around the chair's. He unscrambled his limbs enough to turn and stare at Vi with his odd eyes.

'Since you seem to be the only person, other than myself,

awake in the room, have you any other ideas to enliven the rest with?'

Vi said, still speaking very fast, 'He's imagining a third, um, entity, born from their love, which will unite them so they are no longer alone. A child, really, except . . .' Acute embarrassment made her stop short of saying that the poem was describing a poetic parallel to the sexual act.

'A kind of metaphysical child. A bold conclusion when you press it, as some of us are willing to. Any idea who the poet is?'

'John Donne,' said Vi, longing for a complexion that did not ensure that every private emotion went on vivid display. 'But I already knew it.'

'Don't apologise for knowing Donne,' Edwin had said.

When the class was over, he caught her at the door. 'What's your name?'

'Honour St John. But I use my second name.'

'Which is?' He looked less like a bird of prey when he smiled.

'Violet. My friends call me Vi.'

'Violet suits you.' Vi blushed still more ferociously.

At the first seminar of the summer term, after Edwin had handed round the sheets of purple printed poems, he said, 'Violet, could you kindly read aloud for us the first poem on the sheet?'

At the end of the class he stopped her again as she was trying to sidle out. 'You see. It wasn't so bad.'

'I didn't read it very well.'

'Hopkins is hardly a piece of cake.' The odd eyes held hers. 'You have a good ear.'

'Miss Arnold said that.'

'And Miss Arnold is . . . ?'

'My English teacher. At school. It was her idea I should come to Cambridge.'

'You wouldn't have come under your own steam?'

'I shouldn't think so.'

'Why not?'

'I'm not bright enough,' Vi said, and began blushing again.

'Nonsense,' Edwin said. 'You're shy, not at all the same thing. There's nothing wrong with being shy. I'm shy too, if it comes to that.' Vi, who did not believe this for a second, felt grateful. 'You like poetry.' It appeared to be a statement, not a question.

'When I understand it.'

'If you like it you will understand it. Apprehend it, I should say. Poems are like people: they should not be too well "understood".'

He walked her to the gate by St Benet's church, where blue and white bluebells were still gracing the old graveyard. 'Come and have a drink with me some time and tell me which other poets you like.'

'Bloody hell, I gave my thigh one hell of a bashing on those underwater bars.' Jen emerged like a gleaming sea lion suddenly from the water. 'They should watch that. I could sue. Is it nice there?' She heaved herself up and rolled on to the couch beside Vi.

'It is nice,' Vi said. 'I wouldn't have come if my steward hadn't bullied me.'

'I know what you mean. Sometimes you have to be made to do things which turn out to be the best things you ever do.'

'You think so?'

'Oh yeah. Ken made me marry him. I didn't want to, but he kept on at me, and then he shut me in a cupboard under his gran's stairs and wouldn't let me out till I promised to marry him. He told me it was full of spiders. I was scared of spiders so I said "yes".'

'Heavens.'

'I had my fingers crossed and I wasn't meaning to go through with it. But then, you know, I got to quite like the idea. Funny thing, life.'

'Did you ever regret it?'

'What, marriage? Who doesn't? Goes with the territory. See, look, there's going to be one hell of a bruise there. Ken'll be mad at me. He says I can't be trusted out on my own.'

They showered and washed their hair and dried it with over-efficient blowers provided by the spa.

'It's like school,' Jen said, towelling her back and shoulders vigorously. 'Only the showers work better here and, goody, look, body lotion.' She pumped a palmful of cream from a dispenser and rubbed it over her breasts. 'Never really get rid of stretch marks, do you? Not that you seem to have any. What are you up to now?'

'I might have an early lunch.'

'I'm off to play Scrabble with Ken. It's his turn to win.'

'Do you take it in turns?'

'Not officially. But I let him win every so often. Stops him getting narky. Know what I mean?'

'I think so,' said Vi. Even 'narky' Ken was so obviously a pushover for Jen.

9

Trouble had broken out in the Alexandria Grill. Walter, the German chef, who had fallen in love with Jean-Paul, a waiter from Toulouse, had caught Jean-Paul flirting with Pedro, the Spanish sommelier. Walter, who took pride in being temperamental, had gone after Pedro with a steak hammer, swearing to beat that fucking Spaniard's fucking head in. Luckily, beyond a bad bruise to Pedro's shin, caused by his leaping on to a counter in the course of escape, no real damage had been done. Pedro had withdrawn to his room, where he had locked the door and was threatening legal action.

Walter was indispensable to the restaurant, and the crew purser, after issuing the chef with a curt reprimand, decided to order Pedro to his quarters sick. Meanwhile, a replacement wine waiter was needed. The head sommelier, who had heard that Dino had restaurant experience and a reputation for a good manner, suggested that he might take Pedro's place until things had calmed down.

Des was on his first luncheon duty when he saw Mrs Hetherington. 'Can I get you anything to drink?' he enquired.

'What will you have to drink?'
Edwin and Vi were sitting in the RAF bar in the Eagle, the

ancient inn on Benet Street. Above their heads, on the ceiling, inscribed in soot, candle smoke and lipstick, were the names and numbers of the men and planes of the RAF and the U.S. Eighth Air Force lost in the last war. One evening, one of the fighter pilots, a P. E. Turner of Cherry Hinton, placed a chair on a table and climbed up to write the first sooty inscription on the ceiling with his cigarette lighter, thereby starting a trend.

'I don't know,' Vi said. 'I don't drink much. Not beer, anyway.'

'You don't like beer?'

'I can't seem to.' It was a stumbling-block in her social life that she had never cared for the most popular student drink.

'So what will you have? Whisky? Gin and tonic? Wine?'

'Oh, wine, please,' said Vi, confused by choice. 'I don't like spirits much either.'

'It will be my ruin, if other vices don't carry me off first.' He ordered a double Scotch and had finished it before a quarter of her glass was empty. 'I see you have noticed my eyes.'

Vi, who was in fact trying to look away from the rapidly emptied glass, blushed and said, 'They are like the eyes of a cat I had once.'

'I have no objections to being likened to a cat. What was yours called?'

'Arthur.'

'After the king?'

'No. I don't know why "Arthur". I suppose I just liked the name.'

'I am glad it was not the king. I can't abide grail fanciers. You're not a grail fancier, are you?'

'I don't think so,' said Vi, who had never thought about it. 'This is nice.' She sipped the white wine.

'It's a Chablis.' He ordered one for himself. 'Quite a good one for a pub. It won't make you too drunk.'

Vi, who thought it might be fun to get drunk, asked, 'What do you do when you're not teaching?'

She had meant to ask what his thesis was on but he surprised her. 'I write poetry.'

'Goodness.'

'I shall finish my thesis, which is not very sensational – an examination of the use of Ovid's similes in Renaissance verse, very dull – and then try for a teaching post.'

'In a university?'

'A school. It's harder work in term time but the holidays are longer and there's nothing to do in them but write. What about you?'

'What about me?'

'What do you plan to do when you leave here?'

'Oh goodness,' Vi said. 'I don't know. Survive. If I get through Part One that will be enough to be going on with.'

'Of course you'll get through. You'll get a first.'

'Oh no, I couldn't.'

'I'll show you how,' Edwin said. 'It's not hard once you know the tricks. It's just a matter of practice and keeping your nerve.'

'I don't seem to have much nerve.'

He looked up at the ceiling commemorating the English and American youths, stationed in nearby Debden, Duxford or Fowlmere, who had sat night after nerveless night, ready to take their lives in their hands, and their Whitleys or Wellingtons into the air, against the superior machine-gun power of the German pilots in Messerschmitts and Junkers.

'My father was a fighter pilot in the war,' Edwin said. 'He

was nearly shot down twice before the Nazis finally nailed him. Nerve is practice, too.'

Des, standing by the table, coughed and repeated, 'May I get you anything to drink with your lunch?'

Immersed in her notebook, Vi did not immediately recognise the dark young man who had invited her to dance.

'Sorry, I was miles away.' She was thinking how she had never asked what that loss of a father had meant to Edwin. 'A white wine, maybe.'

'May I recommend the Chablis, Mrs Hetherington?'

It was not much of a coincidence. But it pleased her. 'Thank you, Dino. Chablis is exactly what was in my mind.'

Edwin was wrong. Vi did not get a first in Part I. She got an upper second and was perfectly content with it. With no money to join those of her fellow-students who were off abroad, she spent the summer working for a firm which specialised in the cleaning of seedy London bedsits, employing students for sub-trades-union wages. It was a grim job, involving disagreeable smells, soiled sheets, filthy lavatories and wastepaper bins containing used condoms, sanitary towels and occasionally empty syringes. On the brighter side, most of the bedsits serviced by Blitz were located in the Earls Court area, so she got to see Annie and the Australians.

The Australians, Annie assured her, were very good value. They were dedicated party-goers and easy flatmates, clean and, best of all, generous with the booze. Annie had no complaints and was thinking of visiting Perth, which, one of her flatmates told her, was a paradise for surfers.

'But you don't surf,' Vi objected.

'They say it's full of gorgeous men who teach you in no time.'

Annie was now assistant buyer in Marshall and Snelgrove's shoe department and had many words of sartorial advice. 'Courrèges-style white boots are in next season, Vi. I can get you a pair at cost, or better still, some of the damaged stock we're meant to send back.'

'Is there much damaged stock?'

'There is by the time I've finished with it,' Annie said darkly. 'What size are you?'

Towards the end of the summer, Vi received a postcard of a Greek temple, sent from Sicily. *Sun, wine and ruins (alongside me). Am renting a house round the corner from Newnham next year. Will you share? E.*

The university rules permitted students in their final year to lodge not only with registered landladies but with Cambridge MAs. This implied an unreasonable faith in the moral qualities required for receiving the Master's degree, which involved nothing more testing than waiting five years after gaining a BA. Luckily for Vi, Edwin's thesis on Ovid had taken him well over the five-year requirement so that when she went to clear her new address with her tutor all Miss Greyling said was, 'Be sure to see that there is a functioning bolt on your door. Not that I am suggesting that Mr Chadwick would of course . . .'

There was no fear of Miss Greyling's politely unstated apprehensions being realised. Occasionally, usually very early in the morning, Vi met a young man making his way discreetly out of the green front door of the small house in Church Rate Walk. Since Edwin never referred to his guests, she didn't either. It was, she imagined, why he had moved from his comfortable rooms in college, so as not to be commented or spied on.

Vi entertained a few young men herself. But more because sexual experience, if not expertise, was, she felt, a requirement of her age and position than because of any special liking for any one in particular. Her happiest times were spent with Edwin, either at the late-night pictures, where they saw every foreign film on view, or watching TV.

Edwin was a fan of anything that dealt with murder. His special favourite was *Miss Marple* mainly because he had become expert at second-guessing the murderer. They had a weekly prize of a bottle of wine for whoever was the quickest to spot the villain. Edwin usually won.

'The trick is to spot the person most unlikely to have committed the crime.'

'In that case,' Vi pointed out, 'surely *Miss Marple* should commit at least one murder.' She herself preferred *Dr Kildare*.

The bottle of wine was often drunk over discussions of poetry. One evening, Edwin said, 'I am thinking of starting a poetry magazine. Will you help?'

'How?' Vi was clearing away spaghetti, one of their supper staples.

'Write to people, help with the typesetting, advise the editor . . .'

'That's you, I take it?'

'Who else?'

'How will you fund it? Neither of us has a bean.'

'The Persians debated everything twice,' Edwin said. 'Once sober, once drunk. There's another bottle of Valpol in the kitchen. Fetch it here and we can debate.'

The next morning, hung over from the unaccustomed alcohol, Vi asked, 'Did the Persians really debate everything drunk?'

'Sober as well.'

'How do you know? How is it known, I should say?'

'It's in Herodotus.'

'You've always said Herodotus was fanciful!'

'No more than any other historian.'

Vi had finished her salad and drunk the glass of Chablis and was looking out at the sea which in a mood of gracious gaiety was spangling with light.

'Another glass, Mrs Hetherington? Or can I get you something else?' It was the dancing waiter again.

'Thanks, no. Although, have you any Valpolicella?'

'I believe there is a good one. I'll fetch the list.'

'No, no. I trust your judgment. Just bring me a glass, if you would.'

How funny that Valpol, the very cheapest plonk around when she and Edwin were being Persians, nowadays appeared on grand wine lists.

'Shall I send the cheese board over, Mrs Hetherington?'

'Why not?'

'And will I see you later, for the dancing?'

'You do this as well as dance?'

'The sommelier is sick. I am filling in.'

'You do it very well. The wine was lovely.'

'I am glad. I shall see you later, then, Mrs Hetherington?'

'I don't know, Dino. Perhaps.'

10

The doors to the balcony in Vi's cabin had been shut fast and bolted, top and bottom, and an aggressive smell of synthetic lemon signalled the recent presence of Renato. A leaflet, offering as a 'taster' a free private dance lesson with Marie or George, had been propped ostentatiously against the pile of books on the desk.

Maybe, Vi thought, I should take this as a form of spiritual exercise. She forced back the bolts and opened the doors to the cleansing sea air. What a pity no similar cleanser existed for the heart. Outside, she leaned on the balcony, watching the water and letting Ted's rings slip up and down on her fingers, the way he used always to warn her not to lest she lose them. She was remembering the poetry magazine.

Edwin revealed an unexpected talent for acquiring money for his proposed publication. Whereas he was generally lackadaisical over money, over the magazine he became ruthless. He mounted a fierce campaign for donations, haunting the rooms of colleagues and bombarding their pigeonholes with written appeals until they gave in and coughed up. Retired dons, and their wives, were targeted at their own parties, where an apparently indefatigable Edwin stayed on late, till to get rid of him they pledged their financial support. Under his direction, Vi typed letters to charitable trusts pleading the cause of poetry. The strategy produced enough funds for an estimated print run of two hundred for the first edition of *Mustardseed*.

How to fill the magazine exercised Edwin more. His own poems, some running to several pages, took up much of the space. He had contacts on the poetry circuit to whom, in her capacity as assistant editor, Vi wrote asking for contributions. Many of those appealed to were happy to offer poems which had been turned down by more established magazines. An ad in the university newspaper produced further efforts from aspiring student poets, not all of them bad. Ralph, the sculptor who owned the house and worked in the basement, where he was engaged on a long-term project of casting the Seven Deadly Sins in bronze, supplied some line drawings, and with these and the poetry submissions they got together almost twenty pages.

'We need one, maybe two more poems,' Edwin decided one evening.

They were eating risotto. The peppers and mushrooms were from the market, where fruit and vegetables were sold on weekdays and at weekends varieties of tatty junk were passed off on the tourists as antiques. At the end of the day's trading any produce past its saleable life was sold off at rock bottom prices. Vi and Edwin were well-established 'rock bottom' customers.

One bottle of wine had already been polished off and Edwin had opened a second.

'This is a Persian debate. Anything promising left in the slush pile?'

Vi went to her room and came back with some sheets of paper.

'There are these. I'm not sure what to make of them.'

'Let's have a look.'

Edwin read the papers on which were typed two poems of several short stanzas. 'These are rather good,' he said. 'Here, give me some more of the Valpol. Emily Dickinson–ish but distinctively their own voice. Who are they from?'

Vi began to clear away the plates. The tiny freezing kitchen ran off the room, which acted as their sitting and dining room and also held a sofa bed for guests. Rinsing the plates under the tap, she called out, 'Would you like some fruit? I got a job lot of tangerines at the market.'

She came back into the room with a blue glazed pottery dish piled with the orange fruit. The dish had been her gift to her mother, part of a matching set bought on the holiday in Brittany, where Vi had learned to swim in the biting cold green sea. She could still feel her mother's hand in the water under her stomach, and the feeling it evoked, half comfort, half apprehension, as her mother promised not to let her go until Vi gave the word.

The jug and the plate were almost the only relics of her mother – her father, either through grief, incomprehension or plain meanness, she had never quite decided which, had given almost everything else away. Only these and a small, worn garnet cross, which she believed her mother had been given at her christening, survived.

Edwin was re-reading the poems. He put down the paper. 'Violet St John, tell me the truth, did you write these?'

'Why?'

'There's a smudge on the "m" like on your typewriter. But anyway, I can hear you.'

'I didn't think about the "m". They're probably no good.'

He was quiet for a moment. Far off she heard the tuneless sound of a night bird. Then Edwin spoke.

'They're marvellous.' She looked into his odd eyes and saw that he was serious. 'Here,' he said, and he was smiling as only Edwin could smile. 'Have another drink, Miss St John. You're a poet, and you don't know it.'

Vi, out on the balcony, opened the notebook but the breeze coming in off the sea blew the pages so it was impossible to read and she went inside. Back in the cabin, she read again the poems which, her heart in her mouth, she had shown to Edwin long ago that November evening.

'Will you stay on and help with the magazine after you graduate?' Edwin asked.

Vi had sat her finals, for which Edwin had drilled her. 'Forget any nonsense about developing ideas. That's balls. Summarise as many ideas as you can in advance. It's like doing a jigsaw. You need to put all the pieces of sky together in advance and on no account waste time attempting to form new thoughts. Forget thought. This is about being organised.'

It was always easiest with Edwin, perhaps the least organised person she would ever meet, to do as he said. He was far more thrilled than she was when she was awarded a first.

Miss Arnold, who was also delighted with the news, came up for the graduation ceremony. She had long since instructed Vi to call her 'Theodora', but while Vi was careful to use the name in her old teacher's presence she remained in Vi's mind inalienably 'Miss Arnold'.

Miss Arnold arrived on a motorbike, in leathers, riding pillion behind a much younger man whom she introduced as

'Al, a colleague in the art department'. Vi complimented her teacher on her leather jacket.

'Do you like it? I got it from Annie Packer. She gets samples from her store which she sells off cut-price at her flat. I get all my clothes from Annie. I must say, my pupils have turned out well.'

Edwin was charming to Miss Arnold, to whom he deferred over her dislike of Milton ('Milton is ponderous') and gave her all the credit for her former pupil's success. Miss Arnold accepted the praise as no more than her due. It turned out that Al had been at art school with Ralph downstairs, so all five of them celebrated Vi's success and Miss Arnold and Al spent the night in the basement sleeping between Pride and Envy.

The following day the four of them went punting. It was that rare thing in England, a summer of constant heat. The sky blazed with an almost Italian light. Against the fierce blue, the leaves on the tall poplars fluttered, semi-rotating in the warm air. Edwin poled them expertly along the Cambridge Backs while Vi lay under a sunhat, trailing her hand in the sedate water of the Cam, grateful that it was all over and she could begin her life at last.

Miss Arnold and Al sat fore while Miss Arnold pointed out the sights. 'Queens', over there, is the redbrick one, named for the two queens, King's, you'll recognise, Al, from the twin pinnacles, Clare, small but very well-regarded, that's St John's, the next we come to is Magdalene.'

'Were you at university here?' Al in innocence asked.

Miss Arnold pursed her lips. 'I was at Birmingham. The Shakespeare department is considered the best in the country.'

They returned the punt and sat outside the Granta drinking

Pimms. 'Over there,' Edwin pointed, 'is the notorious Garden House Hotel.'

Earlier that year a 'Greek Week' had been organised at the Garden House, with support from the Colonels' fascist regime. There was a student demonstration and violence broke out when protestors invaded a dinner and did some minor damage. Six students had been arrested, one of them Edwin's, and Edwin had stood bail.

'Ah yes,' said Miss Arnold, who was a Marxist and was pleased to have some political colour introduced. 'I had forgotten about the riots.'

During the course of the afternoon, it emerged that Miss Arnold was living with Al.

'I am not marrying him, Violet. Of course he is very keen.' They had repaired to Vi's bedroom, where Miss Arnold was repacking her body tightly into Annie's leathers.

'You don't want to marry him?'

'I don't want to marry. Quite another matter. I hope you will never make the mistake of marrying, Violet.'

Mrs Viney, when Vi went to say goodbye to her director of studies, offered calmer congratulations. She suggested that with a first – 'a very decent one, I am told, Viola' – Vi would be considered favourably for a postgraduate research grant. 'I always knew you had it in you when you made those clever observations about Sterne in your entrance paper. Sterne would make an excellent topic for a thesis. So few women seem to grasp the humour of Sterne.'

'You need a Bunbury,' Edwin suggested when Vi recounted this conversation.

'What do you mean?'

'As in *The Importance of Being Earnest*.'

'Yes, I do know where Bunbury comes from.'

'So, then. You need an alibi, though as a matter of fact I don't see why you should have any need to explain yourself to a woman who after three years doesn't even know your name.'

'It's my fault,' Vi said. 'I never corrected her at the start. It's because of Honour. People call me Honour, get confused and then no one gets Violet right.'

'Where did "Honour" come from?'

'She was my mother's mother. Her father called all his children after the virtues.'

'Whatever they are!'

'My great-aunts were Mercy, Charity and Prudence.'

'Lucky there wasn't another girl or she might have been Chastity.'

'I think there was but she died.'

'I hope you are making that up!'

Vi said she thought not.

'Poor child probably died of prospective shame. People underestimate the power of names. Anyway, do a Bunbury on Viney. Tell her that you have an important editing job.'

'I suppose I do, in a way.'

'Dead right. I need your good ear and shrewd judgement.'

Even after all this time, Vi, who could not get used to being needed, was still capable of blushing. Edwin went on as if he had not noticed. 'You'd be useless at research anyhow. You can't even use the university library.'

'That's not fair. You wouldn't know if I hadn't said.'

'When has "fair" been anything to do with anything? We are talking about what is the case. Anyway, I loathe writing my thesis.'

'You never write it.'

'That's principally what I loathe about it. But for reasons of sheer selfishness I want you to stay on here. And, by the way, your Miss Arnold is quite right about *Tristram Shandy*.'

A gust of wind through the open doors of the cabin sent Vi looking for something warm to put on, and the interruption led to a feeling that she was in need of tea. If only she had thought to pack her travel kettle as Annie had advised.

Opening the door of her cabin, she saw Renato, who almost sprinted towards her. 'Renato, you couldn't find me a kettle, could you? So I could make tea in my room?'

'I will look for you, Mrs Hetherington. I am sure I can find one.'

'That would be very kind.'

'You need tea now, Mrs Hetherington? I bring you some in your room?'

'No, thank you, Renato. You know, I think I shall go down to the King Edward and watch the dancing.'

11

The critic, with Kimberley Crane hard on his heels, wandered into the King Edward Lounge as George was announcing, 'Are we all ready, ladies and gentlemen? Remember the man leads. No women's lib on the dance floor . . .'

'Delicious.' The critic looked about with mild approving eyes. 'It makes one feel that civilisation has not entirely died.'

Kimberley Crane was overtaken by a thought. 'Would you like to dance?'

'So charming of you but, alas, my heart . . . But let me not stand in your way.'

'No, no,' said Kimberley hastily. 'I didn't want to be a spoilsport.'

'How could you be?' asked the critic. 'Shall we order? While I may be denied the pleasures of dancing there are still cakes and ale.' He snapped his fingers at Boris, who, recognising a fellow whim of iron, stepped over smartly. 'Some of those exquisite sandwiches and a pot of Ceylon for me, please.'

Boris turned the blue enquiring gaze on Kimberley Crane. 'None for me, thanks. Tea gives me a headache. And no sandwiches or cake either. I'm strictly gluten-free.'

'Anything else I could fetch for you, madam?' Boris made a respectful-seeming bow.

'A brandy.'

'Any special brandy that madam would like?'

'A double, with a dry ginger.'

'And not so much of the ginger?' murmured the critic, apparently to himself.

'Pardon?'

'A quote,' said the critic. 'They drop two a penny from my lips.'

The band had begun to play 'Moonlight Becomes You' when Vi entered and was spotted by the critic, who waved at her across the room.

'Come and join us. We are but auditors at the spectacle but you perhaps are an actor if you see cause . . . ?'

Boris, arriving with a tray of tea, two plates of assorted sandwiches, a bottle of ginger ale and a balloon of brandy, set them with exaggerated deference on the table. He bowed to Vi and turned on her the interrogating blue.

'Tea, madam? Darjeeling, Assam, Ceylon, orange pekoe, oolong, Lapsang, Earl Grey, Lady Grey, Russian Caravan or herbal?'

'Thank you. Just ordinary builder's, please.'

'Builder's?' Boris frowned.

'English breakfast,' said Vi, relenting.

The dancers stumbled, strode or glided by as the critic made delighted little interjections. 'See that divine green sequinned frock. My maternal aunt had one just like it. And do look, flowers in the hair. I may be mistaken but I think they might be pansies . . .'

'I'm going to be a bad girl and break my diet,' Kimberley Crane said. 'Can you pass the sandwiches?'

'Certainly,' said the critic, handing her an almost empty plate.

'So sorry, the other, with the cucumber.'

Her sorrow was misapplied. 'I'm afraid I have eaten all the cucumber. I cannot recommend the egg.'

Boris, arriving with Vi's tea, reported that due to unexpected demand the cucumber sandwiches had run out.

'Not even for ready money,' sighed the critic. 'Forgive me, I must be away. I am told that there is a napkin-folding class on Deck Six and I am anxious not to miss a second of it.' He made off with a surprising turn of speed through the tea-tables.

'D'you think he wanted to get away from us?' Kimberley was lifting the bread lids of the relics of the sandwiches, inspecting the fillings.

'Oh I am sure not,' Vi said, untruthfully.

'His trouble is he thinks he's somebody.'

'I suppose we all are, in a way.'

'I wanted to talk to him about an idea I have for a play but he felt threatened, I could tell. People are threatened by creativity.'

'You think so?'

'God, this egg mayo is disgusting. My nutritionist will murder me.'

'Perhaps you needn't mention it.'

'Oh, I tell Karen everything. She's psychic. She thinks I may be too.'

'How nice for you.'

'You might be psychic. Lots of people are without knowing it.'

'Heavens, I hope not,' Vi said.

'I must get going. I'm booked for a massage. The masseur walks on you with bare feet. You have fun, now.'

Vi, left to herself, did have fun. She was enjoying watching the down-at-heels band and the hesitant, elderly dancers in their unaccustomed high heels and spangled frocks and hoped that they were also enjoying themselves.

To Mrs Viney's disappointment, Vi did not embark on a thesis on Sterne. As editing *Mustardseed* could hardly support her financially, she took a job as a gallery attendant at the Fitzwilliam Museum. This allowed plenty of time for reflection, since, as Vi reported to Edwin after the first day, the work involved nothing more demanding than keeping an eye open for unsupervised children, art thieves and lunatics with penknives (with only the first posing any real threat to the peace and quiet of the museum).

She struck lucky and after a few weeks was posted by Samuel Palmer's watercolour *The Magic Apple Tree*. Her working days were spent sitting in the Palmer Room, shrouded for conservation purposes from the everyday sun, with the six black-faced sheep, drowsing under the heavily laden boughs of the prodigal tree, for company. With little to occupy her outer sight, her eyes, in the dimness, drank in the painting's astonishing light and hallucinatory colours: pale gold, gold, marigold, viridian, vermillion, crimson, russet, indigo . . .

The strange anomalous spire, which lent to the painting its air of another world dramatically impinging on this one, became, as she narrowed her eyes, a pathway leading through the fields filled with stooks of ripened corn, over the hills and far beyond.

One evening she and Edwin looked up the psalm that Palmer in his diary suggested had inspired the painting: *The pastures are clothed with flocks; the valleys also are covered over with corn; they shout for joy, they also sing.*

It was, as Edwin remarked, an atmosphere which led naturally to wool-gathering.

* * *

'Mrs Hetherington, oh, please forgive me!'

She had started and almost spilt her tea. 'I'm so sorry, Dino. I was in another world.'

'Happy thoughts, I hope.'

'Maybe.'

'You must only think of happy things, Mrs Hetherington.'

'I'm afraid that is hardly possible, Dino.'

'Will you dance? That will make me very happy. It's the waltz next.'

'That's probably the only dance I can manage.'

'No, no, Mrs Hetherington. I will teach you. Oh, look at your silver shoes.'

'You like them? A friend gave them to me.' Annie would be pleased at her shoes' success.

'They are shoes to dance to the moon in.'

'Dino, really!' But she was laughing.

When Vi got back to her cabin she flopped down on top of the polythene-wrapped dry cleaning which had been laid out on the bed. Renato would have been piqued. If he called by again she must have been oblivious, for by the time she came to, it was too late for dinner at the Alexandria.

She went down, dressed as she was in her jersey and skirt and Annie's silver shoes, to the Bistro, the most unassuming of the ship's restaurants, and ate an omelette and a green salad and drank a glass of white wine, reflecting.

After that first encouragement of Edwin's, other poems, like migratory birds, began to arrive. They alighted in her mind, as she walked to work across Sheep's Green, by the Fen Causeway, or sat in a daze by Samuel Palmer's visionary sheep. Often, very early in the morning, between sleep and waking, she became aware of some unformed presence hovering at the edges of her mind and got out of bed to catch a word or phrase.

Sometimes she used to fancy that it was her mother sending the poems from whatever region she had departed to.

'Why not?' Edwin asked, when she confided this. 'Alph the sacred river runs through caverns measureless to man.'

But rivers dry up, or you lose the way to them.

On the way out of the Bistro, she met the critic. 'Taking an evening off? I've been playing hooky too. The food here's not bad.' He sounded almost human.

'How was the napkin-folding class?'

'Have you any idea what can be done with a table napkin? The Buffet Fold, the Bishop's Hat, the Tuxedo and the Elf's Boot are but a few examples of the art. I am particularly taken with the Elf's Boot. I shall never be able to look without guilt at an unfolded napkin again. How was the dancing?'

'Not bad either.'

'Did you take to the floor?'

'Amazingly I did.'

He nodded approvingly. Vi noticed that behind his glasses his eyes looked tired. 'Gather ye rosebuds while ye may . . .'

'Not very proficiently gathered.'

'If a thing's worth doing it's worth doing badly. Do you feel like a stroll?'

'If you like.'

Up on deck, the critic linked his arm companionably through hers and they set off around the ship, which was almost unpeopled since most of the passengers were busily feeding inside. The moon was sculling behind a racing cloud and had flung around its margin a sinister yellow glow. The critic on Vi's arm was so small and light that he felt like a child.

Other than 'Do call me Colin' he said nothing and seemed content to walk in silence.

At the bow of the ship, however, he stopped and stood looking out over the darkly reflecting water. 'Have you ever considered drowning?'

'Considered what about it?'

'Drowning yourself.'

Vi thought. 'Not drowning, no.'

'I have.'

'Yes?' The admission seemed to demand some form of intimacy in return but it seemed impossible to call him Colin.

'The sea is here. It is, to all intents and purposes, bottomless. Why not immerse oneself in it for eternity and have done?' It was evident that his apparent calm masked a far stormier temperament.

'I've thought about death,' Vi said. Privately, she believed that anyone sensible had. 'But not by drowning. I've heard it's supposed to be very painful.' She had once read an account by a sailor, who had all but drowned but was saved at the eleventh hour, of the excruciating pain he had felt in his windpipe as he went under. She began to recount this but the critic interrupted.

'Oh, pain. Everything is pain.'

Vi understood that conversation was superfluous. It was best during encounters of this kind to say as little as possible.

'No,' said the critic, as if contradicting her, though in deference to his mood she had remained silent. 'I am not a melancholic.'

Vi nodded, hoping that the gesture in the dark would be sufficient.

'In fact, I am a sanguine soul at heart.'

Recalling his vicious reviews Vi doubted that this was the

whole case. She stood beside him, looking out into the obliterating dark.

After some minutes, the fit of melancholy seemed to leave him and they carried on walking, Annie's shoes gleaming like phosphorescent fishes under the ship's few lights. It was growing chilly. Vi shivered as a faint whining hum set up along the ship's cables.

'Do you have family?' the critic asked suddenly.

'I have two sons.'

'And you like them?'

'Very much.'

'Any husband?'

For a wild moment, Vi wondered if he was about to propose to her. She had heard of such anomalies occurring at sea.

'My second husband, the boys' father, died last year.'

'And the first? Is he still with us?'

'I don't know,' Vi said. It wasn't quite true. She was sure that if Bruno had died she would have heard.

'I am also estranged from my first wife.'

'Yes?'

'My own fault. I made an unwise marriage. My third wife was jealous of the previous two wives, who had become great friends. It has created a distance between the three of us. My third wife is a professional hater of men.'

'I'm sorry.' She felt for anyone who had been hated by their spouse.

'I am too,' said the critic. 'But we live and learn.'

Vi, who doubted this was the case, held her tongue.

'You see,' the critic began, 'when I was a younger man I . . .'

A rogue wave smacked against the side of the ship, which rocked violently under the impact, almost toppling the pair of them over on top of each other.

The critic, hanging on to Vi's arm, righted himself, took off his glasses and polished the lenses with a handkerchief. 'Shall we go back inside?'

'It might be best.'

They dragged themselves with some effort through a stubborn door into the warmth and noise.

'Can I get you a drink?' He looked more vulnerable with his hair damp and disarrayed.

Vi, touched by some half appeal in his eyes, was about to accept but hardened her heart. 'I won't, if you don't mind, Colin. I've things to do.'

'You are lucky,' said the critic. 'It is good to be occupied. There are times when I wonder where my occupation's gone. But thank you for our walk. I enjoyed it.'

12

The bed had been turned down, the dry cleaning stripped of its polythene and hung neatly in the wardrobe and the two squares of chocolate placed on the bed with military precision when Vi returned to her cabin. After her late nap, she was not at all sleepy but she changed into her nightdress and put on socks to warm her chilled feet. She wanted to go on reading the notebooks.

'You know what,' Edwin said one evening after she had given him a poem to read over a curry, 'you'll soon have enough poems for a collection.'

Vi had made friends with Mr Jarvis, a taciturn stallholder in the market, who, at the end of the day, donated any vegetables that would be past selling the next. On the days when Mr Jarvis's discards included chillies and peppers, Vi cooked curry.

'They aren't nearly good enough.'

'I disagree. This curry is excellent, by the way. If all else fails, you could always start a take-away. But against that day, would you let me put the poems together for you?'

'If you like.'

'I do like.'

Mustardseed was selling surprisingly well and Edwin's

morale had been given a further boost by a contract with Faber for his own poetry. He went through Vi's poems making detailed suggestions, most of which she followed.

One evening, when she arrived home from work with a tray of aging haricot beans, courtesy of Mr Jarvis, Edwin met her in triumph. 'They are going to publish you in a collection of new poets. Welcome to a life of drunkenness and penury.'

'Hardly "welcome". I've been living that life for the past few years.'

'Don't be a kill-joy. Aren't you pleased?'

'Yes.'

'Well, don't go overboard.'

'I'm just taking it in.'

'Take it in with this.'

He handed her a glass of whisky. It struck Vi that there had been rather more glasses of whisky lately.

'What name will you use?' he asked that same evening, opening a second bottle of wine.

'Ed, do we really need any more to drink?'

'For Christ's sake, Violet!'

'Sorry. I just thought.'

' "Oh reason not the need . . ." '

'OK, I'm sorry.'

There was a pause during which they both tried to think of conversation.

'So what name will you write under?'

'What's wrong with my own name?'

'Don't be obtuse. Your name is capable of several variations. You could be, for example, Violet St John, Honour St John, Violet Honour St John.'

'Honour Violet.'

'You *cannot* have Violet as a surname. It sounds sub-Christina Rossetti.'

'No, I mean I'm Honour Violet St John, not Violet Honour.'

Edwin poured them both more wine. Vi could see that it was going to be a Persian evening. 'How about H.V. St John?' he suggested.

So it was as H.V. St John that she wrote.

'Mrs Hetherington! Coo-ee, Mrs Hetherington!'

'Renato. I'm in bed.'

'I have a kettle for you, Mrs Hetherington.'

'OK, Renato, I'm coming.'

Renato was outside, proudly bearing a laden tray.

'A kettle, Mrs Hetherington. I also find you teapot, tea bags and some fresh milk, skimmed in this jug, and in here full fat.'

Renato sped across the room, laid the tea things out on the desk and stowed the jugs of milk in the fridge.

'Now! Here is the kettle so you have tea when you want.'

'Thank you so much, Renato.' She felt him not quite liking to look at her socks. They were Ted's socks and too big for her. But they were new when he died and warm and she had not wanted to throw them out.

'I have brought you an adaptor, too.'

'Renato, you are an angel.'

'Thank you, Mrs Hetherington.'

When Vi was quite sure there would be no more angelic recurrences she locked the door, put on the kettle and made tea in the chrome-plated teapot. The tea tasted good. Builder's tea. Somehow Renato had divined what kind she liked. In its way, it was a kind of genius.

13

'Bruno,' Edwin announced, 'is a kind of genius.'

They were eating a supper of baked courgettes, tomatoes, onions and cheese. Vi was by now an experienced vegetable cook. They had never wasted much of the household purse on meat. Fish made the place stink, she preferred vegetables and if there was any money over Edwin would spend it on drink.

They were discussing the autumn edition of the magazine and Edwin had passed her some pages to read.

'What do you think of those?'

Vi read the poems. They were long and somewhat convoluted. 'I don't know. They seem . . .' She considered. She had been going to say 'a bit mannered' but instead asked, 'What do you think?'

'They're by a friend of mine.'

She looked at the name. No one Edwin had mentioned. 'Bruno Shilling? Who is he?'

Which was when Edwin made the remark.

'Bruno is a kind of genius.'

Vi ignored this. 'How do you know him?'

'We were at school together. He's one of my oldest friends.'

'If he's a friend and you like his poems of course it's fine by me to put them in. You're the editor.'

'But I rely on your judgement.'

'OK, in my judgement it's fine to publish poems by your friend.'

'You don't like them?'

'I didn't say so.'

'Well, but do you?'

'They are not my kind of thing,' Vi said cautiously. 'But that doesn't mean they are not good. Miss Arnold doesn't like Milton, remember?'

A week or so after the autumn issue of *Mustardseed* was out, Edwin said, 'By the way, Bruno's coming to stay.'

'Your friend?'

'If that's OK.'

'Of course it is. It's your house.'

'No it isn't. We share it. Anyway, it's not mine, I rent it from Ralph.'

'I can't imagine minding any friend of yours.'

'You might,' Edwin said. 'You didn't like his poems. You might not like him either. Almost everyone thinks him charming.'

When Vi returned from work that day a big-boned man with green eyes was reading the *New Statesman* on the sofa. The visitor got up to greet her, holding out a large hand. For all his bulk he moved surprisingly gracefully. 'I am Bruno.'

'Hello. I'm Violet.' She allowed her hand to be held rather longer than she liked.

'So I've been told.'

To her annoyance, the interloper carried her hand to his lips and kissed it.

'Are you in for supper?' Surreptitiously, she wiped her hand on her skirt behind her back.

'If it is no trouble.'

This was annoying too. 'I made plenty enough for three.'

Over supper, Bruno explained that he didn't drink.

'Why not?'

'Because it is a threat to my mental powers, which I value more than mere hedonistic pleasures.'

Vi could not help noticing that Bruno's abstinence made Edwin drink more than usual. He repeated the remark that had annoyed her the first time. 'Bruno is a genius.' Having met the man, it struck her as particularly absurd.

'In what way is he a genius?'

'He spellbinds people.'

Vi looked at Bruno. You may have spellbound Edwin, she thought, but you won't spellbind me.

Bruno, pouring himself water, said, 'It's Edwin's little joke. I've been studying so-called witch doctors for some years. Edwin calls them spellbinders. This here is a very charming jug.'

Vi was taken aback, though whether by the witch doctors or the remark about the jug she could not perhaps have said. 'The jug was my mother's. I gave it to her when I was nine.'

'You had taste as a child, then.'

'Tell her about the sorcerers.' Edwin was now more obviously drunk.

'And your mother . . . ?' Bruno, ignoring Edwin, was looking at her attentively with his disturbing green eyes.

Vi got up from the table and began to clear away. Going out to the kitchen, she called back, 'Would you like some grapes? I get them free from a disobliging man in the market.'

After dinner, Bruno was very attentive in clearing the table.

He offered to dry up and squeezed into the kitchen beside Vi, who washed up with unusual ferocity. The following day he walked with her to the Fitzwilliam on his way to the station.

'What happened to your mother?'

Vi, who at best didn't like conversation too early in the day, was thrown by this.

'Why do you ask?'

'Ed said she died.'

This was doubly aggravating. Edwin was not usually a blabber. 'Yes,' she said curtly. 'She died.'

'Of cancer?'

'Yes.' Inwardly cursing Edwin she asked pointedly, 'Hadn't you better hurry? What time's your train?'

'I allowed plenty of time,' Bruno said. 'I allowed enough to walk you to work.'

It seemed too churlish to continue being openly hostile. Vi asked some token questions about his time in Africa, and with Bruno recounting anecdotes they made it to the Fitzwilliam without any further unpleasantness.

But that evening she said, 'Ed, I wish you hadn't spoken about my mother like that.'

'Like what?'

'To Bruno.'

Edwin looked surprised. 'He asked me about her. Bruno's got an uncanny intuition. He probably guessed you're an orphan.'

'I'm not an orphan. I have one living parent.'

'Not a very salient one. You might as well be orphaned. I don't know why you're being so touchy. It's not a secret, is it?'

'It's private. I don't like people I don't know knowing too much about me.'

'Isn't that a bit paranoid?'

'It isn't at all,' Vi said, hurt that Edwin, who usually understood her so readily, should be so obtuse. 'It's self-protection.'

Edwin laughed and said, 'Oh, I think you're fairly safe with Bruno.'

'I didn't imagine I wasn't safe,' Vi said coldly. She supposed Bruno was one of his lovers but she couldn't have explained why she felt suddenly so put out.

14

Vi lay on the wide bed, feeling the tip and roll of the ship and the churning engines rumble through her body. Fugitive images flittered through her mind. Edwin drunk. Edwin with a hangover. Edwin sitting holding her hand after he had thrown up. Edwin pacing their sitting room, speaking his poems under his breath to hear the rhythm. Edwin the night they quarrelled – their first real row.

Bruno had been with them almost seven weeks. He had announced the evening before, over supper, which was now routinely the three of them, that he would be staying over in London that night, with an old friend, Tessa Carfield. All day Vi had been rehearsing, to the indifferent ears of Samuel Palmer's sheep, what to say to Edwin: Ed, he's your friend and I understand that so perhaps I had better go. Or, simply, Edwin, I think it is time I moved out – or on?

But of course when it came to it none of these things were said.

'Why must you have him here? I loathe him, Ed. Sorry, I just do.' She saw his eyes flicker for a second.

'"Loathe", Vi?'

'Loathe. Sorry, Ed.'

' "Loathe" is a big word.'

'Sorry.'

'I didn't know.'

'You must have guessed.' He had done. She was sure of it.

'I suppose I hoped I was wrong.'

'When have you ever been wrong about me, Ed?'

The ship made a sudden dive into the Atlantic and her glasses, with the notebook, slid off the counterpane. Vi got out of bed and in Ted's large woollen socks padded out on to the balcony.

An eerie light, thrown out by the ship's greenish dimmed lamps, lay diffused over the steel folds of water. It was very quiet. There was barely any sound save for the low lap of the waves, the thrum of the engines and the occasional distant crackle of a disembodied voice. Way down below a glass or a bottle broke and someone shrieked with laugher and then fell silent.

Vi padded back inside and put on Renato's kettle. Had she meant what she had said to Edwin during the row? Impossible now to say. What she recalled was the look in his odd eyes.

'Ed, what *is* it about Bruno? I don't understand. Ralph doesn't like him either.'

'What's he done to Ralph?'

She had come home one evening to hear Bruno's voice raised and Ralph, she noticed, had not spoken to Bruno since.

'They had some argument, I don't know what about. But Ralph is the most pacific of men. Or women, if it comes to that. I can't imagine getting into a fight with Ralph.'

'They weren't fighting, were they?'

'Not physically.'

'Bruno's my friend.' Edwin's eyes betrayed some hidden appeal.

'I don't think I can live with him. Not for much longer, anyhow. I'd better leave.'

'You can't leave, Vi.'

'I can't live here with you and Bruno, Ed.'

It was hard to put her finger on exactly what was wrong except that their old way of life had been set by the ears. Bruno, to all appearances, behaved beautifully: he drank nothing but water, told humorous, even witty, anecdotes, made Edwin laugh and painstakingly converted his bed each morning back into a sofa. He pursued topics of conversation with the kind of energetic advocacy which in another man she would have found appealing. But for all that – or was it because of it? – she neither liked nor trusted him. It troubled her that for once she and Edwin did not agree.

One evening in November, when the wind off the watersodden fens was blowing colder than usual, she came home from work with a newspaper full of leeks. Tough, outsized leeks with dirty hanging roots, from Mr Jarvis. And a head of equally earthy celery and some wizened beetroots. Bruno was lying on the sofa in the warm sitting room, his feet up, reading *The Listener*.

'You should be running a health farm,' he said, watching her put down the vegetables to take off her coat and boots. 'And you ought to be wearing gloves.'

A formless Cambridge had lain all day under a tissue of freezing fog, and her hands were senseless red lumps of jointed cold.

'I've lost my gloves. Or I've lost one of the pair.'

He had a way of watching her. 'Wear one, then. You can put the other hand in your pocket.'

It was an Edwinish sort of remark but coming from someone who wasn't Edwin it irked her. 'I can't be bothered.'

The phone rang. Vi, answering it with frozen hands, dropped the phone and picking it up heard nothing for a second and then recognised the tetchy voice at the other end of the phone. 'Dad?'

'Who is that?'

'It's Honour, Dad.'

Her father was the only person, since her mother's death, who called Vi by her first name. It was perhaps, Vi thought, his way of denouncing the woman who had so selfishly deserted him.

'Honour? Why are you there?'

'You rang my number.'

'No, I didn't. I rang my dentist.'

'Well, you got through to me.'

'How very odd,' her father in exasperation had said and rung off.

She had gone wordlessly into the kitchen and put the dirty vegetables into the sink and run water over them hard so that the noise would be a screen between herself and Bruno. When she emerged, her face red from the effort of suppressing tears and anger, her hands redder still from the cold water, Bruno was standing in the sitting room, just as she had left him.

'Violet?'

'Yes?'

'Why don't you like me, Violet St John?'

'Who said I didn't?'

'Your truthful grey eyes. Honour Violet St John?'

'Yes?'

'H.V. St John?'

'What?'

'You've been crying.'

'I haven't.'

But then she did cry, long and hard.

When Edwin came in, Vi was in the bath. She took longer than usual over it and the three of them ate supper late, leek-and-celery soup and baked beetroots, with cream from the week before that had soured. Vi was unusually polite to Bruno. Neither of them said much during the meal and it was Edwin who talked. As soon as supper was over Vi went straight to bed. She made sure that she left early for work the next morning.

That evening when she came home Edwin informed her that Bruno was moving out.

'Where's he going?'

'To a friend's.'

'Oh, he has another friend, does he?'

'I suppose you'll be glad he is going?'

She had gone to their pub and bought cigarettes, a brand which existed no longer and which, she suddenly remembered, were in a red packet which bore on it the face of a bearded sailor, like a youthful version of Captain Ryle. After that evening she had begun to smoke seriously.

She was visited by a tremendous urge to smoke now. Her smoking had worried Ted, and because it was something she could do for him (with so much that it seemed she couldn't) she had given up. But Ted was dead and could no longer be worried by her.

Crew were forbidden to use the outer passenger decks except while on duty but on the whole Tim Troubridge, the crew purser, who was a fair man, turned a blind eye. Des liked to prowl there late at night, when discovery was unlikely but the slight possibility gave the excursions an edge. He was treading quietly along Deck Three, skirting the dark outline of a shape on one of the benches where a tiny point of light signalled someone trying to light a match.

The quiet voice made him start. 'Excuse me, but have you a light? These matches keep going out.'

'Mrs Hetherington?'

'Who is that?'

'It's me, Mrs Hetherington. Dino.'

'Oh, it's you!' She sounded relieved.

'Here.' He found his lighter and lit her cigarette.

'Would you like one?'

'We aren't supposed to be on the passenger decks.'

'Don't get into trouble on my account.'

'I will have one, if you don't mind. I often come out here. No one notices.'

Des could smell her perfume, Mitsouko, he thought. Unable to find a way into a conversation, he was turning over in his mind possible approaches when she spoke.

'Have you been on the ship long?'

'Four years this May.'

'You like it, then?'

'It's a job.'

'But you do like dancing?'

'Yeah.'

'Where are you from, Dino?'

He had dropped his Italian accent along with his guard. Best to turn the slip to advantage.

'Leicester. But don't tell anyone. They all think I'm Italian.'

'Who would I tell?'

Her voice sounded frosty and he was afraid that he had offended her.

'I'm not really called Dino.'

'No?'

'My real name's Desmond. Des, I was called at home.'

'Ah.'

She did not seem very interested so the honesty was wasted. He tried again. 'My father was Italian so I . . .'

'You know, I've often thought that we married women are lucky because we have the chance to borrow another name.'

'You are married?' She had that big diamond on her ring finger. Whoever had given her that had made sure that it showed.

'My husband died last year.'

'I'm sorry.'

'I'm afraid I wasn't. Or – well, not enough. Does that sound harsh?'

'Not at all.' In spite of himself, he was shocked.

'I didn't love him, you see.'

'Oh. But I expect . . .' He began what he hoped might emerge as words of comfort but she interrupted.

'I married him after I was married to someone else. He was kind – and I was in need of kindness. But it wasn't really fair on him. Are you married?'

'No.'

'Have you ever been?'

'No.' He was used to being the interrogator, not the interrogated.

'Very sensible. It doesn't solve anything. People imagine it will solve their problems, not seeing that it becomes the problem.' She finished her cigarette and tossed the glowing butt over the rail. 'My teacher told me not to marry. It was the one piece of advice of hers that I never took.'

Des said, not really intending to, 'My mother wasn't married when she had me.'

'Did you mind?' At this she did sound interested.

'I didn't know until I was nearly eighteen. I always thought my grandmother was my mother.'

'You must have minded that.'

'My mother was only a kid herself when she had me, so my grandmother and grandfather brought me up as theirs. It was all right.' And it had been, till his mother had dropped her bombshell.

'How did you find out?'

'She told me. My real mother did. I'd always thought she was my aunty.' Des chucked his cigarette end over the railing to join hers. 'I never liked her much.' He'd never liked her at all. 'Her older sister died, so I guess that maybe didn't help.'

'That must have been difficult.'

'I guess. And for my gran. She looked like she was a lovely girl, my Aunty Mel.' There was a picture of her, a smiling girl with long blonde hair. He had climbed up so often to look at it on the chest of drawers in the bedroom of the woman he had thought his mother.

'Another cigarette?'

'Well . . . ?'

'I shan't give you away.'

'You're sure you don't mind?'

'I don't mind.'

Side by side, they smoked in silence. Sitting so close and smelling her perfume, Des became nervous. The old Des seemed to have returned with his unexpected revelation and taken away his confidence. What did she want? He couldn't tell.

'I'm here, on the ship, I mean,' her low voice came out of the dark beside him, 'in order to visit someone I've not seen for years. He lives in New York.'

So that was it. She was looking up an old flame. Well, she still might fancy a fling on the way. Get herself in practice.

'Are you getting off at New York, then?' The *Caroline* docked for three days in New York, where some passengers left the ship while others joined those who had returned to continue the cruise to Acapulco and beyond.

'I might. Or I might come back on board and go on with the voyage. I've not decided.'

'You've paid for the whole trip?' This suggested unusual wealth.

'Yes. I wanted to keep my options open. It's sheer self-indulgence, I know, especially in these times. But it *is* one of the advantages of having no ties. You can do, more or less, as you like. You must know that yourself.'

'That takes money.' The unintended frankness had spilled out and in the dark he flushed.

'Yes, I know I'm lucky. My husband was not what used to be called a millionaire – heaven knows what it's known as nowadays – but he was well off. He left me, not a fortune but enough money to do, within reason, for a while anyway, what I like.'

'And what do you like?' He had spoken unthinkingly and he felt himself flushing again.

'Maybe not what I thought I liked.' She moved the hand holding the cigarette and he saw a crinkle of light reflecting in the facets of the large diamond.

'You're left-handed?'

'Yes.'

'Me too. We're fellow southpaws.'

'My mother was ambidextrous – she could use either hand equally well. I used to love watching her write my name with first one hand and then the other.'

105

She still had a piece of paper with her mother's writing on it: *Honour Violet St John (right hand)* almost perfectly replicated as *Honour Violet St John (left hand).*

'My father must have been the left-handed one,' Des said. 'The Claybournes are all right-handed. But I can't check. I never met him. And not likely to now.'

'You could find him.'

'My mother wasn't even sure of his first name. Anyway, he wouldn't want to know me. He's probably got a fat wife and eleven kids. Probably had them already when he was having it off with my mother.'

'You don't know. We don't really know much about other people.'

'Maybe.'

'Forgive me, I'm lecturing you and all you wanted was peace and quiet after a hard day with people like me.' She got up and with an almost violent gesture flung her unfinished cigarette into the water.

'No, no. It's good to talk.' He couldn't bring himself to say what was in his mind, which was that she wasn't at all like the other 'people'.

'I'm off to bed but perhaps I'll see you tomorrow. Maybe you'll teach me a new dance.'

'Of course, if you like.'

He thought he heard her laugh as she walked away, and as he stood, still smoking, watching her, a shade moving into the shadow along the side of the ship, he saw something glinting on the deck by the rail.

15

Vi's hands were cold from her stay on deck, and back in her cabin she shook the rings from her fingers. They slid off easily and she scooped them into a little glittering heap on the desk by the notebooks while she ran a bath.

Most of the suites were equipped only with showers but Vi had requested one of the few with baths. She had always had a preference for soaking. She got into the bath and lay back, relishing the almost too hot water in which her limbs were immersed. She inspected them now. Her legs were still in pretty good shape. Not that there was anyone to enjoy them nowadays.

'Does Edwin know?' Bruno asked.

Vi's legs were wrapped around his back and she was smoking. It wasn't easy to smoke lying under Bruno's bulk but neither of them was willing to move. She attempted to lock her ankles together while she stretched out for a receptacle for her toppling ash but Bruno's back was too broad and their knit-together bodies toppled over. 'Ouch. You're squashing me. I don't think so.'

'Why haven't you told him?'

'I don't want to yet.'

'Why not? Here, have this saucer.'

'Bruno, you know why.'

Bruno had rented a damp flat at the top of a house in a street off London's Portobello Road, where Vi had begun to visit him most weekends. He had found work organising lecture programmes for the British Council while he wrote a book based on his research on Vodun sorcerers.

He lectured Vi on the topic while in bed. She was, as she remarked, a captive audience.

'Vodun is an entirely benign religion, remarkably like Catholicism, which is why the missionaries were so successful. The element of sorcery is minor. Hollywood loves it, of course.'

Vi's mother had been a churchgoer and therefore religion had been one of the many taboo subjects with her father. 'How is it like Catholicism?'

'Both have one supreme being, both have saints, that is to say venerable beings whose lives have purified their souls so that they enter the heavenly sphere and have influence on the lives of the living, and of course they eat meat and drink blood as part of their sacred ritual.'

'But Christians don't drink real blood,' Vi objected. This seemed to annoy Bruno so she dropped the subject.

When they finally disentangled and got out of bed dark was gathering outside and the streetlights were beginning to glow orange. She began to prepare supper. 'We're out of butter. I'll pop out and get some.'

'We don't need butter.'

'Why not?'

'Butter's bad for you. It'll make you fat.'

Vi said, 'I don't think I'll get fat, I never do, or not so far, and you can't make a white sauce without butter. Anyway, we need wine.'

She returned from the Polish grocer's on the corner with butter, a mammoth jar of pickled cucumbers and a bottle of red wine. 'I do like Vlodek, he's so gloomy. Did you know he'd lost his left foot from gangrene?' She was unwrapping thin brown tissue from the bottle of wine which was Romanian, or of some other indecipherable Eastern European origin.

Bruno said, 'You drink too much.'

Vi, who had been wondering whether this was so, at once turned defiant. 'I don't.'

'It's living with Edwin. You should be careful – it will affect your liver. In any case, you shouldn't drink that rotgut.'

Vi opened the wine, rather ineptly as Bruno's corkscrew was past its best, and downed a couple of glasses in the kitchen while ostensibly grating cheese. There were no wine glasses, so she drank from a tumbler which meant that by the time she served the macaroni cheese she had drunk nearly half the bottle. Perhaps it was the familiar sensation of being slightly drunk, but for the first time she was aware of missing Edwin.

She had told Edwin she was visiting Annie, who was having 'man trouble'. This was indeed the case. The usually efficient Annie was pregnant by an Italian shoe buyer from Milan, who had shown no intention of leaving his wealthy wife.

The phone rang and Bruno answered it. 'Edwin, *amigo*! I was just thinking about you.'

The phone receiver made a reciprocal amicable mumble.

'Nothing special. Whiling away the time with an old chum.' Bruno winked at Vi, who got up and went out of the room. She was making the bed when Bruno came in.

'He wants to come and stay next weekend.'

'What did you say?'

'I said I may have a friend staying.'

'I think he might be missing you,' Vi said, not quite recognising who was doing the missing. 'You're his oldest friend, Bruno. Let him come and see you. I'll stay put in Cambridge.'

But in fact, the following weekend she did visit Annie.

Annie had moved into a new flat near World's End, just off the King's Road, which she was sharing with her latest set of Australians.

'I wouldn't dream of sharing with any other nationality now, Vi. Certainly not the Brits. They use up all the toilet paper and then never replace it. Aussies are born flatmates.'

Annie's current Australians were off somewhere, apparently parachuting, so Annie and Vi had the place to themselves. Vi made a Hungarian goulash, as Annie, from living with Australians, was opposed to vegetarianism of any kind. 'It's fatal for one's teeth, Vi. One of my flatmates is a dental hygienist. Mandy says that teeth simply must have red meat or they drop out in old age.'

Vi opened a bottle of wine, hoping that this would produce no homilies from Annie. 'Are you drinking?'

'I'll say!'

'How did this happen, Annie?'

Annie explained that the shoe buyer was Catholic and had principles about contraception.

'But not adultery, it seems?'

'I don't think the Pope minds adultery.'

'I think he must do, Annie.'

'Well, not as much as murdering children.'

'I don't know that you can call contraception "murder".'

Annie said that in any case she had decided to have the kid. Michelangelo had agreed to support it. At least, his wife would.

'Goodness. Does she know?'

Annie said she thought not but that Michelangelo had a

personal allowance from his wife, which he had offered to share with her for the child.

'I must say that sounds a dodgy arrangement. Is he really called Michelangelo?'

'Michelangelo was a great painter, Vi. I would have thought you knew that.'

'Yes, of course I do. A sculptor too. But it doesn't sound quite right on a Milanese shoe buyer. Are you sure you want to go ahead with this, Annie?'

But Annie, usually so mindful of her material prospects, seemed to have succumbed to the ancient stealthy spirit of childbearing, which can take the most unlikely souls in thrall.

They spent the rest of the weekend happily trawling the King's Road, where the new-style boutiques, which had sprung up like mushrooms, had names so fanciful it was a job for the sign writers to compress them into the space of their tiny frontages. The boutiques were painted in psychedelic colours and from them issued strains of weird Eastern-sounding music and the dubious scent of joss sticks. The assistants of both sexes were long-haired and moody, high-handed to the point of rudeness to their customers, who responded by dropping the garments they didn't pinch on to the floors of the newly democratic communal changing rooms, to be trampled on by other hectic shoppers.

Vi and Annie visited Mad Meg Merrilies Marvellous Mittens, where gloves of no kind were to be found; also the Daughters of Jephthah, where Annie tried on a long red velvet smock with gold lace, tacked rather than sewn on, at the hem. 'What do you think?'

Vi said she thought it made her look Pre-Raphaelite.

'Yes, of course, that's the idea. But do I look pregnant?'

'I should think anyone would, wearing that.'

'Oh you are hopeless, Vi. Try on these trousers. They won't fit me for long but you could borrow them until.'

At Annie's insistence, Vi tried on a pair of blue velvet flares, very tight over the bottom. The zip was already coming away; a result of the rough handling from other customers. 'I don't think they suit me.'

Annie nevertheless stuffed the trousers into her bag.

It was more or less assumed by the entrepreneurs who had set up these shops that at least fifty per cent of the stock would be stolen and the mark-up for those wealthy, foolish or morally behind the times enough to pay for the shoddy goods reflected this. Annie asked one of the bored male assistants, wearing a tie-dyed caftan, if they had any gold tights to match the gold on the velvet dress, which she got out of the bag, where it was stashed, to show him. She was annoyed to hear that gold tights were out of stock and bagged away some silver mesh ones 'in lieu'.

Vi had to dissuade her from adding a set of Indian temple bells. 'They might have made a noise, Annie. They would have given you away.'

'So what? I'm pregnant, I can plead diminished responsibility. Who was Jephthah anyway and who were his daughters when they were at home?'

By this time, they were eating apple pie and ice cream in one of the smart coffee houses which were opening up on the King's Road. Annie had warned that due to her cravings she was prepared to kill for apple pie.

'So far as I know there was only one daughter, or only one you get to hear of,' Vi said. 'And the trouble was that she didn't stay at home. Jephthah promised to sacrifice to the Lord whatever he saw first if he was granted victory in battle, and the first thing he saw was his daughter, who ran out to greet him.'

'I suppose the old bastard kept his promise.' Annie licked her spoon mournfully.

Vi said she seemed to remember that the girl had insisted on it.

'If you believe that you'll believe anything,' Annie declared. 'Can you lend me half a crown, Vi? I'm desperate for more of that apple pie.'

On the Sunday evening Vi and Edwin met up at King's Cross and they travelled back to Cambridge together. Vi asked after his weekend.

'Fine. Bruno wanted to show me his poetry.'

'Oh. How are the witch doctors?'

'He didn't say. I think he's concentrating on the poems. How was Annie?'

Vi, who had not heard anything from Bruno about his poetry since he had left Cambridge, said that Annie had seemed unnaturally maternal. She did not mention the red smock or the trousers, which she had left behind with Annie, who was expecting a visit from Michelangelo. She did, however, refer to Jephthah. Edwin said that the story was the subject of a Handel oratorio. He said very little else for the rest of the journey and both immersed themselves in the Sunday papers.

They walked from the station through drizzling rain, along Hills Road, turning, at the Catholic church of Our Lady and the English Martyrs, down Lensfield Road. Going past the Polar Research Institute, Vi tried to play their usual game, which was to put words into the mouth of Scott, whose bust over the door commemorated the selfless explorer who had walked voluntarily to his own extinction. But nothing apt or amusing came to her and Edwin walked on beside her, seemingly oblivious.

When they got in, Edwin poured himself a glass of Teacher's.

'Vi, how would you feel if Bruno joined us in the editing of *Mustardseed*?'

'Why? Can I have one of those?'

'Sorry. I wasn't thinking. I think it might help him. He's at a bit of a loss with his poems.'

'What would it mean?'

'Only my going down to see him in London from time to time. I know you won't want him here.'

'I don't mind him coming here,' Vi said, drinking the whisky and feeling strangely angry at Edwin's oversight. 'I've got over that.'

The water was cooling and Vi heaved herself out of the bath, wrapped herself in one of the soft white towels and climbed, swaddled, into bed. She'd done this since she was a child. Usually it induced a profound and satisfying sleep.

Edwin and Bruno were still in her mind as if they had never left it. But that was the mind for you. Once in, nothing ever really left it again.

FOURTH DAY

To let the cat out of the bag: *The punishment for the most serious misdemeanours in the Royal Navy was flogging. This was administered using a whip called a 'cat o' nine tails'. The 'cat' was kept in a leather or baize bag.*

16

Vi woke in a fright. She lay still, uncertain where she was. Then the ship's horn let out a steady bittern's boom.

She was lying naked, sweating into a clammy bath towel. The room's thermostat had been turned full up, perhaps by Renato, but she had neglected to open the doors to the balcony, so the temperature had risen to an oppressive heat. She opened the door to a welcome flood of cold air and then went outside, wet with sweat, in her towel.

She had had a bad dream.

First, there was merely a miasma of vague dread. Then elements of the plot seeped back and clarified. She had killed somebody. And she had been arguing, with an unpersuadable presence, that it was not murder. It had been what in the dream she persisted in calling 'accidental murder', as though that were an explanation or an accepted legal term. She had buried, she seemed to think, the body in a thicket but now they were going to clear the land and her dreadful secret was about to be uncovered.

Still damp with sweat from the anxious dream, she unwrapped the towel and stood naked on the balcony, letting the cold air define her body.

Baz Lincoln had also passed a perturbed night. He and his

wife, Martha, had been rowing. As is the way with couples, their quarrels always ran along similar lines and boiled down to the fact that Martha was older than Baz and other women gave signs, more or less visibly, that they were ready to rescue him from what must surely be a youthful error and present source of regret. This, as Baz was tired as hell of pointing out, was hardly his fault. But fault has little, or nothing, to do with rows, which are generated by a clash of world views, which those who hold them expect, against all experience, to be compatible and which only occasionally, indeed rather rarely, coincide.

Martha had vomited after drinking, one by one, the collection of shorts in the minibar, including, as a final act of desperation, the Tia Maria, which had not been replaced in months. She had fallen asleep while delivering a stream of lively invective and had begun to snore.

Baz, angry and without the consolations of alcohol or unconsciousness, had put on his tracksuit and gone out to clear his head. He was sampling the 'Dawn Snack' – mugs of tea and Danish pastries – when he saw Violet Hetherington approaching. Of all their fellow travellers she was the most sympathetic. On the whole, he was relieved to see her.

'Hi there, Vi. A fellow early bird.'

Vi filled her mug and tea bag with scalding water from the huge urn. 'I had a nightmare and couldn't get back to sleep. What are the pastries like?'

'Horrible. Have one.'

'Thanks, I'll stick to tea.'

Dodging the dedicated dawn walkers, they strolled round to the ship's bow and stood side by side looking out at a pale lemon-washed sky.

'Beautiful,' Baz said.

Vi, recognising misery disguised as aesthetic appreciation, said, 'It's funny how beauty can affect you as a reproach.'

'What was your nightmare?'

'I dreamed I had murdered somebody and they were about to find the body.'

'And have you?' He was leaning down and towards her, smiling the smile that so infuriated his wife.

'Oh, I should think if you were to count my crimes against humanity it would turn out that I'm a mass murderer.'

'I know what you mean.' His power of comprehension, Vi thought, was far more seductive than his smile. But it was probably no more controllable.

'I seem to be dreaming a good deal here. It must have something to do with being at sea.'

'I wouldn't know.' Baz smiled again, more distantly this time, as if remembering to get himself in check. 'I hardly ever dream. Martha does.'

'I have an idea that women do dream more. Or, anyway, remember their dreams more.'

'Certainly my Sangoma women do. They set great store by dreams.'

'I bet they pre-date Freud, don't they?'

'Oh sure. But many respectable theories of dreams antici-pate the Herr Doktor. It was only a novel idea to the modern West. Africa has always understood such matters in its own way.'

Vi said, 'I am going to see someone in New York I've not seen for years. Not since I was a young woman, a girl, really.'

'You think this dream was about him?' Baz's eyes without his glasses were nakedly attentive.

'I think maybe it's about something I did when I knew him. Or something I didn't do, rather.'

'To meet someone after a long time, that is scary – if they have mattered to you.'

'Yes.'

'Well, you are brave then.'

'Oh no,' Vi protested. 'I'm not at all brave. That's the trouble.'

The yellow sky raced away from them heartlessly. Baz said, 'Perhaps when you see your friend it will be different from what you expect. He may, well, cast light on things. From another angle.'

'That's true. We forget how we tend to see everything from our own perspective.'

'I wish you'd tell that to Martha!'

Some conviction of his state of mind made Vi say, 'You know, I almost miss quarrelling now there is no one to quarrel with.' She hoped that this was not trespassing.

Baz looked at her with his intelligent brown eyes. 'You are a clever lady. And now, I think I had better go and wake Martha up with a strong cup of coffee. Thank you for keeping me company on the dawn watch.'

He walked away and almost at once Vi began to miss him. Poor Martha. It would be a torment to be married to a man like that if you did not feel quite safe yourself. His magic was artless. In fact, she guessed that he was an unusually faithful man. But that was probably part of his appeal.

A Nepalese boy, his trouser creases sharp as a razor, was setting up striped canvas deckchairs. Vi took possession of one. Thanks to the fellow feeling engendered by Baz, the dream tentacles had relaxed their grip a little. She lay back, lounging in the deckchair, enjoying the weak sun bathing her face.

One of the ship's stowaway sparrows hopped down and began to peck delicately at some crumbs of crisps at her feet and then flew up to the railing and began to utter small sweet sounds which etched her ears, gently rinsing them. She closed her eyes.

She was on her way to London to meet Bruno.

The previous weekend they had spent in Aldeburgh, where they had walked along the steep pebbled shore with a wind like a scythe shaving their cheeks and gulls in their pale winter plumage keening and wheeling overhead.

'Souls of drowned sailors,' Bruno said.

'Are they? I thought that was seals.'

'Gulls, seals, what's the difference?'

Vi was about to say 'Quite a lot' but instead said, 'No difference. I was being silly.'

'You're not "silly", Vi. You know' – he stopped her on the beach and took her by the shoulders, turning her to face his green gaze – 'you could have what ever you wanted.'

'Don't be daft. Now you're being silly.'

'I'm certainly silly about you, Violet St John.'

Her hand in his, they walked along the banks of cruel shifting stones. 'You know,' she said after some wordless minutes, 'when we met I thought you were one of Edwin's lovers.'

Bruno gave a yowl of laughter. 'My dear girl!'

'Are you insulted?'

'Not in the least. An understandable mistake, in the circumstances. But I hope you're persuaded otherwise by now?'

'Oh yes,' she said, 'of course.' And she was persuaded again before dinner when they returned to the inn where they were staying.

'I will meet you,' he had announced as they parted, 'next Friday at one o'clock in the entrance of the Horniman Museum.'

The Horniman Museum is in an out-of-the-way part of

121

south London and even if you know the geography it is not easy to find. By the time Vi had changed trains at London Bridge, caught the wrong bus and then walked after all, it was a minute or so past one o'clock when she reached her destination. It was a Friday, but she had taken a day's leave so that she and Bruno could visit an exhibition of West African art that was showing at the museum.

There was no sign of Bruno in the foyer. Just as well that she was there first. She had detected recently that waiting made him agitated.

Twenty minutes later, when she was beginning to wonder where he was, Bruno appeared. 'What kept you?' His face was pale and glistened slightly under the unflattering museum lights.

'I've been here, waiting.'

'Since when?'

'Since one o'clock.'

Bruno said, 'I said to meet at twelve. I waited nearly an hour for you.'

'But I was here. It can't have been more than five minutes at most I was late.'

'We were meeting at twelve.'

'Bruno, no, we were meeting at one.'

Bruno took a diary from his pocket, consulted it and wordlessly held out to her the page bearing that day's date. She read *V 12 noon Horniman*.

She was sure as sure he had said one. In her mind, she could hear his voice. 'I don't understand.'

'Did you write it down in your diary?'

'I don't keep a diary.'

'If you don't keep a diary how can you expect to keep appointments?'

What ever could have happened that they were standing there wrangling over the merits of diary keeping? Miserably, she said, 'I've never needed one. I have all my appointments in my head.'

'Not those with me, apparently.'

'Especially with you, Bruno.'

By now, Bruno holding her elbow and steering rather than guiding her, they had entered the exhibition and were standing before a case of ungainly little statuettes. The statues had strange distorted bodies, elongated or unnaturally foreshortened. Some were draped with shells and crowned with blackened thorns, or hung about with bits of bone, ropes of dried weed and in one case what might have been a shrivelled umbilicus. 'What are they?' she asked, as if she cared.

'They're empowerment figures, from the Bight of Benin, in West Africa. Here, have the catalogue.'

'What are they empowered with?'

But Bruno did not answer. He was moving about morosely, his shoulders hunched, inspecting the contents of the cabinets with forensic attention.

Vi tried to keep up with him but discouraged by the cold-shouldering began to lag behind. She stopped before a single larger effigy with a wide expressionless face. From its thick neck a tiny bleached bird's skull dangled; a wooden peg attached to a rope had been driven into the forehead between its eyes.

There was something terrible and forlorn about the figure's gaze. Bruno was apparently directing every ounce of his concentration at the other exhibits, but braving she didn't quite know what she asked, 'What are they for?'

'Vi, please, I am concentrating.'

There was a photograph of the figure with the peg in its head in the catalogue. Vi read: *Some 'bo' figures are believed*

123

to act both as protection against the malevolent effects of sorcery and to promote a Vodun sorcerer's own malevolent purposes. With sorcery, the dominant fear is of destruction by the power of revenge. The most feared form of this is transformation.

'But it is all moonshine, isn't it?' she enquired on the bus back to the station. 'Isn't it?' she asked again, more anxiously, as he didn't reply.

'If that's how you wish to see it.'

She had hoped he might have recovered his humour but silence hung impenetrably between them until they reached the flat. It was clear that she was in the doghouse.

'Would you like to eat something?' She was starving. They had eaten nothing for lunch and she had started early from Cambridge.

'As you wish.'

Vi made cheese on toast with chutney. Bruno ate gloomily but devoured the toasted cheese in rapid mouthfuls. He responded to her fragments of conversation with a chilly politeness but otherwise volunteered no remark.

Unable to bear this any longer, Vi said, 'Bruno, look, I'm sorry if I got the time wrong. It wasn't on purpose.'

'It's disrespectful.'

'Disrespectful?'

'To miss appointments.'

She could hardly believe this. 'I didn't mean to.'

'It doesn't matter.'

'Bruno . . .'

Half an hour later, she knocked on the bedroom door. 'Bruno, do you want me to go?' Her real self seemed to have gone into hiding and an unfamiliar, pleading person was speaking in her place.

After a few minutes, Bruno came out holding a small leathery thing with feathers stuck around it. 'Did I show you this?'

'What is it?'

'It's from West Africa. It's made from the wing of a bat. They say it will keep the soul of anyone who loves you.'

'That's a rather worrying idea.'

'Shall I keep your soul in it, Violet St John?'

'If you like.' She was only pleased that they were talking again. 'Shall we go to bed?'

They went to bed and then things were all right again, for a while.

17

The sun had moved round and Vi in her deckchair felt that it must be about breakfast time. Not wanting to face Renato, or the milling crowds in the general dining area, she decided to sample breakfast in the Alexandria.

Miss Foot, in a safari hat, and Patrick and his parents were at the table. Miss Foot was finishing a plate of scrambled egg and gave a nod but did not interrupt her eating. Patrick, his cheeks full and pink as a peony, looked Vi over carefully.

'Do you like Rice Krispies?'

'I quite like the noise they make,' Vi said.

Patrick fixed her with a steady stare to establish her as friend or foe. 'What noise do they make?'

'Eat up your cereal, darling,' his mother interjected.

Patrick's parents had also passed a troubled night. Patrick, who had slept the sleep of the innocent for the first two nights, had been wakeful and recalcitrant, and reason and Calpol (rather more of the latter) had not proved effective. His parents, fearful of waking the neighbours, had suggested a story and Patrick, with a child's quick sense of having gained some advantage, had kept them hard at it half the night.

It has not been established how many times an adult person can read *Skarloey and His Friends* and remain mentally stable.

After four readings, Greg had declared it was bloody absurd to come on a cruise with a child and asked whose idea was it anyway, he would like to know? Heather asked that he please lower his voice and reminded him that he'd got the idea from his stuck-up friend at the office who had more money than he knew what to do with and anyway, who was paying if it wasn't her father? Greg suggested that perhaps her father would like to pay for a vasectomy and had finally fallen asleep wrapped in a towelling robe on the bathroom floor.

'They are supposed,' Vi said, pouring herself coffee from a chrome-plate pot, 'to go "snap, crackle, pop". But I don't know about that myself.'

Greg shot her an admiring glance. Patrick held his level gaze. His clear grey eyes fringed with black lashes brought to Vi's mind, suddenly and acutely, the stern unwavering gaze of the infant Harry.

'What don't you know about it?'

'It always seemed to me that they go more like "snicker, snicker, snicker".'

Patrick's stare collapsed into a rapturous smile. 'Knickers, knickers?'

'Patrick!' said Greg, looking across at Miss Foot, who was impassively chewing toast.

'No,' said Vi. 'Not knickers. Snicker. It's a kind of silly laugh.'

'Can I try?' Patrick lunged at the milk jug, his father nervously tried to move it out of his range and a pool of milk began to spread rapidly over the tablecloth. Patrick burst into tears.

Heather began dabbing at the tablecloth with her napkin. 'Greg! That was your fault!'

Greg said, 'Sweet Jesus, give me a break!' and got up and strode out of the dining room.

'No use crying over spilled milk,' Miss Foot suggested. She had finished her first slice of toast and was buttering another. The level of Patrick's crying rose a notch.

'Listen,' said Vi, who had commandeered the Rice Krispies. 'This is an experiment. Listen hard and tell me what you hear.' She began to tip cereal into a clean bowl.

'Can I do it?'

'Of course,' said Vi. 'Here's the jug. Now add the milk quick.'

Patrick poured the milk successfully into the bowl and they waited. A satisfying sound issued from the cereal.

'They do go "snicker, snicker, snicker".'

'I'm glad you agree.'

Patrick got down from his chair and came round to stand by Vi. 'Have you got something nice for me in your bag?'

'Patrick! We don't ask people for things.'

'I don't know what you'd call "nice",' Vi said. 'I've this.' She opened her bag and found a key ring, on which hung a small plastic Spider-Man and Daniel's spare keys, which she held in case of emergencies. She hoped there had not been any. She had meant to leave the keys behind with the neighbours. 'You can have Spider-Man but let me detach the keys first.'

'Why?'

'They belong to my son, Daniel. He might need them.'

'Can I have Spider-Man?'

'Say "thank you" nicely, Patrick, to Mrs . . .'

'Violet,' Vi said. 'Or Vi, if you prefer, Patrick.'

'There's a girl at my nursery called Violet.'

'Well, it's my name too.'

'She's not old.'

'Patrick!'

'No,' said Violet. 'But you see, I was young once.'

'OK.' It seemed that she had passed a test satisfactorily. 'Violet, will you read me Skarloey?'

'No.'

'Why won't you?'

'I don't much like Skarloey.'

'Why don't you?'

'I don't like his name.'

'Why?'

'Patrick, let Violet get on with her breakfast.'

'I'm fussy about names. Patrick, for instance, is an excellent name.'

'So is Violet.'

'How good that we like each other's name.'

'Come with Mummy, now, Patrick, and say goodbye.'

'I want to stay with Violet.'

'You can see Violet later, darling.'

'Is Daddy still in a bloody bad mood?'

'Daddy's tired, darling. Say goodbye now.'

'Will I see you later, Violet?'

'I am sure you will,' Vi said. 'We can be thinking up all the names we don't like, to tell each other when we meet.'

Miss Foot was spreading Nutella. 'A bonny child. The parents should not put him under pressure.'

'You felt that they were?'

'No child should be made to read before the age of seven. Doctor Steiner was emphatic.'

'I think Patrick wanted to be read to, not to read himself.'

'There was some tension,' Miss Foot pronounced. 'An aura of pressure.' She licked the Nutella from the spoon by the jar and absentmindedly pocketed it.

'You see auras?'

'One was taught.' Miss Foot bent her head and leaned forward slightly across the table. 'Yours is quite striking.'

'Really?'

'Oh yes.'

Vi waited, not liking to ask what it was that Miss Foot saw. But Miss Foot merely continued to eat her toast in silence. When she had finished, she dabbed her mouth with her napkin.

'That there has been pain is apparent.' She spoke in a detached but kindly tone as if she were some eminent medical specialist whose job it was to prepare their audience for the worst. 'But it is good that you are at sea.'

Vi waited in case there was more to come from the mouth of this surprising sibyl but Miss Foot merely rose from the table. 'Goodbye for now,' she said, pocketing the napkin.

Vi finished the pot of coffee and then made her way to one of the stairways to find Links, the communications centre where, she had been advised by Renato, she could send and retrieve emails. She had been putting this off and now the necessity to do it was weighing on her mind. She had in fact no wish to be in touch with anyone.

Links was further down into the ship than she had so far descended. At Deck Two she was directed along a corridor, where passengers at tables placed by convenient portholes were already playing draughts, Monopoly, backgammon and dominoes, while, in the opposite direction, the green Atlantic raced past the heedless players.

At the end of the corridor she found Jen and Ken, with a jigsaw between them. The section they had pieced together so far seemed to be an uninterrupted tract of dull-looking sky.

'Hi there, Vi. How you doing?'

'Fine, thanks. I'm off to try to fathom the email here.'

'It's a nightmare. Believe me, Vi. Ken better help you. Ken, go with Vi and help her with the email.'

Vi said there was really no need.

'You'll need help,' Jen said firmly. 'Go on, Ken. He's no use at this anyway,' she explained. 'I have to keep undoing the bits he's done. Look, see here – a bit of obvious cloud just jammed into this bit of clear blue.'

Vi, who was pessimistic about her ability to grasp an alien email system, was grateful for the loan of Ken. He escorted her along the corridor to Links, where a number of passengers, including Les Garson, were queuing up to abuse a harassed-looking girl in a tracksuit. 'It's no use getting annoyed with me,' she was repeating. 'It's the AOL system that's down.'

'What a nuisance,' Vi said, in truth only too glad of an excuse not to have to bother. 'I'm on AOL.'

'It isn't down,' said Ken. 'She's only saying that.'

'How do you know?'

'One, I'm on AOL myself and had no trouble getting online, and two,' he counted off on his forefingers, 'her eyes looked to the right. That's a sure sign of someone fibbing.'

'Heavens, Ken. What terrifying information you have.'

'It's right, though. I've studied body language. Eyes to the right, he's not all right. It means they're making it up, though from where you're looking it's the eyes moving to the left you have to watch for. Believe me, never fails. Let's have your cabin number and your email address and we'll get you online in no time.'

Vi could overhear the voice of Les Garson. 'I'm going to write in about this. It's daylight robbery after what we've been charged.'

Ken was busily typing away. 'There you go, Vi. Bob's your uncle.'

In the space of two days fifty-seven emails had accumulated in Vi's inbox. Most, it was true, were offering the usual remedies for erectile dysfunction. Also on offer were visits from sociable girls, available in her neighbourhood. Along with these was a touching communication from her 'Sister in Christ, Mary Louise Benedict', who was dying of ovarian cancer and hoped to bestow on Vi a legacy, which, somewhat uncharitably, she had apparently not considered leaving to her own religious order. The other emails were from Harry, Dan and Annie.

Harry wrote to say that Kristina had found her mobile and he had it locked safely in his desk. Dan emailed to say he had lost his keys and, unable to find the spare set in her flat, was staying there, he hoped she didn't mind. Annie asked, *What are they wearing on board? Are you playing poker with millionaires?*

Vi emailed Harry back, asking him to thank Kristina and to say that there might be 'a few numbers she needed' from the phone and she would ring him about this from New York. She emailed her apologies to Dan. *Darling, my fault entirely. The keys are here with me and I'm afraid I've just given away your Spider-Man. Please get a locksmith and I will reimburse.*

She emailed Annie last of all. *So far no poker or millionaires. I have been dancing, though, and your shoes are just the job.*

When Annie rang Bruno's flat Vi knew it must be urgent.

'What's up, Annie?'

'Vi, I'm bleeding. Can you come over?'

'Of course, but shouldn't you ring the hospital?'

'How does she come to have my number?' Bruno asked, but Vi was too busy getting herself together to think.

'Can you lend me couple of quid, Bruno? Annie's not well. I need to get to her fast.'

Annie was still in her flat when half an hour later Vi arrived in a taxi.

'I've lost the baby, Vi.'

'Oh Annie. What happened?'

Annie said that she had had stomach cramps and had assumed it was diarrhoea. 'Me and Mick had mussels for dinner. I've had bad reactions to shellfish before now.'

'Who's Mick?'

'Michelangelo, of course. You're so funny about him, Vi.'

'Annie, we must get you to hospital. Is the bleeding bad?'

But Annie refused to leave. She wanted, she said, to stay with her baby, who had slipped out in the bathroom before she got to the loo. Preparing herself for much worse, Vi found a small, bloody, almost transparent scrap of a human form, lying in a bath hat designed to resemble a cabbage rose. She carried the scrap through to Annie's bedroom. The tiny being, enclosed in the pink plastic petals of the cap, looked like an eerie illustration to a child's fairy tale.

'I didn't like to leave it there and that was all there was to hand,' Annie explained. 'The bath hat's not mine. It belongs to Mandy.'

'Where are your Australians?'

The Australians were off on one of their jaunts, potholing this weekend, Annie thought.

Vi said, 'Annie, what would you like me to do?' She couldn't say more. She didn't want to say 'it' but it was not clear whether the scrap would have been a girl or a boy.

'I don't know,' Annie said and burst into tears.

It turned out that in fact Annie had taken an abortifacient administered by Michelangelo. Or rather administered by some doctor he had put Annie in touch with. The dinner of mussels, Annie disclosed, had taken place the previous evening when Michelangelo had taken her out to break it to her that it was all off.

'I knew I was right to mistrust him, Annie. What was he playing at, a last supper?'

'It wasn't him, it was his wife.'

Vi, who knew this was shame at Michelangelo's dereliction rather than loyalty, did not try to argue. 'Was this so-called doctor qualified?'

'He had some letters after his name.'

'Anyone can put letters after their name. I can if it comes to that. Where did you see him?'

Annie said she had seen the doctor somewhere in Victoria, but she couldn't say exactly where. They had gone by taxi at Michelangelo's expense.

'Big deal. He buggered off afterwards sharp enough. You must see a proper doctor, Annie.'

But the stubbornness with which Annie had met the conception of the child seemed not to have left her with its passing. 'I don't want to see anyone. I'm hardly bleeding at all now.'

Vi rang Bruno to say that she would be staying over at Annie's. She spent the night in Mandy's bed, which was playing host to an alarming number of soft toys.

'I had to pile the teddy bears on the chest of drawers,' she told Annie the following morning when she brought her tea and toast on a tray. 'I couldn't dream of sleeping with them all ranged along the bed.'

Annie was feeling better and said that she had decided in the night that the baby should be buried.

'Where?'

'Well, his father's Catholic.'

'Annie, I think we must stop considering the child's father.

Where would you like to do this? I doubt we can do it in a church.'

In the end, late at night, under the ungentle yellow illumination of the streetlights, they buried Annie's aborted child on Chelsea Embankment, by the statue of Sir Thomas More. Annie had chosen the tough old saint for the baby's namesake. She suggested a nearby bed of wallflowers for the burial but Vi objected.

'They'll want to weed and then someone might dig him up, Annie. Under the laurel bush is safer. Anyway, laurels are evergreen.'

Vi dug as deep a hole as she could manage with a trowel she had bought specially from the gardening department at Peter Jones and they laid the scrap, wrapped in one of Annie's silk scarves, in the earth beneath the dark-leaved shrub. Annie had been wearing the scarf, she said, the evening she and Michelangelo had walked along the Embankment, the same night that she was convinced she had conceived. They had passed Sir Thomas and his golden face, Annie remembered, had gleamed, which she found meaningful.

It was only after all this had been accomplished, when Vi and Annie were recovering back at Annie's flat over a glass of brandy, that Vi thought to ask, 'Did I give you Bruno's number?'

'Why?'

'You rang me there. How did you know where to find me?'

'I didn't. I rang you in Cambridge,' Annie said. 'Edwin gave me your London number. By the way, Vi, I suppose what we did tonight wasn't strictly legal.'

18

Perhaps it was the result of writing the message to Annie but Vi decided that she would after all sample the dance lesson in the Tudor Room. She went back to her cabin to change into the silver shoes. Nothing could be more 'suitable'.

Renato had been in to do the room. There was a welcome absence of synthetic lemon and a note on the desk: *Madam, I have put your rings in the safe. Plese ask me for number. Renato.*

Vi looked at her hands. It was a while since they had been bare of rings. Well, the rings could stay in the safe for now. She could rely on Renato to make sure she did not forget them.

Down in the Tudor Room women and one or two bold – or biddable – men were assembling in versions of 'suitable shoes'. George and Marie arrived lugging a CD player, George in jeans and plimsolls and Marie in a body-hugging wraparound skirt. They were to learn today, George announced, the cha-cha-cha.

'Mrs Hetherington. You came!'

'I did, Dino.' She gave the name a particular articulation so that he would know she was not planning to unmask him.

'I am so glad.'

The pleasures of giving pleasure are often underestimated and Vi was pleased to have so easily pleased the boy. It was such a simple matter, learning a few dance steps. And really, it wasn't difficult, forward, back and three steps sideways – she had the knack in no time.

'Are we all ready then, ladies and gentlemen? Time to put your hard work into practice. Find a partner, please, and remember how it goes, one, two and cha-cha-cha!'

The voice of Sammy Davis Jr issued seductively from the CD player. Des took Vi's hand. 'Follow me.' He squeezed her fingers gently.

The rhythm flowed easily down through her legs onto her front foot – forward, then back and finally onto the balls of her feet as she stepped sideways for the 'cha-cha-cha'.

'That was brilliant, Mrs Hetherington.'

'You flatter me, Dino,' said Vi, secretly flattered. 'But it was fun.'

'No, you are good. A natural dancer. You have rhythm.'

'Perhaps it's because I am a poet.'

There you go again, said the voice. She found to her annoyance that she was blushing.

'"It is part of a poor spirit to undervalue himself and blush." That's George Herbert, in case you don't know,' Edwin said. 'By "poor" he means modest, not inferior. "Blessed are the poor in spirit".'

Vi, back from Annie's, had come in from the long walk home from the station to find Edwin lying on the sofa that had done service as Bruno's bed. A three-quarters empty bottle of whisky was balancing perilously on a pile of essay papers on the carpet beside him.

The kitchen was a mess of unwashed plates, mugs, saucepans, spilled Nescafé grounds, uncooked rice grains, bits of egg-shell and an inexpertly opened baked beans tin. All the glasses were smeared with what looked like tomato sauce. In the brief moment it took to rinse a glass clean, Vi saw, quite clearly, the expression in Bruno's eyes as she had come from the kitchen the day her father rang.

Back in the sitting room, she poured herself a whisky. 'You knew all the time.'

'What did you think?'

'I thought . . .' But she didn't know what she had thought. She felt her face going red again.

'You thought I was blind. Blind as a bat.' Edwin was at the stage of drunkenness when speech becomes unnaturally precise.

'I thought you'd mind, Ed.'

'She thought I would mind, she thought I was blind,' Edward carolled. 'I minded your not telling me more. One hell of a lot more. One – hell – of – a – lot.'

'I'm sorry.'

Edwin leaned down and with insane care poured most of what was left of the whisky into his already full glass. 'I am not quite drunk as a lord,' he announced. 'Ten lords a-leaping, nine ladies dancing – eight . . .? What's eight?'

'You've cut yourself.' There was a bloodied plaster coming adrift on his right forefinger.

'I cut it opening a – can – of – beans.'

'You must have used the wrong tin opener.'

'I used the wrong tin opener!' Edwin suddenly shouted. 'Listen everyone, I used the wrong fucking tin opener!'

Vi said, 'Ed, maybe we should go to bed.'

'Good idea. Why don't you come with me.'

'To bed?'

'Why not? You do it with everyone else.'

'Ed, please.'

'No, I mean it, Vi. If you can go to bed with my oldest friend why not with me?'

There was no help for it. Vi led Edwin by the hand to his bedroom and assisted him in undressing, which took some doing as he stopped at intervals to deliver his views on life and Walter Pater, who, he declared, had been unjustly neglected. Vi held her patience until he started a homily on Platonic love. 'I want to explain this . . .'

'Do you really want me to get into bed with you, Ed?'

Edwin made as if to walk, buckled and then crashed with his whole weight across the foot of the bed. In his vest and under-pants he looked shockingly pale against the white sheets. 'Only to sleep. I didn't mean anything else.'

'Of course I will, if you want,' said Vi, who was always, sometimes disastrously, willing to oblige.

She went into the sitting room, collected their glasses and the bottle of Teacher's, went to the kitchen, rinsed the glasses, poured the residue of the whisky down the sink, went to the bathroom, brushed her teeth and then, still going slowly, undressed and put on her nightdress.

She returned to Edwin's room with a jug of water and a clean glass and got into bed. Once there, it felt surprisingly normal. Edwin had managed to get himself under the sheet and his eyes were closed. But as she wriggled down, as unobtrusively as pos-sible, beside his long form he rolled towards her and held her to him tight. She could feel, next to her own chest, the knocking of his heart.

'Thank you for this,' he said.

'It's OK. It's nice for me too. I think you'd better have some water.'

'I'd rather have whisky.'

'I've poured it down the sink.'

'Cow. Unmitigated cowishness.'

'Have some water, Ed. Come on, drink up.'

'What's eight?'

'Drink.'

He drank. 'What's eight? I think I should be told.'

'Eight maids a-milking, isn't it? Shut up now and go to sleep.'

Even with a strong attraction, it is almost always impossible to sleep well beside an unfamiliar body, and they spent an interrupted night, rolling away from each other and then together again, like porcupines. When Vi woke the next morning she was alone in the bed. She lay observing through the window the tender greening leaves of the horse chestnut tree opposite and listening to sparrows scratching maniacally under the roof. It was the beginning of spring, so they would be busy making nests.

Presently, Edwin appeared in his dressing gown with a tray. 'Service with a smile.'

'I should sleep with you more often.'

'There's digestive biscuits too,' Edwin said, and got back into bed. The soles of his feet, hardened from his habit of going barefoot, scraped comfortingly against hers.

Side by side, they drank tea and ate biscuits until, brushing away the crumbs, Vi grasped the nettle. 'So tell me how you knew.'

'Oh, I can't say.' He sounded quite casual now. 'How does one "know" things? Everyone knows everything, really. We just hide it from ourselves.'

'I'm really sorry, Ed. I didn't mean to hide. It was that I didn't want to hurt you.'

'Why did you imagine I'd be hurt?'

'Weren't you, though?'

Edwin got out of bed and put on his dressing gown again. 'I'm going to make coffee. You'd better get a move on or you'll be late for work.'

That evening it was almost like the old days. Vi cooked mushroom risotto, Edwin opened a bottle of Valpolicella and they talked – apparently easy.

'Vi, what happened? You loathed Bruno, or said you did. You offered to move out.'

'I don't know, Ed. I can't explain.'

'Darcy and Elizabeth Bennet?'

'I wouldn't say that fitted the situation.'

'It's really none of my business,' Edwin said. 'Sorry to pry.'

'Look,' Vi said. 'It went like this. I came home one day from work, with some leeks from Mr Jarvis, as a matter of fact. Bruno was in the sitting room when I came home and I was annoyed to see him.'

'Why annoyed?'

'I don't know. He annoyed me. And then my father rang, which made me angry.'

'Angry with your father or angry with Bruno?'

Vi thought about this. 'Angry with Bruno for not leaving me alone to be angry with my father, I suppose. I went to wash the leeks in the kitchen, there was celery too, now I remember. When I came out of the kitchen, with my hands all wet from the vegetables, he was standing there. Just standing, looking at me. He asked why I didn't like him.'

'And did you say?'

'I couldn't.'

'Because you didn't want to?'

'I just couldn't.'

'So you went to bed with him instead?'

'I don't know,' she said again. 'It sort of happened. I burst into tears and suddenly, there we were, neither of us with clothes on. I know that sounds feeble.'

'No,' Edwin said, 'it sounds true. Sex is a great puzzlement.'

'But I don't know that it was sex, exactly.'

'I can't see what else you could put it down to,' Edwin said, opening another bottle of wine.

You were right, it wasn't sex, the voice said.

'But what was it then?' Vi asked, stripping off in her cabin, for the dancing lesson had made her sweat. She dropped her clothes wantonly on the floor, performed a cha-cha-cha and went into the bathroom for a shower.

19

Out on the balcony, in a towelling robe (monogrammed with the initials of the *Queen Caroline* against potential theft), Vi opened another of the old notebooks. A postcard and a blue aerogram from Australia fell out. Also a small gift card of a picture of some violets.

Annie had implemented her plan to visit Australia and was in Perth staying with Mandy's sister. *Perth*, Annie wrote, *is a massive improvement on London. The surfing's fab and the men are fantastic. Next stop Brisbane!* She sounded extremely happy.

The picture postcard of the Martyrs' Memorial in Oxford was less fulsome: *The teaching here is quite a challenge but I have a lively sixth form class. We are doing 'Antony and Cleopatra'. Come and visit me soon. E.*

The recovered closeness with Edwin, the night of the revelation about Bruno, held together for a while. Vi continued to visit Bruno in London, and once he came up to Cambridge to discuss *Mustardseed*, of which Bruno was now officially co-editor, when Vi was down visiting Annie.

Annie seemed to have got over the perfidious Michelangelo and was dating the gynaecologist from Brisbane who had dated Mandy.

'Is that allowed?' Vi asked.

'Mandy chucked him.'

'No, I mean weren't you his patient?'

Annie declared that she'd only rung him for advice and that he'd never laid a hand on her, save in the way of lust.

But although Vi and Edwin seemed to go on as before, something – neither wanted to admit it – had changed. Bruno telephoned her most evenings and asked what she had been doing. This was not always easy to explain. She felt awkward talking to Bruno in the presence of Edwin, though he never made any remark.

Bruno, however, was curious about Edwin.

'I've no idea,' she said one evening when he asked where Edwin was.

'Didn't he tell you?'

'It's not how me and Edwin are.'

'Edwin and I.'

'What?'

'Not Edwin and me. It's Edwin and I.'

'OK, but I still don't know where he is.'

In May, when the buttercups were pronouncing to any who cared to try the experiment that they liked butter and the cow parsley had transformed the hedges and ditches to a cream haze – and the students were busy taking caffeine and 'uppers' in preparation for their exams – Edwin also followed up an old idea. He applied successfully for the post of Head of English at a large comprehensive in Oxford. Vi, when he told her, gave in her notice at the Fitzwilliam. She couldn't imagine a life in Cambridge without Edwin.

At the end of August, Vi parted from Samuel Palmer's consoling sheep and she and Edwin packed up the flat. The fulsome greens of the lawns and the Backs were on the turn and the whole city had the last-ditch stand of the final stretch of an English summer.

Vi and Edwin ate a picnic of leftovers from the fridge off the crates into which their few possessions had been crammed. The crates and boxes were a parting donation from Mr Jarvis, who also presented Vi with an unexpected bunch of blue, mauve and dark crimson asters. He had become uncharacteristically loquacious when he learned that Vi was moving and confided that she reminded him of his dead sister.

'A somewhat barren compliment,' was Edwin's verdict when Vi showed him the flowers. He had met Mr Jarvis, who had lost all his natural teeth as a boy.

Bruno had said, when she told him, 'You must come and live with me.' He seemed to think this was settled and somehow it therefore seemed to be although the subject had never been discussed.

So now Ralph downstairs, who was taking one of his Deadly Sins to show at an exhibition and had promised to drive Vi and her crates of books down to London, was at the door with his Dormobile van. The night before, Vi and Edwin had drunk a valedictory bottle of Valpolicella and tried not to be maudlin. As a result, they were brisk with each other, which is never very satisfactory for partings.

When, accompanied by Avarice, Vi arrived at Bruno's flat, she found the place filled with red roses. No scent, or thorns, but that perhaps was to be churlish. She was touched that he was so manifestly glad to see her.

Bruno greeted Ralph like a lost friend and insisted on pouring him a glass of champagne. But Ralph, who was usually so polite, said he had to be on his way and left most of his glass of champagne untouched.

* * *

Although Vi was not easily bored and, as Bruno said, the nearby Portobello Market was enough like the market in Cambridge for her to feel at home, she was unused to being without an occupation. To her surprise, Bruno seemed dead set against her looking for a job. 'I can support you,' he said and Vi, who was not yet experienced enough to know when to take someone at their word, was gratified that he seemed to want to look after her.

Most days, when Bruno went off to his job at the British Council, she drifted down the Portobello, passing the time of day with various itinerant stallholders, usually ending up at Mr DellaCosta's stall, which sold varieties of exotic fruit and vegetables quite beyond the scope of Mr Jarvis.

Mr DellaCosta had a pale fudge-coloured whippet called Cleopatra who, during working hours, was tied by a dressing gown cord to the corner post of the stall. However, when Mr DellaCosta's brother Petey played the steel cans, which, when the mood took him, he did outside the Salvation Army on the Portobello, Cleopatra sat by his cap looking wistful and encouraging the punters to part with their loose change.

One day, when Petey was playing, Vi, who liked buskers, had stooped down to place money in the cap and Cleopatra licked her wrist.

'She don't do that often,' Petey said. 'She's nervy. Bet you're Pisces, aren't you?'

Vi said that her birthday was in November.

'Your moon'll be in Pisces. I'm never wrong. I'll do your chart for you, if you like.'

The dog, Petey explained, was on loan from his brother, and Vi, whose moon turned out not to be in Pisces but quite elsewhere, got into the habit of dropping by Mr DellaCosta's stall each day to buy veg for supper. Although she did not recognise this she was lonely and, unlike Mr Jarvis, Mr DellaCosta was chattily companionable.

A section of the library served as the ship's bookshop and Vi, her hair a little wild from drying in the salt breeze, found it packed out with people.

The critic was seated at a table, set with a jug of water and a plate of biscuits, behind a placard of his name, written in Gothic script, and the legend 'Signing Today'. Beside him, on display, was an edition of his latest collection of theatre reviews, *Slings and Arrows*.

When he saw Vi he waved. 'I expect you have come to buy my book?'

Vi shook her head. 'I'm here to look for something in the library.'

'Can I tempt you to a biscuit? We have shortbread or custard creams?'

'No thanks.'

'Spurned,' said the critic, affably.

Disapproving murmurs rose from the bevy of waiting admirers. The bookseller looked uneasy. There had been a small unpleasantness at Kimberley Crane's signing, when a so-called fan had confused her with Philippa Gregory.

Vi, who had found what she was after, had ordered lunch in an out-of-the-way spot in the Bistro and opened the frayed-at-the-edges volume, which she had tracked down in the section of the library marked 'Hobbies and Reference'. To her irritation, she saw a figure approaching.

'Is it all right if I join you?' The hovering presence resolved into Valerie Garson, in a trouser suit which, in the white piping, suggested a naval allusion.

Vi summoned politeness. 'Of course.'

'Only, Les is having a Thai massage.'

Vi closed the works of William Shakespeare. 'Honestly,' she untruthfully assured, 'it's fine.'

'Oh, were you reading?'

Vi said she could always read later.

'Anything good?'

'Not bad.'

Valerie Garson settled down to study the menu, which offered continental snacks, light meals and today's specials. 'I've not tried here before. What have you ordered?'

Vi tried to think. 'A salade niçoise.'

Valerie Garson said she fancied a salad too, though she was also tempted by the crostini. She plumped finally for one of the specials, fillet of sole on a bed of warm pear and arugula.

When Vi's plate arrived Valerie Garson said, 'Those anchovies look nice. Makes me wish I'd had a salad after all.'

'You can always order one.'

'They'll have started on the sole and it's a waste, isn't it?'

'Well,' said Vi, 'a drop in the ocean, perhaps, when you think about it.'

'Are you enjoying it?'

'The salad?'

'No, all this – the cruise.'

'I seem to be. How about you?'

Valerie Garson lowered her head confidentially. 'To tell you the truth, I'm not enjoying it that much.'

'Oh dear.'

'Don't tell Les I said so.'

'Of course not.'

'Would you like some wine? I'm going to have some.'

'OK,' said Vi. 'I'll have a glass if you like.'

Valerie Garson beckoned the wine waiter and ordered a

bottle of Pouilly Fumé. Her French accent, Vi noticed, was flawless. 'Les has prostate cancer and it makes him tetchy. You wouldn't notice it maybe but he turns quite nasty with me.'

Valerie Garson's unremarkable blue eyes dampened and then filled. 'I sometimes wish I'd divorced him. I nearly did once. But he persuaded me to come back. He said he'd treat me like a princess if I stayed.'

'Ah yes.'

'I shouldn't have listened,' Valerie Garson said, pouring them each a large glass of wine. Her small, plumpish, well-manicured hand shook a little.

Vi said, 'It's a nuisance how these things become clearer with hindsight.'

'You can say that again. This isn't bad.'

Vi sampled the wine. 'It's excellent. You know about wine?'

'My pen pal's family ran a vineyard in the Loire. I went on an exchange there when I was a schoolgirl. I fell in love with her brother.'

'A happy experience?'

'It was bliss,' said Valerie Garson. 'To tell you the truth, it was meeting him again that made me nearly leave Les.'

'I see.'

'My pen pal and I had a reunion in Paris, and Jules came along too. He'd got a photo of me in his wallet, in my bikini, as a matter of fact. You wouldn't believe it but I was the runner-up in Bournemouth's beauty queen contest in 1965.'

Vi said that she could well believe it.

'He took the picture, the one he had in his wallet, when we hitchhiked down to St Tropez together. He got me to thumb the lifts while he hid, and then when a lorry, or whatever, stopped he jumped out of the bushes and got in the cab too.'

'Did the drivers mind?'

'What could they say? Own up they had designs? Jules introduced me to St. Raphaël – that's an aperitif, quite classy. We took a bottle with us on the beach and slept there in sleeping bags. Well, one sleeping bag, to be honest. My pen pal came out in a funny rash and couldn't come with us. Just as well, really.' Valerie Garson giggled. 'The sky down there's ever so clear because of the atmosphere. He showed me Orion's Belt. I always think of St Tropez when I see it.'

'I should think you do.'

'I kicked myself that I didn't, you know, but I was still a girl and it wasn't like it is now. But to tell you the truth, Jules and I had a bit of a reunion in Paris.' Valerie Garson coloured; for a fleet second, behind the furrowed, heavily powdered face, Vi saw the fair young girl who had slept on the beach at St Tropez and had not known that this was the best life would offer her. 'His wife had gone off with a wine taster from Rouen. He wanted me to go back with him and help to run the vineyard.'

'But you didn't?'

'I was going to, but Les came home from a golfing weekend – it was raining and they left early – and found me packing. Lucky I hadn't written the note I was going to leave him. More wine?'

'Thanks, I'm fine. What would the note have said?'

Valerie Garson poured herself another glass. 'I'm leaving you, you big bully. Or fat bully, I hadn't quite decided.'

'Ah.'

'That sole's taking its time. They must be out with a net catching it. Anyway, I couldn't leave him now, with the cancer.'

Vi considered whether or not to say, You could, of course, and said it.

'I don't think I could live with my conscience.'

'Well,' said Vi, 'forgive me, because it is not my business, but I think consciences are more elastic than we imagine. And cancer is no excuse for bullying.'

'I know that,' Valerie Garson said. 'But you know, I haven't got the gumption to leave now. Pathetic, isn't it?'

'No,' said Vi. 'It's quite understandable.'

'I shouldn't be saying all this.'

'It's OK to say it.'

'It's nice of you to listen. Les says I ramble.'

Vi said, 'Yes, well, he would, wouldn't he? I'm really very sorry, Valerie. I'm glad you told me and I think you're brave. And thank you for the wine. It was delicious.'

In the lobby by the lifts, she met Les Garson, rather more glistening than usual. 'Have you seen my other half?'

'I think,' Vi said, 'I spotted her on the way up to the Alexandria.'

'She'll be at the trough, the little piggy-wiggy. Fancy a quickie?'

'Thanks, I've had a drink.'

'Go on. Spoil yourself. I've been. I had a young woman with legs up to her armpits walk all over me this morning. Mind you, it cost an arm and a leg! Black girl, but very attractive.'

'Really?'

'Got a book there, have you?' Vi pressed the button for the twelfth floor. 'See you tonight, then?' As the lift arrived, Les Garson stood, smelling of an aftershave heavy with phero-mones, not absolutely blocking her path. 'Did anyone ever tell you you're a very attractive woman, Vi?'

'No one I wanted to hear it from, Les.'

20

Vi, in her room, opened the doors and went out on to the balcony. She breathed in the clean air to expunge the lingering scent of Les Garson's villainous aftershave. The mercurial sea had turned a darkly brooding green. Above it, as far as sight could reach, stretched a taut white sky. With any luck, she thought, we shall have a storm.

Back inside, she opened the library copy of Shakespeare at *Antony and Cleopatra* and found the line she was looking for: *Sometimes we see a cloud that's dragonish.*

The clock on the church tower of All Saints, along the road towards the Portobello, struck the half hour.

'Oh shit,' Bruno said. 'I'm meant to be meeting La Carfield for lunch.'

Tessa Carfield, who had been a year or so above Bruno at the LSE, was a partner in a headhunting firm and had found him his job with the British Council. 'I'd better fly or I'll be late and then she'll moan like buggery.'

Seeing him off at the door, Vi met the postman with Edwin's card. As she came upstairs, the phone was ringing. Someone from Tessa Carfield's office. So Bruno had been late after all. In the afternoon she took Cleopatra to Kensington Gardens.

A fondness had sprung up between Vi and Mr DellaCosta's fudge-coloured whippet. Vi had got in the way of liberating the dog from her post at the stall and taking her for an afternoon run in the park. Cleopatra chased grey squirrels, not too successfully, and sniffed the bottoms of other dogs while Vi stood about, mindlessly gazing, or sat on benches beside chatting women, discontented au pairs, lovers necking and dozing old men. Usually the two of them walked down to the lake, where Cleopatra pursued and then retreated from the vicious, over-fed swans.

She was chopping vegetables, still in a reverie, when Bruno returned. 'That looks good.'

'Ratatouille, or will be, courtesy of Mr DellaCosta. He's given us some chrysanthemums. I wish I liked chrysanths better. There's not much else by way of flowers at this time of year.'

Bruno said, 'It's the smell you don't like. It's funereal.'

'But also the colours. I ought to like them. But I don't. How was lunch?'

'Fine.'

'There was a message from Tessa's office.'

Bruno had gone into the hall and was hanging up his coat. He called out, 'What was it?'

'From Tessa. You must have been late.'

He came back into the kitchen and kissed the back of her neck – where babies are kissed, as he'd said once. 'No, she was. She'd got the time wrong.'

Vi, chopping garlic, felt a small cold spot in her stomach. 'How do you mean?'

'She'd written the time wrong in her diary. She's all over the place, that one. And boring! God, I couldn't wait to get away.'

Over supper Bruno said, 'You not hungry, my pet?'

Vi said she wasn't really and thought she might go and lie down.

At night the flat made strange clicking noises as the poorly fitted joinery of the house conversion eased itself back on to old accustomed planes. That night, Vi, who had always slept well, lay awake listening to the noises of the shifting house and the traffic outside. Bruno, by her side, was breathing heavily. She slid from the bed, stole into the sitting room where she found her notebook and shut herself in the bathroom, wrapped against the draught in an old dressing gown rescued from Edwin.

Towards Christmas, Edwin visited them. He wanted to discuss the future of *Mustardseed*, of which Bruno was now the official editor. Edwin, who had a new poetry collection coming out, seemed to have lost his old enthusiasm for the magazine and even spoke of selling it.

Bruno occasionally asked Vi's opinion about a poem but since Edwin's abandoning of the role of editor no poem of hers had ever appeared.

On the last day of his visit, when Bruno was at work, Vi introduced Edwin to Mr DellaCosta and they took Cleopatra for a walk in Kensington Park. London was experiencing a cold snap and Vi wore a hat knitted in the colours of the rainbow, bought in the Portobello Road. Edwin borrowed the matching scarf and wound it round his head and ears like a turban. Neither had gloves and they walked in the freezing air, making dragon's breath and blowing ineffectively on their fingers.

Their cheeks and noses grew visibly pinker as they stood watching Cleopatra snuffle about in the roots of a horse chestnut. It put Vi in mind of the morning she had woken in Edwin's bed to see the pale fawnish backs of the unfurling horse chestnut leaves outside.

Perhaps it was this which made her say, 'Ed, are you really OK in Oxford?'

'As much as I ever am. How about you here?'

'I think so. Mostly.'

'Are you writing – don't say if you'd rather not.'

'I am, I think.' Vi placed a superstitious hand on the horse chestnut's venerable grey bark. 'Actually, it was Cleopatra that got me going. And then the coincidence of your card.' She told him about the poem she had written in the night.

'Well, the night's a good time for working. Safe. Are there others?'

'There seem to be.'

'What does Bruno think?'

'I've not mentioned them.'

'Ah well.'

Following Cleopatra's lead they strolled towards the lake, where the ducks and geese were shoving each other, greedily angling for bread or whatever else that was edible they could get their beaks on. Cleopatra made a few sallies and then stood stock-still, staring at the milling fowl, apparently hypnotised.

'You know, I'm afraid she is rather a stupid dog,' Edwin said. 'Not a bit like her namesake.'

'We don't know that the original wasn't stupid,' Vi said. 'We only have Shakespeare's version.'

'No, there's Plutarch too. I've got my sixth formers reading him at school. The North translation anyway.'

'Ed, what was Bruno like at school? I never hear much about his past, nothing at all, in fact.'

'As you'd expect, stroppy, definitely not stupid. Remember, he only arrived when we were in the sixth form.'

'How would I remember that? Neither of you talk about

it. I don't even know much about his family, except that he seems to dislike them. You know, I've never met them.'

('You must have had a mother and a father,' she had said to Bruno once, but his face had set pale in the expression she was learning not to question.)

'What were they like, Ed?'

But Edwin said that he had never met Bruno's family either, nor, so far as he could recall, had Bruno ever discussed them. They had been too taken up with French existentialism and alcohol.

'So he drank then?'

'Oh God yes. We always met in the pub.'

'A bit different now!'

'He's a convert. You know how converts always tip into their opposite.'

Vi stood, looking out over the wintry lake at the herring gulls, sailing in their ease on the far reaches of the silvery water. It might be no bad thing to be a gull. She said, 'I don't know if I should say this', and told him about Bruno's lunch with Tessa Carfield.

'People do lie about being late.'

'Yes. But the other thing is I looked in his diary.'

'Aha.'

'I shouldn't have done, of course, but I had such a strong instinct.' The best thing about Edwin was that, even implicitly, he never reproved. 'He'd written twelve thirty in his diary. I know this sounds bonkers, but I'm pretty sure they were supposed to meet at one and to save face he changed the time. He did the same to me once – changed the time we had agreed to meet and then wrote it in his diary.'

'To prove that he was right?'

'Or me wrong.'

Edwin frowned. 'Have you raised this with him?'

'I don't like to. It'll put him in a mood.'

'Don't you think you should?'

'But I may be wrong,' Vi said. 'I probably am. I can be vague.'

'You know you aren't really,' Edwin said.

They returned Cleopatra to Mr DellaCosta, who presented Vi with some figs, a bag of over-ripe tomatoes, a bunch of parsley and the tail end of a rope of garlic. 'The trouble is,' said Vi, 'I can't ask to buy anything now because he always gives it to me for nothing. Even the good stuff.'

'Not like Mr Jarvis, then?'

'I miss Mr Jarvis.'

'Is it the teeth you miss?'

'You know what I mean.'

That evening, she cooked tomato sauce for spaghetti, their old favourite, while Edwin went out to Victoria Wines in search of Valpolicella. They had drunk most of a bottle by the time Bruno came home.

'You've got tomato on your cheek.' Vi wiped her face with her sleeve. 'Now you've got sauce on your jumper.'

Over the spaghetti, Edwin and Bruno discussed what to do with *Mustardseed*. Vi's own contribution to the magazine had practically dwindled to that of copy editor. This mostly meant checking the poets' punctuation, a delicate task since some were quite unclear about their punctuation, and indeed might never have learned its rules, while others held eccentric, if not quite untenable, and fiercely defended views. Bruno said nothing about her poems, or his own, but divulged to Edwin that he planned to borrow a cottage from Tessa Carfield in order to finish his book on sorcery. Tessa had a cousin in publishing to whom, when it was written, she had said she would direct the book.

At about ten o'clock Bruno announced, 'Some of us have to work tomorrow – I'm off for a bath.'

Vi, who wanted to talk more to Edwin, said, 'I'll come soon.'

Twenty minutes later Bruno put his head round the door. 'Are you coming to bed?'

'In a bit,' Vi said.

Bruno left, not quite closing the door. Edwin waited and then opened another bottle of wine and refilled their glasses.

'Ed . . .'

'What is it?'

'I don't know, really . . .'

'I do,' Edwin suggested. He got up and walked over to the door, listened a moment, closed it and returned to his seat in the armchair. There was a burn mark on the armrest where someone had once either stubbed out or incautiously left a lighted cigarette.

Vi said, 'What is it?'

'You're frightened of him.'

Vi had a sensation of being slapped across the face. 'Am I?'

'Well?'

'Well what?' She was annoyed: to be frightened seemed humiliating.

'Bruno can be kindness itself.' She was conscious that this was a desperate comment.

'No one kinder – provided you meet him on his own terms.'

'What do you mean?'

Edwin put his finger on the mark on the chair and frowned. 'This was the result of a row we had once.'

'Ed? What happened?'

'There is a "kindness" which shuts up leopards for their protection in narrow cages.'

There was something almost thrilling in this. 'I'm hardly a leopard.'

'You know best.'

'Why d'you say that I am?' Now that the idea had been raised she did not like its being dropped too readily.

'He calls you "pet" and "lamb", doesn't he?'

Vi flushed. 'They're terms of affection.'

'They hardly seem to fit.'

'I like lambs.'

'Who doesn't? But if you don't mind me saying so you are not much like one. Not at all lamb-like.' He looked at her unblinkingly with his odd eyes.

There was a pause in which Vi had a sense that something might happen. What did happen was that Bruno reappeared at the living room door.

'What's going on here, a meeting of minds?'

Across the way an engine was gagging as someone tried and failed to start a car.

Edwin got up. It was apparent from the care he took in rising that he was drunk. 'I'm going for a piss.'

Vi said, 'We've been discussing *Mustardseed*, me and Ed.'

'Edwin and I. Are you going to bed, Edwin?'

Edwin, on his way to the bathroom, stopped and stood looking at Bruno, as if waiting to see if he had anything to add. 'Any second now, Bruno.'

Bruno stared at the two of them. To do this he had to move his head slightly from side to side.

Like a cobra, Vi thought. She was calculating whether or not he had overheard.

'Well, well,' Bruno said finally. 'Well, well, well.'

'I'm going to do the washing up,' Vi said, hoping that her feeling of panic was not apparent to either man.

Two nights later, Bruno rolled towards her in the darkness. 'Shall we get married?'

'Why?'

'That's not a very gracious response.'

Be careful, said a voice.

'I'm just taken aback.'

'I wanted to marry you the moment I saw you.'

'Why?'

'When I was a boy I had a secret companion who went everywhere with me. I knew you the moment I set eyes on you.'

'What was this companion called?'

You're not going to believe this, said the voice.

'Guess.'

'I can't.'

'Violet. A violet by a mossy stone . . .'

Oh really! said the voice.

Vi said, 'But I annoy you. I'm always annoying you.'

A police car shrieked past close by. Then there was one of the odd silences which can fall suddenly, even in London.

'You're a nuisance.' Bruno patted her bottom. 'But you have a nice arse. Never fuck a woman with a big arse.'

Vi squirmed around so that he was lying behind her and pushed her bottom into his belly. 'I'll think about it tomorrow.'

You better had, said the voice.

21

Dark purplish clouds were amassing high in the sky, as if, but not in fact, reflecting the darkening water. Vi found Annie's shoes in the wardrobe and went down to the King Edward Lounge. Fewer people than usual had collected for tea but among them she saw Baz and Martha, holding hands.

Baz beckoned. 'Come and join us for tea.'

'I'm here for the dancing.'

'Brave lady!'

'I learned the cha-cha-cha this morning so I'm keen to put it into practice.'

Martha said, 'I wouldn't mind a dance.'

Baz pulled a face.

'Balthazar Lincoln, you always do that. You danced at our wedding. I have pictures.'

'That was a million years ago.'

Vi said, 'I picked it up quite easily and if you know the steps already . . .'

'Martha was the three-times jive champion of Kansas City when I met her.'

'Me and Bobby Crawshaw.'

'I'm a horrible disappointment after Bobby Crawshaw. Her mother told her we had rhythm.'

'Baz! She never did.'

'She thought it, though. You can't deny it.'

Martha said there was no doing anything with him and Baz said she might as well accept that he was a lost cause and have done.

'Lost cause for what?' Martha smiled admiringly at her husband.

'Dancing anyway,' Vi said. She was pleased she could still be pleased to see a couple happy and this made her like them more. 'I should dump him, Martha. That's my dance teacher, Dino, coming over. He'll dance with you. He dances like Fred Astaire.'

'That I can *not* resist.'

'Look, he's even Fred Astaire's shape.'

Vi, watching Martha, in the arms of Dino, being swung expertly around the tilting floor, said, 'Baz, do you remember I mentioned someone I knew who had studied African religion?'

'Sure. May I pour you some tea?'

'Thanks. Milk, please, no sugar. He had a – a purse, I suppose you'd call it, made out of a bat's wing and feathers of some sort, I don't know what exactly. He said it had the power to keep the soul of anyone who loved the owner.'

'I've not heard of that one. It sounds like one of the dodgier elements of Vodun.'

'Yes, it was supposed to be Voodoo, sorry, I mean Vodun.'

'It's not my area. But there are, or were, some spooky aspects to Vodun. Of course, this always gets grossly exaggerated in the popular imagination.'

'How does it work, would you say?'

'Suggestion.' Baz helped himself to a cucumber sandwich. 'The power of suggestion. A much underrated power. You know, I never get over my love of cucumber sandwiches. I

162

think of them as quintessentially English but none of my London colleagues ever ate them except at our house. Martha says they would have much preferred her brownies.'

Watching Baz contentedly chewing the sandwich and idly watching his wife, happily enjoying a small freedom, Vi was overcome with the thought that she should have been with just such a man.

'Baz.'

He returned his courteous gaze to her. 'Yes?'

What she had it in mind to say, to him, a stranger, already sounded impossibly foolish, mad even, but she knew him to be kind.

'Do you think, I mean, could someone actually be . . .' but the tango was over and a flushed and jubilant Martha was greeting them excitedly.

'That was just great.'

'Bobby Crawshaw standard, sweetheart?'

'You bet,' Martha said. 'I hope you've left me some of the cucumber.'

Vi didn't quite know what was happening but she knew she was scared. Her heart was not exactly banging but it seemed to be giving out a low juddering moan, not unlike the sound which had issued from the chain on the bicycle that she jettisoned in Cambridge. It seemed also to be hurting in her chest. Extraordinary that the heart – if it was the heart – really did that.

'They aren't that good,' she said miserably. She and Bruno were walking, more like marching, home from the park. Bruno had instigated a fitness regime which entailed walks after meals. 'I didn't say anything about it because I was sure they would turn them down and then you'd be cross.' It was one of the notable things about him, his habit of getting cross on her behalf.

'You should have told me.'

They were crossing Moscow Road by St Sophia's, the Greek Orthodox church. Traffic had been diverted from the Bayswater Road and a stream of vehicles thundered past, among them a large truck carrying McVitie digestive biscuits. A vision of putting an end to all this by stepping out in front of the biscuit lorry flashed across Vi's mind.

'You should have told me,' Bruno said again. 'I am a poet too after all.'

'Yes,' Vi agreed. She didn't see the relevance of this but what could be gained by questioning it? As people do when feeling hopeless, she repeated herself. 'They aren't that good, the poems.'

'That's not the point. The point is you didn't discuss this with me. I am a figure in this arena. As a simple act of courtesy – bear in mind that the editor is a personal friend – you should have discussed the matter accordingly.' He seemed to have become someone who spoke like a nineteenth-century bureaucrat.

'Listen,' she said, 'I didn't think, that's all. It wasn't directed against you. I just did it.'

'But you should have done. You should have thought. What do you think I feel not knowing that you are to have your poems published by the publishing house where I'm to be published too?'

How could I know that? she thought. You never told me. And the editor is not a 'personal friend' of yours, he's an acquaintance of Tessa Carfield's cousin.

'I have to ask why you have done this.' Now he had turned into an investigative journalist or policeman. 'You of all people.'

'Listen,' she said again. 'I'm sorry. Really. I didn't mean to make you angry.'

'I'm not angry.'

Clearly that was not the case. 'I didn't mean to hurt you, then.'

'I'm not hurt.'

They had reached the flat and were up the stairs and in the kitchen before she spoke again. 'I was going to talk to you about the book.' She lit the gas, clumsily filling the kettle. 'Bruno, please.'

'Yes, Vi?'

'Don't be like this.'

'How do you expect me to be?'

'Not like this.'

'I wasn't aware that you had the right to dictate my responses.'

'Of course not, but . . .'

'Vi, you must act as you choose. But if you choose to act in certain ways there are going to be consequences.' He seemed to have metamorphosed into counsel for the prosecution. 'You're an adult woman, you know that.'

Vi, who did not feel at all adult at that moment – in fact quite the opposite – tried her hardest not to cry. Desperate to smoke but unable to lay her hands for the moment on the matches, she lit a cigarette from the gas ring so that her hair caught in the flame and flared up dangerously. Bruno stood there, watching her rinse it under the cold tap.

Sink or swim, remarked the voice.

'Bruno . . .'

'You smoke too much.'

'Bruno . . .'

'Yes?' The prosecuting counsel had been promoted to a high court judge, about to pronounce sentence.

'Please let's not quarrel.'

165

The judge's face wavered, decomposed and then reorganised itself into an interrogation officer, who looked into Vi's face with terrifying calm. 'I have no idea what you mean.'

'I mean this.'

'This is not a quarrel, Vi. It's a statement of feeling.'

Bereft of words she stood there, water from her wet hair running into the tears which dripped from her chin.

'Please don't manipulate me, Vi,' said the interrogation officer. He spoke more in sorrow than in anger. 'You know how I dislike tears.'

'But of course I'm upset to have upset you.'

Don't grovel, said the voice.

'Then why do it?'

'Why do what?' The kitchen smelled horribly of singed hair.

'Upset me. You know what you are doing.'

She didn't. Or rather she did, but she didn't know why it mattered. No, that wasn't true either. She understood that it mattered but for reasons that would not have mattered to her, and this frightened her. Ed was right.

'I love you,' she announced bleakly.

Fool! said the voice.

'And I love you, Vi.' Bruno's face had shifted fractionally from interrogation officer to dispassionate surgeon.

Liars, both of you, remarked the voice.

'So, if we love each other . . . ?' Vi had gone across and was squeezing his shoulder.

He placed a big enfolding hand over the crown of her head. 'Poor hair . . .'

'Do you still want us to marry?'

'My violet by a mossy stone.'

Blinking idiot, you mean, the voice said. It sounded more weary than accusing.

22

As Vi was leaving the King Edward Lounge, Des caught her at the door. 'You never danced, Mrs Hetherington.'

'I'm sorry, Dino. I was talking to Doctor Lincoln.'

'While I danced with his lovely wife.'

'She told me to tell you that you're a neat dancer. You'll have had a much better time with her. She seemed to know all the steps.'

'She is a very good dancer. But you will be a very good dancer too, Mrs Hetherington, with practice. Believe me, I know. I hope you will come to the ball tonight.'

'When is it and where?'

'In the Queen Victoria Salon, Deck Eight, nine till midnight. You may want heels, though maybe not if it gets any rougher.'

'I'll do my level best to rise to heels.'

When she returned to her room a bowl of crystallised ginger was on the desk, with a note propped against it: *Madam, for see sickness.*

As far as Vi was aware she had never in her life suffered from seasickness but she was grateful for the ginger. Her mother had liked ginger and consequently it was another thing her father would never have in the house. Vi had often bought her mother chocolate ginger for her birthday, August the sec-

167

ond, the day after they were to dock in New York. She tried to open the doors to the balcony but they blew back in her face so that she had to lean all her weight against them to force them open.

White spume was riding crazily along the tops of racing waves below and gobbets of foam were being thrown about pell-mell by a wind sweeping the face of the water with the long arm of an angry demon. She dragged over a chair to prop open the doors.

'It's your life,' Edwin said. They were in the park. Cleopatra was sniffing round the roots of the horse chestnut down from which occasional conkers were plummeting softly to the grass. Edwin picked up a couple, still half encased in their pithy green armour. He peeled away the spiked overcoats and extracted the gleaming mahogany conkers, balancing them on his palm.

'They're like us,' Vi said. 'Immaculate and beautiful and shining in glory when they emerge but very quickly dulled.'

'In my day these would have been baked in the oven to be strung on strings for lethal battles. Boys are no longer boys.'

'The world is going to the dogs.'

'Speaking of which, if fair was fair, which we know it never is, you would dedicate your book to Cleopatra, not to me.'

Cleopatra, who had found a molehill, was exploring it busily but not too effectively.

'I would never have written a line but for you, Ed.'

'You would so.'

'No, you have to accept that. You and my mother made me write.'

'Then you should dedicate the book to her.'

'She's dead,' Vi said. She tossed a conker high into the

bright autumnal sky and caught it in one hand. Conkers always reminded her of the silky heads of newborn babies. She tossed the conker up again, in an arc over her head, and caught it, like a novice juggler, not quite ambidextrously, in her left hand. 'Anyway, that would upset my father. He can't bear for her to be mentioned.'

'And this won't upset Bruno?'

'I can't dedicate the book to Bruno.'

'Is that why you are marrying him?' He looked at her in his quizzical unblinking way.

'I love him.'

Nonsense, said the voice.

'I wouldn't know about that,' Edwin said. 'I am no expert and I am quite certain I don't understand love, especially not love between a man and a woman. But who says you have to marry someone because you love them?'

'Bruno seems to want it.'

'And that's a good-enough reason?'

Of course it isn't, said the voice.

'I can't put it off now. It's all planned.'

'What is planned? A brief registry office performance somewhere in the Marylebone Road, with me and Tessa Carfield as witnesses and lunch after. It's hardly holy writ. I bet the lunch hasn't even been booked.' Vi, who had been delegated to arrange the wedding breakfast, looked guilty. 'It hasn't been, has it?'

'But you've come down specially.'

'For God's sake, Vi. I can go away again. You cannot make my presence in London a reason for marrying.'

Listen to him, said the voice.

'I thought Bruno was your oldest friend,' Vi said.

* * *

The wind was working up a plaintive howl. Vi opened her notebook and took out the small card with the picture of violets on it. Inside she read, 'To my Violet by a mossy stone.' There was also a lunch menu, with four signatures: her own, Edwin's, Bruno's and Tessa Carfield's. Tessa Carfield had written, 'To Bruno and Vi, who deserve one another.'

She tore the menu and the card into very small pieces and threw them overboard. A shred of violet blew back on to the balcony. She took it inside and burned it in an ashtray. Then she read the poem which she had written, in Edwin's dressing gown, in the draughty bathroom of that old flat. A flat now worth several hundred thousand pounds. She had driven past the house, done up in an extraordinary candy pink, quite recently. But even the vast shift in the flat's monetary value did not come near to the distance she felt from the girl who had written the poem. She had no idea any longer whether the poem was any good. The best of it was the opening line that she had stolen from Shakespeare: *Sometimes we see a cloud that's dragonish.*

Antony, at the close of his life, contemplating his love for Cleopatra, who has deceived him, fatally; contemplating the mutability of love, the mutability of everything apprehended by human consciousness with its power to affect the shape of reality, its aptitude for perceiving the reflection of its own desire and not what is really there.

But what *is* really there? she called out, in the face of the demon wind, to the unanswering, unanswerable sea.

In the wardrobe, beneath the line of hanging frocks, stood a pair of shoes with heels a good six inches high. Vi put them on and appraised her lengthened image in the mirror. Annie would approve. It was thanks to Annie, who had insisted on supervising her packing, that she had packed them at all. There was also Annie's old silver strapless ball gown, passed on to Vi when it no longer fitted Annie and never yet worn. That would do nicely with Ted's diamond. But the diamond was in the safe where Renato had locked away her rings and she hadn't bothered to ask him for the number. She rang the steward's line and, getting no response, left a message.

Dinner that evening was a muted affair. Aside from Vi, only Baz and Martha, the captain and the critic were at the table. The rest of the company had presumably retired to their rooms to batten down. Towards the end of dinner, Miss Foot arrived and ordered a bowl of chicken broth. 'I am fairly well acclimatised but it is advisable to take some light nourishment in the face of any physical perturbation.'

'A glass of wine?' offered the critic. He had ordered a very superior claret for the whole table which only he and Vi were drinking. Martha had abstained to keep Baz company and the captain had explained that you couldn't teach an old dog new tricks and if they didn't mind he preferred to stick to lager.

Miss Foot calmly accepted the wine. 'Claret is a good tonic for the stomach.'

Baz said to Martha, 'You'd better have a glass, then, sweetheart. It might keep you from throwing up,' and winked, which made Martha laugh.

'I assure you, it is a proven prophylactic,' said Miss Foot, possibly misreading their mirth.

'A little wine for thy stomach's sake,' agreed the critic, smiling with his customary seeming-benevolence.

Miss Foot turned her head. 'I don't know if you are familiar with the work of Rudolf Steiner?'

The critic, under the influence of the excellent claret, allowed that he had heard something of the spiritually minded Austrian educationalist but would be intrigued to hear more.

171

By the time the claret was finished, Miss Foot, with the ruthlessness of the innocent, was still expounding the principles of anthroposophy.

'May I get you more wine, sir?'

'Thank you, no,' said the critic. He was looking a little pale. 'I think I'll go to my room.'

Dino waited respectfully while the critic excused himself from the table. Vi also pushed back her chair.

'Hoist with your own petard?' she suggested quietly as, staggering slightly from the motion of the ship, he began to weave a progress through the tables.

The critic grinned at her, not a bit benign. 'Cow.'

'Shall you be coming to the ball later, Mrs Hetherington?'

'If there is still to be one, Dino. In this weather surely it will be cancelled.'

'Oh no. We will be available for any of our guests who want to dance.'

'Come hell or high water?'

'That's us, Mrs Hetherington.'

'Excuse me.' Miss Foot had also risen and, clinging to the chairs at the next table, was making her way awkwardly round to where they stood. 'You don't know the number of that man's cabin? I have some literature which he might enjoy.'

Dino said he was so sorry, he didn't, but in any case they were not permitted to divulge passengers' details.

'I'll leave a note for him at the purser's office.'

The two women left the dining room together. Miss Foot took Vi's arm. 'I heard you mentioning dancing just now. Perhaps you have heard of Doctor Steiner's system of dance. He was a great advocate of the curative potential of movement, to balance the forces within.' Waiting for the lift, she added, 'I notice that your aura has altered.'

'Really? In what way.'

Miss Foot stepped back a little, apparently scrutinising a point just above Vi's head. Her eyes, Vi observed for the first time, were, disconcertingly, somewhat the green of Bruno's.

'It's brighter,' Miss Foot concluded. 'Brighter and clearer. Indigo, perhaps verging on violet.'

23

Vi's walk back to the cabin was unsteady and therefore laborious. The ship had begun to roll and plunge in earnest so that it was difficult not to appear drunk – in fact it was possible that in such conditions only those who were habitually drunk could readily negotiate a straight path. When she reached her room she found a note propped on the desk: *Madam, have unlocked safe. To close plese use own number. See card.*

Reaching into the safe Vi brought out the ashtray in which the conscientious Renato had placed her rings. She tipped them out on to the gold counterpane, all of them, save the solitaire diamond.

She got up again to search the safe, groping in the corners. Nothing to be found but an old black hairgrip.

A strange feeling of lightness came over her. I have lost it, she said to herself. I have lost Ted's ring. And a part of her thought, Oh well, never mind. But not to mind was disrespectful to Ted. Anyway, she was planning to leave it to Harry's wife, when he had one. If he were to marry, she supposed she should say.

Rather shakily, she went to the phone and rang Renato.

'Renato, sorry to bother you but could you come?'

'Of course, madam.'

He was with her in a moment.

'Renato, I can't seem to find my diamond ring.'

A look of quite appalling terror ran like a live current around Renato's face. 'I have not seen it, madam.'

'No, look, it's OK, I'm not accusing you of anything . . .'

'There was no diamond when I put your rings in the safe, madam.' The pupils of his dark eyes had contracted alarmingly.

Vi tried to take hold of the situation. 'Renato, please. Of course I know you have not taken anything. I simply need to establish – to find out when the ring disappeared.'

Renato darted to the safe and began frantically fishing about. 'Look, no diamond. Nothing in here.'

'Yes, I've looked.'

He dropped to his knees and began rummaging under the bed. 'We move the bed.'

'OK.'

Together they shifted first the extraordinarily heavy bed and then the equally cumbersome sofa. Renato trawled the floor on his knees and then scoured the balcony and the bathroom. 'It not go down the plughole?'

'It's too big, I think.'

'I have the plumber look in the pipe.'

'I don't think that's necessary.'

'I fetch him now, madam.'

In no time, Renato was back with man in a boiler suit, a yellow protective helmet, a bucket and a roll of tools. Vi sat on the bed, trying not to mind this well-meant invasion. 'Renato, I am going down to the dance soon.' The awful truth was she would rather not have to bother to search for the ring, though she was ashamed of this and knew it to be wrong-headed.

'No dancing,' said Renato. 'Ship moving too much.' As if to a backward or wayward child he made a see-sawing gesture with his hand.

'I'll go down to see what's going on.'

'No dance tonight, madam.'

Oh dear, Vi thought. We've got into one of our tug of wars but now I seem to be on the other side.

The plumber had unscrewed the U-bend under the wash-basin and retrieved nothing more substantial than a toothpick and a mass of dental floss. Renato began to try to persuade him to delve into the plumbing beneath the bath.

'Honestly, Renato. It wouldn't go down a plughole. I know that ring very well. It was my engagement ring.'

This was a bad move since the admission brought on a further flap.

'Oh, madam, your engagement ring. We find it. I promise. I promise we find it.'

'Renato, I am going to dress for the dance and then I shall go down and report the ring lost at the purser's office.'

But this only threatened to make matters worse. 'Madam, they will ask me about it. They will think . . .'

'It's all right, Renato.' It was necessary to become firm. 'I shall not mention you at all. I shall explain that I put the rings in the safe myself.'

Renato seemed a little mollified. 'Thank you, madam. And I look around your room again. Undo the bed in case the ring in mattress.'

Vi, carrying the heels for balance, and walking warily in Annie's strapless dress, called in at the purser's office on Deck Three. The business of reporting the lost ring was, as she feared, lengthy and tedious. Since she had decided, for her own sake as much as his, not to involve Renato – for really she could not bear to provoke any more anxiety – her account, speedily improvised, created certain problems. Yes, her jewellery had all been locked in the room safe (she did not own up to the shoe bag in the suitcase), but since she had removed all the rings and placed them in the safe without checking them it was possible, even likely, that the diamond had been lost before this. Did anyone other than herself have the safe combination number? Not as far as she knew. Could she give some indication of the number in case they needed to check on security? In view of the loss, she felt it best not to reveal these details for the moment (memo, remember to ask Renato what number he used). When was the last time she was aware of wearing the ring? She had no idea but would try her best to recollect. Was the ring insured?

Oh Christ, thought Vi, I don't believe it is, for when, after Ted's death, she had discovered how much he was insuring it for she had allowed the insurance to lapse.

This is the story of my life, she decided, taking the lift up to Deck Eight. I let all insurances lapse.

At Deck Five Ken, in evening dress, got into the lift. 'Ken, how dashing.'

'You too, Vi. You look sensational.'

'I'm off to the ball.'

'You *shall* go to the ball,' said Ken. 'Jen's in bed, stuffed to the gills with seasick pills. She said I was getting on her nerves. She insisted I come dancing.'

'Well, I'm sorry for Jen but very glad for me. I need an ally. I'm a complete novice at dancing but I am rather loving it.'

'It will be a pleasure, Vi. I'll need protection from some of those single ladies. I don't feel quite safe. Some, I swear, have beaks.'

Vi, relieved not to be thought to have a beak, said she could do with some protection too. 'A nice man at my table in the Alexandria, who studies traditional African healers, says that his healers prescribe lion's fat for courage.'

'You don't need lion's fat, Vi. You've got me.'

Because she was grateful she told him about the ring.

'That's terrible. I hope you're insured.'

'Well, that's the thing, Ken. I'm not sure I am.'

Had the missing ring been Jen's Ken could hardly have looked more aghast. However, not even mutely did he convey reproach. The world, thought Vi, might be divided into those who on receipt of news of any personal disaster reach for reproach and those who reach first for sympathy. It occurred to her that that was what had been wrong for her with Ted. For all his kindness, he could never resist saying I told you so. He was saying it even now from the grave.

'It was my engagement ring,' she went on. 'It is so valuable that I couldn't bear to think about it, you see.'

Ken, who didn't at all see, nodded but his forehead was still furrowed in the odd V shape that in a man denotes real concern. I mustn't spoil his evening, thought Vi.

'I expect it will turn up. My poor steward is even now on his knees, I would bet, going over my room with a fine-tooth comb. A strange thing to search with, don't you think?'

Ken was not so easily distracted. 'When do you remember wearing it last?'

'I've been racking my brains. But my mind's a blur.'

'That's shock,' said Ken, glad to have found a handle on the situation. 'Come on, you need a brandy.'

He marched her to the bar and ordered two large brandy and sodas.

The numbers toughing out the weather were noticeably sparse. Most were downing folk remedies against potential sickness, Fernet Branca, for example, or drinking with the bravado of those hell-bent on throwing caution to the winds.

'You wouldn't like a Fernet Branca, Vi?'

'Frankly, Ken, Fernet Branca is more likely to make me sick.'

'You're a good sailor though, you said.'

'Well, that's my boast. Though I suppose I've never been thoroughly tried.'

Despite the weather, the dance had drawn quite a number of people in evening wear especially dry-cleaned for the occasion and eager to get their money's worth. When Vi and Ken reached the salon, the ball was in full swing.

'Righty-ho, then, Vi. Time to face the music. Shall we waltz?'

'I can just about manage that.'

'Put yourself in my hands. Dancing's a man's responsibility.'

Ken, as she might have expected, turned out to be a first-class dancer. They danced a waltz and then a foxtrot, over which, recalling her dance with Dino, she managed not to make too great a fool of herself. At Vi's request they sat out a couple of dances but, seeing Martha Cleever hovering at the edge of the room, Vi said, 'Ken, come and meet Martha. You must dance with her. She's a champion.'

Martha said, 'Hey, I'm really just poking my nose round the door. Baz has gone to bed with a book and I was wakeful and kind of drawn by the music.'

'It's as well you're here or poor Ken would be saddled with me for the duration.'

'Very happy to be, Vi.'

'Yes, but you should be dancing with an equal.'

'I'm not properly dressed. I can't dance in tracksuit pants and these.' Martha looked down at her rubber flip-flops.

'Oh go on,' said Vi. 'What does it matter? What size are you? You can borrow my shoes if you like.'

Vi, barefoot, watching Martha, proficient on the borrowed

heels, and the other women, more splendid but maybe less original in gauze and satin and sequins, the chandeliers making an artist's brightness of their hair, was overcome by a fugitive exuberance. Only the thought of Renato searching, she feared fruitlessly, for the diamond brought on a lowering of spirits. What ever could have happened to it? She knew in her bones that Renato had not pocketed it. And no one, the purser's office had assured her repeatedly, had handed in jewellery of any kind.

'Mrs Hetherington?'

'Dino.'

'It's the cha-cha-cha next.'

'But look, I have no shoes.'

'You must dance the cha-cha-cha, Mrs Hetherington. I insist.'

Martha, passing Vi on the tilting floor, cried out, 'I must give back your shoes,' and Vi in reply called, 'It doesn't matter,' which was as well since both were ignored by their partners. Ken, red-faced and sweating, was flicking Martha cavalierly from side to side, as Des, with equal efficiency but more decorum, swung Vi back and forth.

At the end of the dance the two women dropped down together, panting.

'Wow! I've not had such fun since I was a kid.'

'According to Miss Foot, dance balances the forces within the body.'

'She may be right!'

The ship made a sudden lurch, causing a general stumbling and from some quarters delighted squeals. When the next dance was called Ken stood up again. 'Come on,' he said to Martha. 'Tomorrow we may all be in Davy Jones's locker.'

'But Vi'll want her shoes back. Vi?'

'Really, I'm not bothered. I'd lend you my dress too if it wouldn't cause a commotion.'

She watched them executing a scintillating quickstep. The two of them looked in their element.

'Mrs Hetherington. You're not leaving?'

'No, I'm going for some air and a cigarette.'

'But your feet . . . ?'

'Oh, my feet are fine.'

'You'll be blown away in this wind. May I come with you to see that you are safe?'

'Of course, Dino.' Though she hardly cared if she were blown to the ends of the earth.

The wind had got up a vicious speed and they had to creep, heads bent, round to the smokers' corner, the semi-protected area aft.

'You don't happen to remember,' Vi asked, as he was trying to light her cigarette, 'if I was wearing a diamond ring when we sat and smoked outside the night before last. I suppose as it was dark you wouldn't have noticed.'

Des had turned up the flame of his lighter and his face was briefly illuminated. The pupils of his eyes looked startlingly black. In the sudden flare of light Vi observed something.

'I'm afraid I don't, Mrs Hetherington.'

'I just wondered. Only it's lost. I don't know where or when. I'm trying to retrace things in my mind.'

'Is it valuable?'

'Very valuable, I'm afraid. My poor husband would be distraught.' She remembered that she had told this man that she had not loved Ted and felt remorseful. It was not the price of the ring that mattered – it was that Ted had given it to her, with love and pride.

It was not much fun smoking in the wind. Vi tried to

throw her cigarette overboard but it blew back on to the ship. 'Goodness, it really is getting rough. Shall we go back in?'

'If you wish, Mrs Hetherington.' He held her arm as they fought their way back to the door, holding fast to the handrail.

'Do call me Vi.'

Inside he asked, 'Will you dance, Vi?'

'One more dance, maybe.'

'The night is young.'

'But I am not.'

'I think you have a young soul.'

'I'm afraid my soul is as old as God.'

He seemed distracted as they waltzed. She said goodnight and thanked him and went across to Ken and Martha, who were sitting at a table over a bottle and a couple of glasses. 'Violet! Some bubbly?'

Martha said, 'Ken's leading me into the path of temptation.' It did not look as if she had put up much of a fight.

'OK, I'll have a glass.'

'Atta girl, I'll fetch one over.'

The ship made another sharp lurch, producing more staggering and excited screams. 'Davy Jones's locker, here we come,' said Ken, arriving with a champagne glass held aloft.

The ship was moving closer to the waters off Newfoundland, not far from where the *Titanic* had sunk. Several of the more ghoulish passengers, furnished with this information, were busy spreading it about, gleefully depriving others of their blissful ignorance and in some cases a good night's sleep.

The band had started up with the syncopated rhythm of the samba and Vi, feeling suddenly weary, said, 'I'm off. Keep the shoes, Martha. You can return them in the morning.'

'Don't turn into a pumpkin,' Ken called after her.

At the lift, however, she stopped and then turned back to

the salon. Ken and Martha were hugger-mugger, engaged in what you could tell at a glance was an enthralling conversation. Vi, unwilling to break in, stood there until Martha, sensing eyes on her back, turned round.

'Sorry, but I forgot there was something I wanted to ask you, Ken.'

'We've discovered that we're the ship's ghetto,' Ken announced. His face, Vi observed, was flushed.

'We've been comparing notes about our families' lives,' Martha said. She was looking slightly awkward.

'And deaths. Our parents were four that Hitler missed. Lucky for them.'

'And us,' Martha added, with a hint of reproval. She moved just a fraction away from Ken's arm, which was resting easily along the back of her chair.

'Well,' Vi said, 'compared to that I have a very trivial question. What was it you told me about people's eyes, Ken, when you helped me with my email?'

'Eyes right he's not all right, you mean?'

'That's it.'

'It goes like this: when you try to tap your memory, your eyes involuntarily shift to the left. If you're tapping into your imagination – or making up a story, or telling porky pies – then they move to the right.'

'And that's tried and tested, is it?'

'Well, I won't say it would stand up in a court of law.'

24

There was a vase of pink and yellow carnations on the desk in Vi's room and propped against it a note: *Madam I have undo the bed. No ring. Very sory. Renato.*

She went out on to the balcony. The ship, for all its tonnage, was rocking like a toy boat in a baby ogre's bath. There was a sudden tremendous crack overhead and the sky blazed in a brilliant awning of light – behind it there followed a deep violet glow. She breathed in the powerful smell of the sea, whose moods and ancient vicissitudes no one has yet learned to control. There was something marvellous about standing there in bare feet, bare-shouldered in her silver dress to the heavy-shouldered wind. She would stand there. Stand there in the weather. Perhaps she would be struck by lightning?

'Congratulations,' Tessa Carfield had said.

She was hosting her Midsummer's Eve party. Vi had not wanted to go to this. She did not shine at parties and had never warmed to Tessa Carfield. She was there on sufferance because Bruno had accused her of jealousy.

'How can you be jealous of Tessa Carfield? She has an arse like a juggernaut.'

'I simply suggested that you were spending rather a lot of time at her cottage.'

Bruno's habit of rating women according to the size of their bottoms was one of the things she had left without comment too long. To do so now would provoke an almighty row.

'It's my work, Vi. You, as we see, manage to get your work done with no trouble. I have to find some place of asylum for mine.'

'Fine.'

The notion of 'asylum' was not reassuring but she was by now too wary to question it.

Bruno said, 'I can't deal with your possessiveness,' and ignored her for the evening.

And now she was reporting for duty, as agreed, and he hadn't even arrived. She had talked for a while to a tall, grey-haired solicitor called Edward, whose wife, he explained, had multiple sclerosis. He fetched her a drink and told her about Peter Brook's production of *A Midsummer Night's Dream* which was causing a stir at the Roundhouse. 'Do go. The fairies swing on trapezes and make extraordinary sounds through plastic tubes. Look, here's my card. Give me a ring. I'm angeling the show so I can get you a couple of tickets any time.'

But he had left early to get back to his wife and now Vi was left stranded without support with an unmediated Tessa Carfield.

'Congratulations on what?' Vi hoped this didn't sound too rude. Tessa Carfield was always very polite. Too polite, on balance.

'On your prize.'

'What's this? What's this? What prize?' Bruno had arrived and come up behind them and was digging his chin, in a way he supposed amusing, into Vi's shoulder.

Before Vi could say, 'Hello, Bruno' and steer him away Tessa Carfield had gathered momentum. 'I've just heard the news from Duncan.' Duncan Bredon was a poet, widely tipped for the Oxford Poetry Chair. 'Duncan was one of the judges. He told me in strict confidence, of course, knowing what close friends we all are.'

'I don't know how you could have done this,' Bruno said for what might have been the sixth time.

They had caught the last tube and were walking down Kensington Park Road from Notting Hill. Vi had taken off her shoes. If asked why, she was planning to say it was because they hurt her, but it was a measure of the disgrace she was in that Bruno had so far made no comment but walked on wearing, she knew without looking, a face of unflagging resentment. In fact, she had taken off her shoes because she needed some sort of physical discomfort to distract her from this other awful pain.

'How could you enter for a poetry prize and not tell me? Unless it was that you didn't want me to compete.'

This was dreadful. She did not say, You couldn't have entered, or been entered (for it was not her idea after all but the publisher's), you've not published a collection of poems, because now, suddenly, the greater terror was not what she might have done to him but that he might recognise that he was not a poet and never could be one.

'I hadn't realised you were so competitive,' he continued.

They carried on down the hill in single file, tears like acid channelling Vi's cheeks. Bruno had withdrawn into one of his unnerving silences. They passed the Corinthian-columned orange church, which announced on a neat green notice that a private service of exorcism was available on request. Vi could not bear it a second longer.

'I don't give a monkey's fuck about the prize. I didn't enter it myself, the publishers did, and I didn't tell you because I knew you'd mind and I never thought I would win. I didn't know myself until this morning. And you've been out all day. I was going to tell you this evening if that bloody cow hadn't stuck her barge arse in.'

In a blind fury she flung her shoes into the road.

Bruno walked into the road and picked them up. He began to walk back to the pavement, slowly and deliberately, almost into the way of an oncoming car, which swerved wildly as the driver, understandably furious, hooted repeatedly.

'Bruno, for God's sake, what are you doing . . . ?'

He returned to the pavement as if sleep-walking, his face white and grim, and handed her the shoes. 'I can't live with this, Vi.'

Vi felt frightened. 'What does that mean?'

'What do you think it means? I need space. I need to go away to be by myself.'

'Where?'

'I can go to Tessa's cottage. She's not going to be using it for a while.'

Vi wanted to say, Don't leave me, Bruno. I am scared. I can't seem to manage things as I did. Instead she said, 'Oh. Well then, that's fine.'

'I have to do this, Vi. Otherwise, it's going to kill me.'

'Of course I don't want to kill you, Bruno.'

Why not? asked the voice.

'I don't think you know what you do to me.'

'OK,' she roared, 'I don't. I don't know at all what I do, or am supposed to have done. You can have your fucking space.' She hurled the shoes one by one back into the middle of the road.

Bruno stopped dead. 'Go and pick those up.'

'No.'

'Pick them up.'

'They're my shoes and I can do what the hell I bloody well like with them.'

'I'm not walking home with you in bare feet.'

'Why not?'

'You look like a tramp or a gypsy.'

'What's wrong with gypsies? It's dark anyway.' As if that mattered.

'I don't wish to walk down the street, even in the dark, with someone in your condition. And, so this is clear, I want to live with a civilised woman who knows how to behave. Not a wild-cat.'

'Like Tessa Carfield, I suppose?'

'I knew you were jealous.' Vi hit him. 'And violent.'

Vi took off the silver dress and stood in her knickers on the balcony. Then she took off the knickers and stood there naked. Despite the thunder and lightning, there was no rain. She wished there would be rain so she could be drenched through. She felt that to be thoroughly drenched by rain would help.

After a bit, she went inside and extracted from the pile on the desk a book with a torn brown dust jacket.

Dragonish by H.V. St John. Under her name in smaller type she read: 'Winner of the Warner Hepplewhite Prize'. She opened the book and looked at the dedication: *For Edwin: Love Always.*

'Ed?'

'Vi, what time is it?'

'I don't know. Two, maybe.'

'What's up?'

'Could I come to stay?'

'Of course. When are you coming?'

'How about right now?'

Vi walked to Paddington Station and caught the milk train

to Oxford. From the station she walked down past the Randolph Hotel, where she encountered a tousled young couple in evening dress, the girl carrying a single red rose. At the Martyrs' Memorial, nowadays a useful point of contact for bicycle thieves and drug dealers, she stood, looking at the spiky memento of the place where Cranmer and his colleagues had been burned to death for protesting, remembering how Bruno had filled his flat with roses for her arrival.

At the foot of the memorial, a couple of tramps were huddled in thin sleeping bags, as much victims, perhaps, of their own convictions as the martyrs. She was observing them, with fellow feeling, when one woke and beerily requested money for a cup of tea. Vi gave him five pounds on condition that he spend it on drink. Then she set off up the Banbury Road.

Birds in the well-tended Oxford gardens, ecstatically celebrating the heartless summer, harbingered her progress up the long walk to Squitchy Lane, where Edwin had rented a flat. She rang the bell and waited, steeled for there to be no answer. And then Edwin was at the door in a shabby dressing gown. Somehow, all his dressing gowns managed to look shabby.

'Hello. Coffee's up.'

'I don't know what else you would have expected,' he said as they drank the coffee in his kitchen. It was not too clean, with the kind of grease that is ingrained and depressing. Not a patch on Church Rate Walk. 'Bruno believes he is a poet and you go and win a prize for poetry. It's a catastrophe for him.'

'And me.'

'Only if you let it be.'

'He's gone off to Tessa Carfield's cottage to write about his horrible sorcerers. I can't bear those creepy sorcerers.'

'He won't enjoy it. Bruno hates to be alone.'

That was true. 'How do you know that?'

'Oh, you know, we were at school together. He needs an audience, if only for his moods.'

When Edwin had left for work, with a copy of *The Duchess of Malfi*, which he was teaching his sixth formers, Vi walked back into town down the Woodstock Road, more verdant than its counterpart, the Banbury Road. Passing a narrow street, she saw some students drinking from cans of lager, singing 'The Times They Are A-Changin'' and throwing cigarettes to each other across the road. One dropped a tobacco tin from an upper window to a friend below. The carnival atmosphere suggested that the exam results were out and they were celebrating, still on the far side of worldly responsibility.

Vi walked on past the Martyrs' Memorial. What ever could it be like to be bound to a stake, waiting for an intolerable heat to render to ashes your living flesh and bone? Her tramp had left the other asleep in his skimpy tartan bag. She hoped her one was off buying drink.

Reaching Christ Church Meadow, she took off her shoes and went barefoot over the still dampish grass. The shoeless late-night walk with Bruno had been a successful punishment and a large blister had formed on the ball of her right foot. She found a patch free of fresh cowpats and lay down on her back, smelling the inimitable scent of living grass.

Above her smarting eyes wheeled a cacophony of rooks, their ragged wings etched sharply against the virginal blue sky. A little way off, cattle lying in gleaming shapely heaps cast cool compact shadows in the uncompromising June sunlight. There is something peculiar, she thought, about the way a shadow is and isn't the thing it is a reflection of.

After a while she fell asleep, worn out by the early start and the crying. She dreamed of Bruno but when she woke she could not recall any fragment of the dream.

FIFTH DAY

First rate: *Until steam-power took over, British navy ships were rated according to the number of heavy cannon they carried. A ship of a hundred cannon or more was known as a First Rate Line-of-battle ship.*

25

Although Vi had been awake since dawn, she felt no inclination to sleep. Putting on trousers, a sweater and plimsolls, she let herself out of her room and walked down the now familiar red-carpeted stairs.

Outside the Atlantic was thrashing the ship for its life, throwing up spectacular plumes of spray which, blowing on to the deck, were leaving the boards wet and perilous. Good. Perilous was what her spirit craved. Remembering the strange night stroll with the critic, she recalled his desire to become immersed in the ocean – or his expressed desire, since for all she knew this was a pose. No, not a pose. He wasn't posing with her then, maybe a mood of the moment.

She knew these moods of the moment. But there were more enduring strains: repeated discouragements which grow to tidal waves of devastation, more lasting in their consequences.

('Large things are bearable,' Edwin had said, when he came home that evening after she had taken flight to his flat in Oxford. 'It's the small things which break us.'

'Is this a small thing, Ed?' she had asked him, pitifully.

'An accumulation of small things, I would say.')

Reaching a sheltered area, she stopped for a cigarette and found she had left the packet behind in her room.

She was regretting the forgotten cigarettes when Miss Foot, in a mackintosh cape and sou'wester, came round the corner clinging to the handrail. She stopped and stood, rain running from her sou'wester, catching her breath.

'I felt that I must come out and witness the spectacle in all its glory. I have no balcony, you see.'

'Me too,' said Vi. 'Though I'm lucky, I do have a balcony.' For some reason, she did not seem to mind the arrival of Miss Foot.

'I expect you've earned one, my dear.'

'Oh, I don't imagine so,' said Vi hastily. 'It's my husband's money. My late husband, I should say. I'm giving most of what he left me away to our sons but I kept enough for this voyage.' How strange that she should be confiding this to Miss Foot. Not even Harry and Dan knew her plans for Ted's legacy.

'I meant in a previous life.'

'Oh.'

'Perhaps you don't believe in other lives?'

Vi considered. Miss Foot was not Kimberley Crane. 'Not really.'

'Nevertheless you experience them. I expect you think I'm a batty old woman.'

Vi, not knowing how to answer this, took the coward's way and laughed.

'People do,' Miss Foot continued. 'They suppose I am off my rocker but I don't mind. Provided one doesn't mind what people think, one is free. Or comparatively free, don't you agree?'

'I do,' said Vi, endeavouring to make up for the laughter. 'Most definitely.'

'I can tell you have had a past life. A troublesome, even a troubled one. But I believe that it is about to change.'

'Goodness.'

'Goodness has something to do with it, yes. You attract the destructive but you also attract the good. It is a question of discrimination, of distinguishing between the two conditions. They can, as I am sure you are aware by now, look alike.'

'I see.'

'But do you, my dear?'

The dim lights under the shelter cast a disconcerting halo about Miss Foot's flat undistinguished face.

Vi said, 'What you say about my life having been troubled is quite correct.'

'There you are,' said Miss Foot as if an important point had been settled. 'But that will pass, is passing. I hope you don't mind my approaching you. I had half a mind to say more earlier but I followed my instinct and waited. And now, you see, here you are. The world always responds if we listen.'

'Thank you for approaching me,' said Vi, unlike the world unsure how she should respond.

'No need for thanks. The benefit is mutual. Real benefit always is. One can never know how things may turn around.'

'No,' said Vi. 'That is true.'

She was wondering whether it would be nosy to ask Miss Foot why she was on the ship when her companion said, 'I am travelling to New York to visit my sister. We've not met for fifty years. She has cancer and would like to see me again. I shall try to help her but I fear she is resistant to help. That is the true sin against the Holy Ghost – the refusal of grace and mercy.'

'Yes,' said Vi. 'I think you might be right about that.'

'She is intense,' Miss Foot went on. 'But intensity is not an index of spiritual depth.'

'Certainly not.'

'I would not be surprised, though naturally I shall not say this, if it were not the intensity that led to the cancer. Misdirected, it can be malign.'

'I am sure.'

'Well, I'll be off to my bed. I am reading *Moby-Dick*. I felt I should acquaint myself a little more with the Americans in preparation for this trip. The writing is very energetic – the Americans are energetic, I admire them for that – but it could do with some editing. There is far too much about harpoons.'

'Yes,' said Vi. 'I agree with you about that too.'

Miss Foot stood looking out at the raging sea. Her lips were working and she appeared to be murmuring silently to herself. At last she said, 'I saw you dancing with that poor young man.'

'This evening?'

'Yes. You may remember I said that Doctor Steiner was a believer in the virtues of dance. I dropped in to watch the dancing for a while and I saw you. Grace and mercy, remember.'

'I'll try to remember.'

'Well, goodnight, dear.'

Vi made her way round to the port side of the ship, where the force of the wind was less fierce and the deck a little dryer. Before she drew near enough to be sure, she had guessed the identity of the figure standing smoking under the shelter.

'Dino? I was just thinking about you,' she said.

Vi, alone in the flat, with no job, no Bruno, Annie in Brisbane, where things were apparently going well with her gynaecologist, and Edwin in Oxford till the end of term, was unbearably lonely. Her solitary state was brought home to her by Mr DellaCosta, who noticed the reduction in her fruit and veg purchases.

'You on your own, darling?' he asked one day.

Vi explained that Bruno was away working.

'He don't want to leave a lovely girl like you on her own too long.'

The next time she saw Mr DellaCosta he presented her with a bunch of fat spears of asparagus. 'That's what my ma give my daddy when he look to stray. You give him some of that, sweetheart. Your man come back to you, you see.'

Vi ate the asparagus alone. She had had no word from Bruno and could only suppose that for the time being he did not want to come back.

In a fit of worse-than-usual despondency, she arranged to visit her father, who seemed almost offended at the prospect of having his evening interrupted by his only child.

'I'm afraid I cannot have you spend the night, Honour. My daily's on her annual leave and there is no one to make up the bed.'

Vi did not say that she could quite well make up the bed herself. She had, in any case, no desire to spend the night. Her father had taken to using nylon sheets in insipid pastels, which he boasted of buying by mail order from Brentford Nylons on the Great West Road. Her old bedroom, which for a time had served as the spare, had begun to do duty as the repository of his bulk buying, which, she concluded, was another means of fending off guests, if it wasn't a symptom of him going out of his mind. When she had visited last, the room had been stacked with rolls of bargain lavatory paper, catering-size boxes of soap powder and, more puzzling, jars of English mustard, pickled onions and salad cream. Also, quantities of 100-watt light bulbs, particularly bizarre since her father was fanatical about turning off electricity and for some years had lived in almost perpetual semi-darkness.

The morning after her doleful attempt at igniting familial

affection she woke with a sense that she might also be in danger of slipping towards some fatal point of disintegration. For all she could tell, she too might be quietly going out of her mind. It was this fear that prompted her to ring the agreeable-seeming man she had met at Tessa Carfield's party. That it was the last occasion on which she and Bruno had been some sort of a couple was in her mind when she rang the firm of solicitors named on his card.

He answered the phone himself so it must have been a direct line. 'I was just thinking about you. Funny how that sometimes happens and then the person you're thinking of rings.'

Her first thought was that he had confused her with someone else. 'Edward, it's Violet St John.'

'Yes, I know.'

'Oh. I was ringing about *A Midsummer Night's Dream.*'

'You would like tickets?'

'If that's really OK,' Vi said, relieved to be so readily remembered.

'Indeed it is,' he had said. 'How many would you like? It seems to have become incredibly popular, so I doubt I could get hold of more than two.'

'Oh, one's enough, honestly. It's just me.'

'Let me have your number and I'll call you back.'

He rang back almost at once. 'I can get two tickets so if you really have no one you would rather bring I might come along myself, if I can get someone to look in to see to Margaret.'

'No, there's no one. That would be fine. Thank you.'

He named a day the following week adding, 'If you fancy a bite afterwards there are some fairish places to eat in Primrose Hill.'

'That would be very nice.'

'Good. Shall I meet you there or would you like me to pick you up?'

Vi, too unused to being chauffeured to be at ease with this idea, said she would meet him at the Roundhouse before the start of the performance.

Two days later, a letter from Bruno arrived:

Dear Vi, If you would like to come down here I can now see you. There are trains from Paddington, via Newport. If you come, could you bring the catalogue for the exhibition we saw at the Horniman? It's in the bookcase somewhere. I can meet your train if you let me have times. B.

Vi rang Edward's office and got his secretary. She asked the secretary to give Mr Hetherington her apologies and explained that she had been 'suddenly called away', which struck her as the sort of language a solicitor would understand.

She packed her better summer clothes in some excitement and had her hair done and, in a reckless mood of anticipated happiness, her nails, bright red. She hunted for the catalogue from the Horniman exhibition and finding it flicked through to the picture of the bleak figure with the peg through its head. It stared blankly out at her and she was suddenly reminded of the little bat-wing purse Bruno had shown her that day they had quarrelled.

Slightly guiltily, she searched for the purse in Bruno's desk and chest of drawers. But with no luck.

On the morning she was due to leave she woke at four, choreographing in her mind the meeting with Bruno: he would sweep her up into his arms, they would make love by the side of a mountain stream, he would apologise, confess his faults and they would live happily ever after. Maybe that was going a bit far . . .

When the phone rang at just past five a.m. she answered in trepidation in case it was Bruno calling to put her off. But it was not Bruno, it was Edwin.

'Vi?'

'Ed!'

'Vi. Can you come.'

'Where? Why?'

'To Oxford. I need you.'

'What's up?'

'I'm at the police station.'

'What's happened?'

'I'll tell you when you get here. Get a taxi when you arrive and ask for the St Aldate's police station.'

26

'Do you think I could have one of your cigarettes?'

'Sure.' Des tried to light it for her. 'It's not the best weather.' He was wary, Vi could tell, of using her name.

'I rather like it,' Vi said, thinking that the wind had so blown about her hair that she might well look a little deranged.

'Me too. I like all weathers as a matter of fact.' He had dropped his dance host manners with his Italian accent and sounded younger, less sophisticated.

'Desmond,' Vi said. 'Would you like to come up to my room for a drink?'

'It's not really allowed. I could get into trouble for less.'

'How about if I were to say, if asked, that I was overtaken with sickness and you were escorting me to my room?'

'Right. If you like.' His reluctance was almost palpable.

They walked up the red-carpeted stairs with Vi, for the sake of show, holding on to his arm. There was no one about, and they made their way along the corridor to Vi's room without meeting a soul.

'Nice flowers,' he said, looking at Renato's ice-cream-coloured carnations.

'My steward left them for me. He is mortified about the ring.'

'The ring?'

'My diamond,' said Vi. 'Which has gone missing. What would you like to drink? I have a complete minibar here which is woefully untouched.'

'I'll have a beer, please.'

'You can have a short if you'd prefer.'

'No, beer's fine, thanks.'

'A glass, or do you prefer the bottle?'

She suspected he would prefer the latter but he accepted a glass.

Vi poured herself a brandy. 'I've been thinking,' she said, 'and I feel sure that I was wearing the diamond ring when we smoked that evening on deck. Would you have a think for me and see if you can remember it?'

'I'll try.'

'Thank you. Only my poor steward is in a state over this. He's afraid he will be accused of theft. But I know that he didn't take it.'

'Who else could have?'

'Well, you know how it is, Des. Some things you do know. I don't always trust my instincts but in this case I am and I know Renato did not take my ring.'

Des shifted in his chair. 'So who did?'

'I've been pondering. I think it may have dropped off my finger. My hands tend to shrink when they're cold. My husband used to warn me that I might lose a ring one day. Of course, when he was around I had the wedding ring on to secure the diamond. He would say it's my own fault for taking my wedding ring off.'

'But it's insured?'

'Oh yes,' said Vi, 'it's insured, as you would expect. My husband saw to that. But with something like this it is not the money which matters.' She looked levelly at Des. 'Do you see?'

'Yeah, I do.'

'So what I thought was this: you might very kindly institute a search among your colleagues, in case some sharp-eyed person spots it, on a ledge or under something. The ship's so big I can't possibly undertake to search everywhere myself. There would be a reward.'

'Sure,' said Des. 'How much would that be, if you don't mind my asking?'

'The amount it is insured for.'

'And that's . . . ? Just so's I can say.'

'I don't have the insurance papers with me. But you have my promise that whoever finds the ring will get the same sum.'

'Righto. I'll ask about.'

'You see, there is only the rest of today left, really, before we reach New York. So if I'm to have any hope of finding it I need to get a move on. You might start looking around the area where we were sitting that night. Would you do that for me?'

'Sure.'

'Thank you. Another beer?'

'No, I'd best be getting back.'

'I'll check to see that all's safe.'

When Vi opened the door she saw Renato hurrying down the corridor. 'Renato.'

'Madam, you have found your ring?'

'Sadly not. One of the dance hosts has just escorted me to my room. I went dancing, perhaps unwisely, and wasn't feeling too well.'

'Oh, madam. You like I fetch the doctor?'

'I'm fine now, thank you. He's just leaving. And he has very kindly offered to help in the search for my ring. Dino,' she called into the room where he was standing looking awkward, 'I've explained to Renato that you kindly saw me back to my room.'

He had jumped up and was smiling with a dreadful desperate eagerness. 'Are you sure you are all right now, Mrs Hetherington?'

'Thank you, Dino. Renato will see to me if I need anything.'

Vi rang directory enquiries and asked for the number of St Aldate's police station. When she got through, half an hour later, she asked for Edwin.

'I'm afraid you can't speak to him, miss.'

'He rang me from this station about half an hour ago.'

'Mr Chadwick has been detained, miss.'

'Can't I speak to him?'

'I'm afraid not, miss. He's detained in the cells.'

'My God. Why?'

'I'm afraid I can't answer that, miss.'

'Will you give him a message?'

'I'll make a note you rang, miss. May I take the name?'

Bruno was waiting on a deserted platform at the station in Knighton. He looked thinner and had gone quite brown. He kissed her distantly on the cheek and picked up her bag.

'I'll take this to the car.'

'Does the car go with the cottage?'

'You couldn't manage here without transport.'

'Bruno,' she said. 'Listen, I'm going to have to go back – well, anyway to Oxford. Maybe at once.'

'Why?'

'Edwin's in trouble. He rang me from an Oxford police station just before I left.'

They had reached the car, a pale blue Morris Hillman. Bruno put down her bag with great deliberation and stood with his big hand placed flat on the car's roof. 'What kind of trouble?'

'They wouldn't tell me.'

'They?'

'The police. The one I spoke to was a pig.'

'Edwin didn't tell you?'

'I got the impression he couldn't talk for long. He sounded frantic. I must go to him.'

'Why?'

'Well . . .'

'No, Vi, I mean this. Why do you have to go running to Edwin? If he's in trouble he needs a solicitor, not you. What can you do?'

'He didn't ring a solicitor, he rang me.'

'Either he's been had up for drunkenness or it's some sex thing. He's probably been caught picking up boys.'

'So?'

'So are you going?'

'Well . . .'

Bruno picked up her bag from where he had placed it and moved it about a foot to position it at her feet. 'If you go then take that.'

'Meaning . . . ?'

'I don't want to see you again.'

'Bruno, Edwin's your friend too.'

You knew it would be like this, said the voice.

'He didn't ring me.'

'How could he ring you? You're not on the phone. I haven't been able to ring you. No one has been able to ring you for weeks.'

'Please don't embarrass me in a public place, Vi.'

'For Christ's sake,' she yelled, 'you can't call this a public place. There's not a living soul in sight.'

An elderly man in a uniform came out of the station into the yard and looked over to see what was going on and then went inside again.

Bruno said, 'Either you get in the car and come with me to the cottage, or you catch a train to wherever in the world you please. And if you do that I shall not see you again.'

Leave, said the voice. Get on the next train.

'Bruno, please listen . . .'

'No, Vi, you listen. Either get in the car – or go.'

Go, said the voice. Go *now*.

She got in the car.

27

When Vi woke, the storm had passed and the ship was cradled in a muffling fog. She could see nothing beyond the lifeboat hanging just beneath her, ready for disaster.

She dressed and went down for breakfast in the Alexandria. Patrick was there, spooning in cereal.

'Patrick, I hoped you'd be here.'

'Violet, are you going to say all the names you don't like?'

'Do you want to go first?'

'I don't like Jaiden or Lucas or Charles.'

'That's interesting. I quite like Charles.'

'He's a boy at nursery I don't like. So are Jaiden and Lucas boys I don't like.'

'Any others?'

'I don't like Jodie or Tina.'

'I agree.'

'Or Gabriella.'

'Not nice girls?'

'Jodie pinches people. Gabriella had nits. Tina spits at me.'

'How horrid of her. Do you spit back?'

'We don't spit at people do we, Patrick?' his mother re-monstrated.

'Your turn to say what names you don't like.'

Vi said, 'OK, I don't like Samantha, Sandra, Lulu, Kylie or Kim . . .' She stopped short, aware that she was on the edge of an indiscretion.

Patrick looked at her sharply. 'You were going to say Kimberley.'

'I said Kim,' said Vi.

'There's a lady called Kimberley here on the boat. I heard my mummy and daddy talking about her.'

'And I don't like Roy, or Karl, or Eric, or Justin or Rex,' Vi continued, feeling the best policy was to press on.

'Rex is the name of a dog!'

'Well, I don't like it.'

'You don't like Skarloey either, do you?'

'Most definitely I do not like Skarloey.'

'But you like Patrick.'

'I do.'

'Because you like me.'

'Exactly.'

'I don't like poo poo or bum bum,' Patrick confided. 'Do you?'

'Time we went, Patrick. Say "bye bye" to Mrs Hetherington.'

'She's not called Mrs Hetherington. She's called Violet. She's my friend.'

'Thank you, Patrick,' Violet said. 'I am honoured. Goodbye for now.'

'Bye bye poo poo wee wee bum bum.'

Vi was enjoying a pot of coffee to herself when Martha Cleever, her hair in a soigné French pleat and wearing lipstick, arrived. She had on a short skirt which revealed a pair of sturdy legs.

'Oh hi, Vi, if I'd known you were here I'd have brought back the shoes.'

Vi said it didn't matter a scrap as she had no plans to wear the shoes. Any time before that evening would do.

Martha seemed a little ill at ease. 'I'm glad to have found you. Baz will be along any minute.' She paused to pour herself coffee.

Vi, who had an inkling of what was coming, offered to pass the milk and sugar.

'Thank you, I take neither. I wanted to ask you, I was very late back to our room last night. Ken and I got talking and the time just flew by.'

'I'm glad you both had such a nice time.'

'Oh we did,' Martha said. 'Not that there was any, you know. We just talked.'

'Well, that's often the best fun.'

'Oh yes. We found we had a lot in common. Ken's grand-mother died in Ravensbrück and both my grandparents died in Dachau. It kind of made a connection between us.'

'I can see how it might.'

'Anyway, before I knew it, it was three a.m. and Baz was kind of worried, so I told him, well, to be honest I said that I'd been up talking with you.'

'Ah.'

'I said I'd gone with you to your room.'

'I see.'

'I don't know why I said that,' Martha said. She frowned.

'You were helping me to my room because I was feeling unwell, perhaps?'

'You know, I did kind of intimate something like that. It wasn't that anything happened with Ken but Baz said he'd got-ten worried and come looking for me.'

'And he couldn't find you?'

'I kind of panicked and said I was with you . . . and

then there were your shoes,' Martha added, not entirely logically.

'Well,' Vi said, 'since last night you were talking to me and, as it happens, I was helped to my room, I think if need be we can reassure Baz.'

'There wasn't anything . . .'

Vi interrupted. 'It doesn't matter. It's not always a good plan to speak the truth. It can be misleading. People misread the truth quite as often as they believe lies. But my guess is that Baz won't ask.'

'He was very pleased to see me last night, I mean this morning,' Martha said. 'That was kind of nice.'

'Good,' said Vi. 'Then I suggest we stop worrying. You had a nice time, Ken had a nice time and Baz was very glad to see you. What can be wrong with that?'

'I hope *you* had a nice time?' Martha asked.

'Very nice,' Vi said. 'I chatted to Miss Foot.'

'Oh but . . .'

'Don't worry,' said Vi. 'She won't give us away. And someone did come to my room with me, and he is not likely to spill the beans. So our stories tally.'

Martha looked pleased. 'I hope it was someone nice.'

'I am not sure that I would call him nice,' Vi said. 'But it was interesting, certainly.'

On their last day at sea, the passengers due to disembark at New York were for the most part in the unsatisfactory half-hearted state of anticipating the end of an event and thus being unable to enjoy the time remaining. They roamed aimlessly about the ship, picking up the extensive trivia sold, at grossly inflated prices, by the ship's many franchised retailers. Vi, catching sight of her hair, which looked, as her mother would have said, like the wild woman of Borneo's, went to We Are Hair, where it was washed and blow-dried by a cheerful New Zealander called Avis.

'Nice and full we're doing it today?'

Vi, who had a horror of big hair, said she liked her hair smooth and very simple.

'Not a problem. Ever thought of having some nice highlights put in to hide the grey?'

'There's not a lot of grey, is there?' Vi was perhaps a little vain about her natural hair colour.

'Why let the men know our age? Keep them on their toes, I say. Still, yours isn't too bad.'

Coming out of the salon, she met Ken and Jen, Jen handsome in brief white shorts and high-heeled mules and Ken in dark glasses, burdened with plastic bags marked 'Duty Free'.

'Vi, we were just talking about you. Your hair looks nice. I like it full like that. Have you recovered from last night?'

Ken took off his sunglasses.

Vi said, 'Thank you, yes. I'm afraid I was an awful bother but Ken was kindness itself.'

'He'd have got the rough side of my tongue if he hadn't been.'

'I got it anyway,' said Ken, looking relieved.

Vi said, 'Can you do me a favour, Ken? I want to buy someone I'm seeing a special whisky.'

'He'll go with you,' Jen said. 'Give me the bags, Ken, and take Vi down to the Duty Free.'

Ken squeezed Vi's arm going down the stairs. 'That was sweet of you. Very quick.'

'Ah, well.'

'That Martha's a nice woman.'

'Yes.'

'Not that there was anything . . .'

'I know that,' Vi said firmly. 'Now, about the whisky. It's for a friend I've not seen in years and I want to take him something really special.'

There was some discussion among the cognoscenti in the Duty Free over the best malt to buy a whisky drinker with form. Vi left Ken debating with a Greek Orthodox priest from San Francisco, returning, he explained, from a retreat on Mount Athos, about the merits and demerits of single malts from various unpronounceable Scottish islands. She wandered off to look for something suitable for Annie. A Gucci bag? But Annie already had any number of bags and these all appeared hideous. In the end, she bought a plastic train filled with Smarties for Patrick, no less hideous but more reliably acceptable.

On her return to the drinks section, she learned that the priest, who turned out to be a bishop, perhaps pulling rank, had swung the choice of whisky to a sixteen-year-old single Islay malt. Vi paid and then helped him with the choice of stole he was buying for a nun friend.

'But surely she would only wear black?'

'I think she likes a spot of colour in private.'

They finally settled on a discreet azure and the bishop gave Vi his card. 'Do look us up if you are ever in California. I hope your friend enjoys the malt.'

Ken carried the bottle of Lagavulin up to Vi's room. 'Honestly, Ken, I can manage.'

'I'd like to be able to say I'd been in your room with a clear conscience, Vi. Not that Jen would ever suspect anything.'

He prowled about the room inspecting the balcony and even the bathroom. 'I'll mention the swans. Jen'll like those.'

'Don't overdo it,' Vi advised. 'Too much detail sounds suspicious.'

*　*　*

'Will you accept a reversed charge call?' asked the operator. It was hard to imagine where they acquired such voices.

'Yes.'

Thank God it was Edward Hetherington himself at the other end.

'Go ahead please, caller.'

'Edward?'

'Vi. Are you all right?'

'I am but a friend of mine isn't.'

'What's up?'

'I don't know exactly but he's in a police station in Oxford. He's being held in the cells.'

'Give me his details. Can I ring you back?'

'I'm in a phone box. There's one at the bottom of the road near where I'm staying. I can call you back but at present I've got no change, only a pound note.'

'That's all right. Reverse the charges.'

'Are you sure you don't mind?'

'Quite sure. Where are you?'

'It's Tessa Carfield's cottage in the Welsh Marches. Near somewhere called Knighton. Why?'

'It's nice to know where you are. I'll get on to this. Call me back in an hour.'

Vi walked into Knighton and had a cup of coffee in a depressing hotel. The coffee was mostly milk and tasted of chicory essence. There was a jukebox which took her money and didn't play 'Heartbreak Hotel'. When she asked the man behind the bar for her money back he grinned unsympathetically and said she would need to come back Wednesday and have a word with the manager.

She walked up the hill to the chemist, where she bought

some Nivea cream for her face, which was smarting dreadfully. There was still twenty minutes before she was due to ring Edward back. So she went into a second-hand bookshop and loitered there, reading one of the various second-hand copies of *A Shropshire Lad*.

'Will you accept a reversed charge call?'

'Yes.'

'Go ahead please, caller.'

'Vi? It's Ted Hetherington.'

'Oh, Ted. What's happened?'

'A colleague's on his way to Edwin in Oxford.'

'Why is he there?'

'We don't yet know. It's usually best to sort that out in person. If you ring me later today I can tell you more. Say, between four thirty and five p.m.? I'll need to leave here by five thirty. Margaret's not too well.'

Tessa Carfield's cottage stood by itself on a low rise reached by a long track. It was small and whitewashed and had a large stone fireplace and a flagged floor. There were only two rooms, a living room with a small Belling stove and a primitive sink with a water heater, and a bedroom with a bed with a painted iron frame, the bed-head worked in the form of a Welsh harp. There was no bathroom, but an outside WC with a wooden seat that had long lost its varnish and a door that swung open to Housman's hills. In other circumstances it might have been idyllic.

Bruno was typing frenetically at the only table when Vi came back from the phone box. 'Shall I unpack?'

'If you're staying.'

'I seem to be.'

'That's up to you,' Bruno said.

'I've rung a solicitor for Edwin.'

'Who?'

'Someone I met at Tessa Carfield's party.'

'I don't remember any solicitor.'

'It was before you arrived.'

'So what's Edwin been up to?'

Vi, who hated that form of question, said, 'I don't know. I'm ringing Ted back later this afternoon.'

'"Ted"? I see. Very matey.'

'I brought the catalogue for you from the Horniman exhibition,' Vi said.

'Yes, I saw.'

So he'd been through her bag. 'Bruno, what happened to that strange purse you showed me once? The one made of out of a bat's wing?'

'It's here. Why?'

'Why is it here?'

Bruno stopped typing. 'Vi, is it your intention in coming here to interfere with my work?'

'You asked me to come.'

Bruno got up and went into the bedroom. After some minutes, he came out again. 'So where is it?'

'What?'

'You know.'

'I haven't a clue what you're talking about, Bruno.'

'The soul-keeper. What you choose to disparage by calling a purse.'

'I don't know where it is. You said you had it here.'

Bruno walked into the bedroom and came out with her notebook. 'If you don't return the soul-keeper I'll burn this.'

'What?'

'I'll put your notebook on the fire.'

'Bruno, I haven't seen your horrible little purse since the day we went to the Horniman exhibition. This is mad.'

'You have fifteen minutes to return it. After that, the book goes into the fire.'

Vi began frantically opening the few cupboards and shifting the armchair. She dug her fingers down the crack at the back of the sofa. Nothing but ancient fluff and burned-out matches. She went into the bedroom and searched through all the drawers and then took up the rugs. The only thing she found was any number of woodlice.

This is a set-up, the voice said.

Finally, she felt under the mattress. 'The missing item seems to be here.'

'I'm glad you came to your senses.'

'Bruno,' she said. She was overcome by a sudden appalling weariness. 'I didn't take the bloody thing. I loathe it, as a matter of fact. You know I didn't take it, nor would I ever hide your possessions. It's not in me to do that. I can't believe this is happening.'

Just as you like, the voice said. But he put it there.

'Will you accept a reversed charge call?'

'Yes.'

'Go ahead, caller.'

'Ted, I hope you don't mind all these reversed charge calls. I do have some change now.'

'I think the firm can absorb a few reversed charges. Now then, about your friend . . .'

When Vi returned to the cottage Bruno was lying on the bed, listening to the news on the radio.

Vi said, 'Edwin was arrested for picking up a man in the

public lavatories. The man, may he rot in hell, was a plain clothes detective. I think that is utterly, utterly vile, to trap people deliberately like that.'

'So what follows now?'

'What "follows" is that Ed has been charged with gross indecency.'

'Are you surprised?'

Vi stared. 'Bruno, you are Edwin's oldest friend.'

'He's a faggot.'

'I can't believe you said that.'

'No? Let me say it again.'

Vi put her hands over her ears and went, 'Wurra wurra wurra,' as she had done as a child so as not to hear what was being said. But the device no longer worked. She knew what was being said.

She took her useless hands from her burning face and stood looking at Bruno lying on the bed, looking at her with expressionless green eyes.

Vi, on her way to the morning dance class, met Martha wearing a red flounced skirt.

'Hi there, Vi, I hear they're doing jive today so I thought maybe I'd come along and brush up my technique.'

'It's the only dance I really know,' Vi said. 'I'm too young to have learned ballroom, but I just caught the tail end of jive.'

Martha spent some time looking over to the entrance to the room but there was no sign of Ken. Nor of Dino. The dance hosts appeared to be having a day off.

Marie put on 'Jailhouse Rock'. 'Now has everyone got a partner?'

'D'you want to dance with me, Vi?'

'OK, Martha, if you're willing to put up with me.'

'Sure. I'll lead.'

Towards the end of the class, Patrick and his parents appeared. 'There's Violet,' Patrick called, pulling Greg's hand. 'Can I dance?'

'Of course you can, Patrick. Come and dance with me and Martha.'

'I'm shy of Martha.'

'It's OK, you guys.' Martha had spotted a tall figure hovering near the doorway. 'I've just remembered I've an errand I need to run.'

Greg and Heather took snaps with their mobiles of Vi and Patrick dancing to 'Living Doll' and Vi explained to Patrick that while she liked Elvis as a name she didn't care for Cliff.

'Why not Cliff?'

'He's not a good singer. Elvis isn't a great name in itself but Elvis Presley's the absolute tops so you have to like his name.'

'My friend at nursery is called Elvis.'

'How sensible of his parents,' said Vi.

Les and Valerie Garson came by, Les walking ahead of Valerie, who nodded. 'That's a nice young man you've found to dance with.'

Les Garson stopped. Ignoring Vi, he walked across to Patrick and ruffled his hair. 'Are you going to dance with me, young man?'

'No I'm not.'

'Why's that?'

'Because you're too fat.'

Valerie Garson had a sudden fit of coughing.

'That Heatherfield woman's a snob if you ask me,' Les said as they entered the casino.

'Hetherington.'

'What?'

'Her name is Hetherington. I must say she was very pleasant to me when we lunched together.'

'For my money she's a dyke. Probably make a pass at you. I'd watch yourself.'

'You won't anyway.'

'What?'

'I said we had a nice meal anyway. You're going deaf, Leslie.'

Martha returned from her errand looking quite pink. 'Will you be coming to the "Swinging 60s" dance tonight, Vi?'

'Well, if you're game I am. Where is it?'

'The Prince of Wales. I'll tell Baz.'

'I see,' said Vi.

'Who's Baz?' Patrick asked.

'He's Martha's husband.'

'Do you like his name?'

'I do,' said Vi. 'I like Martha's name, too.'

'As much as you like mine?'

'No,' Vi said. 'I like your name best of all. Now, if it's OK with your mummy and daddy I've got something for you in my room.'

'Is it something which is good for me?'

'Not at all good for you, Patrick, no.'

Des, on his way to serve lunch at the Alexandria, ran into Boris.

'How's Mrs Hetherington?'

'Fuck off.'

'I hear you were seen going to her room.'

Des stopped. This might be the case or it might just be Boris trying to wind him up. Boris had the uncanny ability of those who grew up in the long shadow of the KGB: the ability to see round corners.

'Yeah, well she was ill and asked me to help her.'

From the satisfaction in Boris's smile Des could see that the dig had been a lucky strike.

'She's lost some ring. Asked me to spread the word there'd be a reward. It's valuable, she says.'

Boris grinned. 'I will keep my eyes peeled.'

'Keep them peeled, Boris, yes.'

'I will tell Sandy. She has the sharp eyes, that one.'

28

The plastic Smarties-filled train went down well with Patrick until Vi made the mistake of pretending that it was Skarloey.

'Skarloey doesn't look like that.'

'Sorry. I was being silly.'

'Were you making things up?'

'Yes.'

'Daddy says it's naughty to make things up.'

'Well,' said Vi, cautiously, 'perhaps it is sometimes, but other times it's a very good idea to make up a story. It all depends.'

'What does it all depends on?'

'That's too difficult for me to answer.'

'Why is it too difficult?'

Luckily at this point Renato knocked on the door. 'Any news of your ring, madam?'

'No, Renato, sadly. But may we have some fresh orange juice and biscuits, please?'

'Of course, madam. For the little one?' Renato bared his teeth at Patrick, who shrank behind Vi.

'I don't like that man,' he said when Renato had closed the door.

'Why not?'

'I think he bites children.'

Patrick ate the plate of biscuits but explained that although he did like orange juice, because it was good for him, he didn't want any right now. He might like a Coke, though.

'I'm awfully sorry, but my minibar has no Coke.'

Patrick sighed philosophically. 'That's what my mummy says.'

Vi took him back to his parents' room.

'I expect Mummy has a headache,' he suggested as he and Vi raced each other down the two parallel flights of stairs.

'You've won, Patrick. Why?'

'Usually when I go to see my Aunty Chris she does and my daddy lies down with her to make it better. Is that a story?'

'It's really very kind of you,' Heather said when Patrick showed her the train. 'Sorry about the mess. You know what it's like packing. I hope he wasn't too much bother.'

'I wasn't too much bother,' Patrick said. 'Have you and Daddy been having a headache, Mummy?'

Passengers disembarking at New York were kindly requested to leave their luggage outside their rooms by four a.m. The luggage was sorted through a complicated colour-coding system and Vi, queuing up at the desk for her label, found herself behind the critic.

'What colour are you?' he asked.

'Purple, I think.'

'I'm pink. Does it have any significance, one wonders?'

When they had been issued with their respective labels he said, holding open the door for her, 'If you're at a loose end in New York do call me up and I'll take you to a show. There are several I'm lined up to see. They all sound quite dire.'

Vi took his card. 'You're not coming to the "Swinging 60's" dance tonight? I see they've added in an apostrophe.'

'I am tempted to if only to see if the rogue apostrophe is maintained.'

It did not take long to pack. Vi left out jeans and T-shirt for the dance, Annie's shoes and a blouse, a skirt and underwear for the following morning. She packed all the books and the notebooks, except for one. Then she went down to the library to return the works of William Shakespeare.

'Funny,' the librarian said. 'You're the only person who's taken this out since we started the Atlantic run.'

'You don't have a copy of John Donne, by any chance?'

'He's a thriller writer, isn't he?'

'In a sense.'

'I'm afraid we can't allow any further loans till we leave New York.'

'It's OK,' said Vi. 'I just wanted to look something up. It doesn't matter.'

Lying on the hard mattress on the iron bedstead, Vi heard an engine starting up and then the sound of the Hillman driving off down the uneven track. She got up and went into the other room. The fire had died down but the ashes were still warm. There was a note from Bruno on the table, saying that he was returning to London. When she was ready, she could come and collect her things.

Towards lunchtime, she walked down the track to the phone box and called Edward Hetherington but he was out.

'May I take a message?' asked his secretary. She sounded almost friendly.

Vi said there was no special message but to tell Mr Hetherington that she had called. She walked on into Knighton, cashed a cheque at the local Barclays and bought a few supplies from the Co-op.

The following day she rang Edward Hetherington again. He was still out of the office but there was a message.

'His wife's had one of her poorly turns, I'm afraid,' his secretary explained. 'So Mr Hetherington's off for a few days. He asked if you would kindly ring him when you get back to London. Meantime, he says you're not to worry, everything with Mr Chadwick is in hand.'

Not knowing what to do or where to be, Vi set out to walk up the lane which ran on beyond the track. She walked uphill until she came to a high ridge, where she climbed through a fence into a field, scraping her scalp and wounding her leg on the barbed wire.

Sheep were standing, or lying in heaps, in Samuel Palmer's incredible light. Beyond them, the land mounted, gathering in light, to hills and valleys within hills. Fields of ripening cereal stretched far behind her. For a moment, she was back in the shrouded room of the Fitzwilliam, from where, each evening, she went home to the little house in Church Rate Walk. But she wasn't there. She was here, and alone.

She walked on for what seemed like miles and lay down at the edge of a field of barley, overcome by a searing exhaustion.

A lark shot like a bolt into the terrible blue above and opening its throat sang relentlessly into the bounding light. The lines from Donne's poem were running through her brain:

> *When love with one another so*
> *Interinanimates two souls,*
> *That abler soul which thence doth flow,*
> *Defects of loneliness controls.*

But she had betrayed Edwin and there was no soul in all the world able to counter her terrible loneliness.

When she opened her eyes Edwin was there. He was standing a little way off, where the line of hedgerow ran, but she saw him, quite distinctly against the hilly skyline, with the noonday sun making a halo of his long hair. She stumbled to her feet and hurried towards him, but the figure dissolved into the half trunk of a burned-out tree, which must have been struck by lightning or suffered some other natural disaster. Looking through the cage of her fingers, her fingernails and the poppies among the yellowing barley were bright beads of blood.

It was dark by the time she found her way back to the cottage, her skin torn by barbs of wire and brambles and with an itching rash down the length of one arm. Unequal to undressing, she fell asleep on the bed, hardly able to pull the musty-smelling eiderdown over her tired body.

She woke next morning, stiff and cold, feeling that she had been in a bad accident. The rash had developed into a series of ugly wheals and her eyes were red and swollen from the damp feather eiderdown. She tried to boil an egg but the pan boiled dry and the egg, black and cracked, smelled vile. She set out down the track but turned back not knowing what she had set out for. That evening she burned her hand on the kettle trying to fill a hot water bottle.

Fool, fool, fool, the voice tolled.

Several days later, she was not at all clear how many had passed, she heard a car coming up the track and then the sound of a door slamming. A feeling, half joy half terror, seized her. She got up from the bed and walked to the doorway, swaying from dizziness and lack of food. For many days after, she retained the delusion that it was Bruno who had caught her as she fell and carried her to the car.

As the fog lifted, the passengers due to disembark strolled about on deck taking in last impressions, or photographs, quarrelling over the packing or how best to get into Manhattan, via taxi or coach. Vi ate lunch uninterrupted, reading her notebook. In the afternoon, she went to her balcony and sat outside, watching the sea.

Renato called in to see if she needed any help. A form on which it was possible to nominate crew who had shown 'exceptional service' had been placed, prominently, at the front of the information folder giving details of the procedures for departure.

Vi tried to reassure. 'You have been wonderfully attentive, Renato. I shall certainly make sure to say so.'

'Thank you, madam. But your ring?'

'I have a hunch it will turn up, Renato, and if it doesn't, well . . .' She shrugged.

Renato smiled obligingly. Surely it was impossible for a sane woman to be taking the loss of a diamond with such calm.

The question of her emails had been pushed guiltily to the back of Vi's mind. She had been failing, on a daily basis, to check them since the day Ken had helped her. By good fortune, on her way to Links, she found Ken and Jen at their jigsaw puzzle, which, nearly complete, now extended to almost as much sea as sky.

'What is it?' Vi asked.

'It's the *Titanic* going down, but at a distance, see?' Jen pointed to a small perturbation in the upper left-hand section of sea.

'It's like Breughel's *Icarus*.'

'We've not seen that one.'

Ken said, casually, 'You coming to the hop tonight, Vi?'

'You'd better,' Jen said. 'Or I'll have to go and I want to finish *The Young Queen's Secret*. Kimberley's going to sign it for all the girls in the book club. I promised I'd tell her what I thought of the ending. She thinks it's her best yet.'

'OK,' said Vi. 'But in return, may I ask for Ken's help getting online?'

226

'Of course he'll help,' Jen said. 'Go on now, Ken. Go and help Vi.'

Before they had quite reached Links Ken said, 'Would you mind looking at something for me?' He rummaged in his pocket and produced a small envelope from which he extracted a pair of earrings, each a large silver treble clef dangling from a long wire. 'What do you think?'

Vi hesitated.

'I got them in one of the boutiques on Deck Five.'

'They're most unusual.'

'Would you say they were memorable?'

'Definitely memorable.'

'Thanks, Vi,' Ken said. 'Only I'm not much of a hand at knowing what women like.'

'I think you do pretty well, Ken.'

Fewer emails had collected in Vi's inbox. One was from Annie, asking to be remembered to New York: *There's a guy I dated there once who's in real estate. Jim Sands. He's divorced. I'll text you his number.*

The next was from Harry with the news that he'd been *offered a job at the firm of solicitors in the City where the senior partner had worked as a junior with Dad.* Vi had to suppress a certain irritation when she read that Harry had FedExed her mobile to her hotel, having *taken the precaution of copying the SIM card first.*

The third email was from Dan.

Dear Mum, Tanya's pregnant so we're getting married. Still staying at your flat as T likes it better here than at mine. When are you back? Lots of Love, D xx

'You all right, Vi?'

'I think so, Ken. I've just heard I'm going to be a grandmother.'

'Never mind, no one would guess it.'

The 'Swinging 60's' dance was well attended. For those leaving the ship, the tiresome business of repacking, squeezing in the extras acquired over the course of the voyage in a mood of mindless extravagance, had been accomplished and there was a general atmosphere of celebration. When Vi arrived at the Prince Charles Salon, the voice of Lonnie Donegan singing 'Hang Down Your Head, Tom Dooley' was being imperfectly imitated by the energetically swinging crowd. Looking around for the critic she met Ken, in jeans and a black T-shirt bearing the legend 'Bob Dylan for President'.

'You look dishy, Vi. What'll you have?'

'You know, Ken, I might stick to water.'

'It's not that bad, surely? You'd win the Glamorous Grandma contest hands down.'

Martha appeared in a pair of new sneakers and wearing the treble clef earrings which swung when she made an impatient little gesture with her head. 'Baz says he's coming to watch.'

'For anthropological reasons, purely. I'm afraid the sixties passed me by.'

Martha said shortly, 'Yes, honey, we all know you're the youngster out with the geriatric ward.'

'Baz, there's something I wanted to ask you,' Vi interposed. 'Would you mind?'

'It would be a pleasure, Vi.'

'Maybe Ken would dance with you, Martha?'

'It would be a pleasure, Vi.'

Really, thought Vi, I am turning into an elderly Emma. I must watch out. She steered Baz through the heaving mass of dancers, by now collectively swinging to the Beach Boys' 'California Girls', and out of the over-heated room into the Mary Queen of Scots Bar.

'It's quieter here and cooler. May I buy you a drink in return for your time?'

'A tomato juice on the rocks would be great. But there's no call for any returns. I'm grateful to be out of that hellhole. I only came to keep Martha company. She's very patient with me. I can be something of a pain in the arse.'

'Ken will look after her. He's exceptionally gentlemanly. I wanted to pick your brains a little more about your traditional healers. What were you saying about suggestion?'

Baz, relieved to be on familiar ground, slung an elegant ankle over his knee and grasped a grey silk sock with an equally elegant hand. 'It's like I said, the human organism is infinitely suggestible. This is how hypnosis works, and in fact I would say most upbringing. You could even say that much of what is commonly called civilisation is born of the power of suggestion. Look at advertising.'

'You mean we simply believe what we are told?'

'Not always so "simply" but yes, that's about the size of it. If for some reason the defences are down, or not yet formed, suggestion has quite magical effects. A parent tells a child that he or she is clever or beautiful, or stupid or ugly, well behaved or badly behaved, and nine times out of ten that is what the child will obediently become. Teachers are the same. Children who excel, as is well known, do so because their teachers believe they have talent or promise. Shamans or healers activate cures in the human system in the same way.'

'And harm?'

'Same principle. Kids who are trouble-makers or failures of some sort are most often told this by significant others from the start. You can make someone ill by suggestion if there is sufficient belief. It's the power of projection. The power is really the subject's own, but if it is projected on to someone of significance it can be turned for or against the subject's person. That's how possession works. It's what the shrinks call transference, but really it's as old as God. Or the gods, as I prefer to say.'

'I suppose in a way it's obvious.'

'You don't need me to tell you, Vi, that what seems obvious may not be so easily grasped.'

'Or avoided?'

'Or avoided.'

'So the bat-wing purse?'

'Remind me what your friend said about it.'

'He was not a friend.'

Baz looked at her hard. 'In that case I'm sorry.'

'He said it had the power to keep the soul of anyone who loved its owner.'

'You know, I would say that if someone loves you, or is in some way powerfully attached to you, then naturally you have the power to entrap their soul.'

Baz walked her to the stairs. 'You're not going back to the dance?'

'I think I've had enough for tonight. The stairs to Deck Twelve will be enough exercise.'

'In case we miss each other tomorrow, I hope if you're ever Harvard way you'll call us up. Martha has taken to you. She doesn't always like the women I like.' He put a hand on her shoulder and smiled his heartening smile. 'You know, I'm pretty weary myself. Do you think I can safely leave Martha with Ken?' The brown eyes were wryly humorous.

'I would say she's in safe hands.'

'I think so, too. It's good for her to be admired a little. Husbands are lousy at that. I'll go let her know I'm off to bed and she can let her hair down.'

* * *

Renato had already shifted Vi's case outside the room, ready for collection. She went out on to the balcony, her last chance to be alone with the Atlantic. The moon was not quite full and was floating, an eccentric luminous yellow disc, in the indigo sky. She went back inside for her notebook and a pencil. She had just finished writing when the phone rang.

'Mrs Hetherington? Sorry to trouble you, ma'am, it's Tim Troubridge the crew purser here.'

'Oh yes, about my room. I'll let you know as soon as I can whether I'll be wanting it for the next leg of the voyage.'

'It's not about your room, ma'am. It's about your ring.'

'Has it been found?'

'If the one I have in my hand is yours, I'd say so. I would be surprised if there were two missing diamonds like this on the ship.'

'That's marvellous.'

'Would you mind coming down to my office, ma'am? There's a couple of things I need to ask.'

When Vi left the purser's office, she returned to her room, where she contrived to squeeze her jeans and T-shirt into the suitcase outside. Now there was nothing but the clothes she stood in, her nightdress and her spongebag to remember tomorrow. And Ted's ring.

She looked fondly at the ring glinting in its familiar place on her left hand. Ted would be pleased. He would say that he had been watching over her, like Providence.

There was a tap at the door and she called out, 'Hello, Desmond. I'm just coming.'

His naturally dark skin had gone quite pale. Poor boy. It wasn't such a crime, the sin of omission. 'The crew purser said you wanted to see me.'

'Come in. Would you like to sit out on the balcony?'

'If you like. I'm not fussed.'

'Have you a cigarette to spare?'

'Sure.'

The Atlantic, having shown who was master, had subsided into a gentle threshing roll. Moonlight glanced off the water. As if in response to the lulled weather the ship was unusually quiet. Those who were not preparing for disembarkation by having a few last drinks for Auld Lang Syne, or dancing to the Supremes, had sensibly gone to ground.

Des lit their cigarettes. His eyes, she saw in the lighter's flare, were tiny points of black fear.

'I wanted to thank you for finding my ring. I explained to Mr Troubridge that I'd particularly asked you to look for it and that you had tried to find me earlier but that I wasn't in.'

Des, quite at a loss, resorted to a dumb nod.

'The message, you know, that you left on my phone.'

He hadn't the faintest idea what she was talking about but he had to say something. 'Is the message still there?'

'I erased it. But as you only said that you had some news for me of course I didn't immediately understand. I explained to Mr Troubridge that we have been dancing partners, and that I had spoken to you about the ring's importance to me, so it was highly understandable that before saying a word to anyone else you wanted to give me the news in person that you had found my ring.'

'And what did he say?' Des was now totally out of his depth.

'I gather you'd put my ring away to keep it safe. It seems an old girlfriend of yours found it among your things and handed it in, hoping, I dare say, for the reward which you know I'd offered. She told Mr Troubridge that she was looking for something she'd left in your room. I expect that was a story.'

He might have known it. Sandy. 'It's a bloody lie.' How did the fucking little bitch get into his room?

'She does sound like trouble but perhaps in the circumstances you will be lenient. I expect she was angry with you for dropping her.'

The penny dropped. Boris. That was how the little cow had got in. He'd heard a rumour that mother-fucker had a spare set of keys. 'She was a mistake and a half all right.'

'We make them, I'm afraid. Long ago, I made a terrible mistake and let down a very dear friend, very badly. He's a poet now, rather a famous one. And for a time, while we were friends, I wrote poetry too. I gave up writing, largely, I suspect, because of what I did to my friend. And because of a foolish liaison I made. But tonight I managed a poem.'

Des, preoccupied, said, 'A poem?'

'I wrote one this evening.'

'That's great.'

'It's a start. So this is a double celebration. Would you like a drink? I can offer you almost any drink under the sun except Coke.'

'A beer would be great.'

Vi went inside to the minibar.

'Stella Artois or Beck's?'

'Beck's, if there's one going.'

'A glass?'

'I'll drink from the bottle, thanks.'

They sat outside with the moon sailing alongside them, its imperturbable face shredded into myriad darting gleams on the petrol surface of the water. Des wondered whether to raise the question of the insurance money but thought better of it. He would make sure to see that cunt Boris got what was coming to him, though.

29

The passengers leaving the ship for good were mostly fractious, setting themselves apart from those for whom a stay in New York was a mere interlude in the round of pleasures to come. The majority had been up early in order to look into the blank eyes and uncompromising face of the Statue of Liberty and be the first to spot the Brooklyn Bridge suspended, as if by gigantic elastic bands, across the East River, and were already worn out from the unaccustomed exertion and consequently taking it out on one another.

Vi met Ken and Jen in the line for disembarkation. Ken was wearing his dark glasses and seemed subdued. Jen gave Vi their address and asked her to look them up in Basingstoke. But they all knew she never would. Heather and Greg were also in the queue, Greg carrying a sleeping Patrick, his peony cheek resting, with the peerless trust of childhood, on his father's shoulder. Vi was almost glad that there was no opportunity to say goodbye.

The luggage for those leaving the ship was piled, according to the colour coding, in the custom sheds at the dock. As Vi was extricating her case from the stack Captain Ryle appeared, dragging a candy-pink suitcase which, decorated with cartoon bears and rabbits, could only be Kath's.

'Glad to spot you, ma'am. I looked high and low for you last eve but you'd vanished into thin air.'

Vi took his hand, offered in the spirit of pure uncomprehending good feeling. 'I was spending a quiet evening on my balcony.'

'That's the ticket. Saying goodbye to the sea. How did the poems fare?'

'Do you know, I wrote one.'

The captain was doomed to be disappointed by her. 'Just the one?'

There were complications at Immigration about the date of her departure from the U.S. Vi explained that she had an open return airline ticket as she was visiting a friend and the length of her stay was undecided. On the other hand, she might be leaving with the ship in a few days. Luckily, Harry, in anticipation of difficulties, had organised the appropriate paperwork through a friend of Annie's husband's in the diplomatic service.

When at last the grudging Immigration officials released Vi on the city of New York to do her worst, Miss Foot was waiting for her.

'I spotted you in the line for Immigration and wanted to bid farewell.'

'Thank you,' said Vi. 'I hope everything goes as well as it can with your sister. It was very nice to meet you.'

'We shall meet again, my dear.'

In the taxi queue Vi encountered the bishop, trundling a compact valise and with a smart laptop case slung over his shoulder.

'Where are you off to? Shall we share a taxi downtown?'

Vi gave him the address of the hotel in the Village where she was booked to stay.

'I can drop you off. I'm overnighting at the Holiday Inn.'

He requisitioned a cab and bargained briskly with the driver, helped her inside and regaled her with stories about Mount Athos until they reached her hotel, where he refused to accept any contribution for the fare.

'Your company was compensation enough. Have you got the Lagavulin safe, now? If your friend doesn't enjoy it I'll eat my episcopal hat. Remember, if you make it to the West Coast there's always a big welcome waiting for you there.'

The reception at the hotel, where her mobile had arrived with a postcard from Harry, felt almost unfriendly after the attentive service on the *Caroline*. Vi unpacked, and then, feeling remorse for her churlishness, tested her phone by sending a text of gratitude to Harry. It was too early to call Edwin so, with nothing else to do, she went out.

New Yorkers are early birds and the great city was already alive with dogs and their walkers, babies in strollers and their minders, and people hustling their several ways to gainful employment, or otherwise. Vi had been warned that the weather would be humid and had changed into a cotton blouse and skirt. In spite of this, she was already sweating when she turned off by the Chelsea piers to walk alongside the Hudson.

There was a sluggish riverish smell coming off the slight breeze, so different from the whistle-clean smell of the vigorous Atlantic. Piles from one of the old piers made jagged ranks of rotting black teeth in the milky turquoise water. Across, on the far shore, splashes of light, reflections of the morning sun, showed on the windows of the impressive line of lofty buildings.

On her way back to the Village, Vi stopped for a breakfast of coffee and pancakes. But it was still only nine fifteen. Too early to call.

Several refills later – and how blessedly liberal Americans

were with their coffee – she plucked up courage and rang
Edwin's number.

'Hello, it's me.'

'Hello, you.'

'I'm here.'

'Well, come on over.'

When he answered the door of the brownstone house
in Christopher Street he was smaller and thinner than
she remembered, and his hair, once long and fair, was iron
grey and cut fashionably close. But the quizzical stare of the
odd eyes, one blue, one greenish hazel, was just the same.
And his voice. Only the slightest tincture of the New York
cadence.

'So you made it.'

'I made it.'

'Come on up. It's four flights, I'm afraid. But very good for
the legs.'

The apartment was small but light. In the corner stood a
familiar priapic bronze figure.

'Isn't that . . . ?'

'Lust, yes. Ralph had him shipped over for me.'

'I brought you this. A Greek Orthodox priest advised me on
the brand, if that's what you call it. A bishop, actually.'

Edwin examined the label. 'The bishop has taste. But I no
longer drink.'

'Oh, I'm sorry.' She was blushing.

'How could you know? And I still have friends who drink,
though New York has grown quite puritanical. Very few of my
friends smoke these days.'

'I'm afraid I've started again.'

'Feel free.'

'I wouldn't here.' She looked around at his lovely things:

a polished walnut table, an elegant sofa, two green leather arm-chairs, a Turkish rug, a jug of tall lilies.

'Really, it's fine. I quite enjoy the smell. How about coffee or would you like some of this?' He held up the whisky and smiled.

'Not quite yet.'

He made coffee and she looked about his apartment. He had changed. Or his way of living had changed. The place was orderly. Calm.

A dove of the palest coral fluttered down on to the window-sill outside.

'They nest there, on the window ledge, in spring. I keep the window permanently open so as not to disturb their visitations.'

'Isn't it cold in winter with the window open?'

'The heating here is ferocious.'

They smiled at each other, not yet at ease. Not at ease at all.

Vi said, 'It's good to see you.'

'It's good to see you, too.'

Now she had to be brave. 'It's good of you to see me.'

'Why so? I was delighted when you wrote.'

'Well . . .'

'Well?'

'Well, you know.'

'I've often meant to write to you, Vi.'

'But you didn't.'

'No, I didn't. You know, bad times, new life. And then you were a respectable married woman.'

'I don't think I've ever been that!'

'No, I can see that now.'

They sat in silence until Vi said, 'I really came to say some-thing to you but now I feel rather foolish.'

He laughed, sounding nervous. 'Whatever it is I expect I've heard worse.'

'I'm sure you've got over it long ago but I wanted to say I know I let you down. Shockingly.'

Edwin frowned. 'How so?'

'When I didn't come that time. When, you know, you rang me.'

'From the police station?'

'Yes.'

'But you organised that solicitor chap to come, didn't you?'

'Yes.'

'Well, then. Much as I may have wanted to see you, he was of more practical help.'

'You didn't mind?'

Edwin frowned again. 'I don't remember. I don't remember very much about that time. Too pissed too much of the time. What I do remember is him, quite brilliantly, getting me off the charge: procuring the commission of an act of gross indecency with another male contrary to section thirteen of the Sexual Offences Act. There is something particularly threatening in that "procuring".'

'But you lost your job.'

'Oh, that. I hated that job. But anyway, that wasn't affected by your not coming.'

'You told me you liked teaching.'

'I was probably pretending – to myself as much as to you. And then losing the job brought me here.' Edwin waved his hand, encompassing, in the gesture, the tiny apartment and the vast body of New York. 'I've been very content here. They like my sort.'

Outside someone speaking into a phone was saying, 'It's all about you. You, you, you. You and your fucking shrink.'

Edwin said, 'I heard that the man you married was my solicitor chap's boss.'

239

'Ted? Yes. He came and found me after Bruno pushed off. I was in rather a state.' That was an understatement. 'His wife had multiple sclerosis and when she died, not very long after that, he asked me to marry him. It seemed a good idea at the time.'

Another silence fell. Vi thought how her mother would have said a wicked fairy was passing over.

Edwin got up, pushing his hands into the pockets of his jeans, and crossed the room apparently to examine a Chinese ink drawing on the wall, of a long-legged stork. It looked, Vi observed, not unlike its owner. He turned round and said, rather curtly, 'All this is nonsense. There was nothing for you to feel bad about.'

He sat down on the arm of the green leather chair and grimaced as his phone began to ring.

'Do you want to answer that?'

Edwin looked at the phone as if he were weighing up from the tone of the ring whether it was worth answering. When the ringing stopped he said, 'You shouldn't have been berating yourself. It was me who owed you an apology.'

'Why?'

He got up again and went over to the window. The dove, accustomed to his presence, did not stir.

'When you didn't come, after I rang you from that awful place, which still gives me the willies when I think of it, which I try not to, I assumed you'd guessed or that Bruno had spilled the beans. But then later I realised you knew nothing.'

'What?'

But suddenly she did know and a flood of light was being poured over her past.

'Bruno and I were lovers.'

You knew this, said the voice.

'Meaning what?'

'Meaning he fucked my arse. Sorry to be so crude.'

'But when?'

'Pretty much any time we could manage it at school.'

'And later?'

'For a while.'

'D'you think I could have some of the bishop's malt?'

'Sure.'

'And would you mind if I do smoke?'

'Go ahead. I told you, it's fine.'

She lit her cigarette and as she did there came to her mind the figure of the young dance host, who had tried to escape what he was, and who he was, sitting abject on her balcony. Grace and mercy. She might send him a bit of money after all. 'So did you and he . . . ?' she began, but Edwin interrupted.

'Only once. You were at Annie's and I went down to London to Bruno's flat.'

'I remember that time.'

'How is Annie?'

'She's just the same, but stouter.'

'I can't picture Annie stout.'

'It hasn't changed the essential Annie.'

'No, Annies are built to last. And your glamorous teacher, I forget her name?'

'Miss Arnold. Only she's not a Miss any more. She married.'

'The art teacher on the motorbike? I rather fancied him.'

'He was cashiered long ago. She married a Muslim dentist. Very dashing. I shouldn't be surprised if it wasn't bigamy.'

'On his part or hers?'

Vi looked over to where the dove's mate had joined it on the windowsill. One of the birds was calling a soft 'caroo caroo'.

'They're very beautiful. You're lucky.'

Edwin looked across at the doves as if for counsel. Then he came over and sat down on the arm of her chair. 'I should have told you. I'm sorry. I was jealous – of you, of him, of the two of you together. But in the end, so you know this, in the end it was you I was more concerned for. I was never in love with Bruno, it was only sex with us.'

'I don't think I was either.'

'But he hurt you pretty badly. I should have told you.'

Trying to take this in she said, 'But I let him hurt me. I could have walked away.'

'He's dangerous. See, that's my weakness. I like them cruel.'

'I don't think I do.'

'No. With you it was different. I'm sorry,' he said again. 'You see there was nothing for you to be bothered about. I was the one at fault.'

'I let him hurt me,' she said again. 'I wish I understood why.'

'Do you need a top-up of the bishop's malt?'

'Frankly yes,' Vi said. 'Though I seem to be becoming something of a dipsomaniac. I think quite soon I'd better join you on the wagon.'

'For me it was that or die penniless in urine-stained rags in a New York gutter. Which would be marginally worse than a London or Oxford one.'

'I'm glad you didn't die, Ed.'

'I'm glad you didn't too, Vi.'

'I wish I were dead,' she had said to Annie. 'I don't mean I want to kill myself. I mean I wish I had died.'

She was lying in bed in Annie's spare bedroom, for once free of flatmates. The last batch of Australians had left and the new intake had not yet been installed.

Annie was brisk. 'Good riddance to bad rubbish, I say. If

anyone ought to be dead by rights it's that bastard. He'd better keep out of my way, that's all. I never saw what you saw in him. Big blubbery baby.'

'I don't know either.'

'You're best off not knowing.'

'I don't know,' Vi said again. 'How did I get here? Did I ring you?'

'That solicitor bloke brought you. Nice of him. Mind you, he fancies you. He's rung up enough times. I told him you weren't well enough to take calls. Best to keep them waiting. It keeps them keen.'

'Don't be daft. He's old enough to be my father.'

Annie gave her an old-fashioned look and said, 'So? Your own dad's pretty naff.'

And soon after, at Annie's discretion, Ted had called by with a bunch of royal blue delphiniums and the offer of dinner when she had recovered.

Annie, now head dress buyer at Liberty's, had got her a job working in their book department and the summer seemed to pass by in a fog. Once, during this period, where but for Annie she would have been homeless, Annie had come in and found her lying on the kitchen floor.

'What on earth are you doing, Vi?'

'I can't seem to function.'

'Get up and wash your face and tidy your hair. You look a mess and that Ted's coming round and I want you looking nice.'

She had gone out with Ted, obediently dressed in Annie's purple Biba frock and Day-Glo orange platform heels.

Only much later she asked, 'What happened to your Australians?' and Annie said, airily, 'I cancelled them. I said my sister was having a breakdown and needed a room.' And when she had tried to protest, at Annie's loss of funds, not her diagnosis, Annie said, 'Oh, shut it, will you? It's not so far from the truth.'

'Is it too early for you for lunch?' Edwin asked. 'I get up at five so by noon I'm ravenous.'

'I'd love lunch.'

'So,' he said, a little later, when he had walked her round the corner to a local place on Bleecker and they had ordered, 'what are your plans?'

'Oh dear. I do hate that question.'

'Sorry. I was forgetting myself, or rather I was forgetting you.' He smiled at her and for a moment she saw the Edwin with whom she had sat all those years ago in the RAF bar. But we'll never be quite the same again, Vi thought. Nothing ever is.

'I may go back on the boat. I may stay here a while. I'm not sure. I suppose –' She halted. 'I suppose I wanted to find out what happened – to you, but also to me. But I still don't really know.'

'Perhaps you never will. For myself, I've stopped hunting for reasons. What happened to Bruno?'

'He married Tessa Carfield. I don't suppose you ever slept with Tessa Carfield?'

'What a horrible suggestion!'

'I was thinking that if you had then everyone at our wedding would have slept with everyone else.'

'I swear, you are the only woman I have ever slept with, Violet St John.'

They laughed, enjoying the gradual recovery of intimacy.

'He'd been with her all the time at that cottage where he had me come and visit when I should have gone to you – to demonstrate his beastly power, I suppose.'

'Well, you know, Bruno never could tolerate a universe that didn't count his wishes as inviolable laws. What does Carfield do nowadays?'

'She still runs her headhunting firm, quite successfully, I believe. Bruno's a partner, or was when I heard last.'

'Never mind. I expect he's irredeemably promiscuous.'

'Who cares?'

'As long as you don't.'

'Not that, anyway.'

You knew, said the voice. That's what you should care about.

'Do you have anyone now?' she asked.

'I have a young man who is kind to me. Kind, I mean, in the particular ways I want him to be. He's very handsome and quite fickle. But I don't ask too much of him. And you?'

'Ted only died last year.'

'And there was never anyone else?'

'There were a few offers. One man I liked a lot, and he me. Or so he said. But after Bruno I was too timid. And, you know, although he sometimes drove me to distraction, Ted was very good to me. He was an utterly decent man. I'm glad for my sons' sake that I was loyal to him.'

'Yes, I'm sorry I shall never have a son. Your sons are his?'

'Very much so. My elder son, Harry, is the dead spit of his father.'

'And the younger one?'

'Daniel? A bit too much like his mother.'

'He's lucky, then. His mother's OK.' He was looking at her with the old unblinking gaze. 'What do they do?'

'Harry is a solicitor, like his father. Dan, at present, writes lyrics for pop songs.'

'Any good?'

245

'I think so, yes. But then . . .'

'Then they will be. His mother always had taste. And your own writing, Vi?'

'Oh, that.'

'Well . . . ?'

'Well, nothing. I've not written a line since we last met.'

Edwin frowned. 'That's seems a pity.'

'I lost . . . I don't know. I lost something.'

'Not for good, I hope. So what did you, do you do?'

'Oh, this and that. I worked for Tate Britain for a while.'

'Not as a gallery attendant?'

'Slightly more elevated. Though, you know, that time, working for the Fitzwilliam, remains my happiest time of employment.'

'You and Samuel Palmer?'

'I missed him too when I left.'

'Yes, he was good company for you.'

There was something else she needed to ask.

'Ed, those witch doctors of Bruno's. Were they real? I mean . . .' But she didn't quite know what it was that she meant.

'He certainly studied them, But then he used them.'

'How, would you say?'

'The quickness of the hand deceives the eye. His witch doctors acted as a kind of decoy. They sound scary but . . .'

'There was an anthropologist on the boat who knew about them. He said they're basically projections of our own psyche.'

'That figures. But that is, or can be, a snake pit.'

'There was this horrid little purse thing, made of a bat's wing, that Bruno had. It frightened me.'

'The creature you should feel sorry for there is the bat.'

'That sounds very sane.'

'It is sane,' Edwin said. 'But that doesn't mean that you didn't

246

come a real cropper. I mean we aren't sane, are we? I don't mean just you and me. You know this but I am going to say it anyway. The only way someone like Bruno feels they exist is to try to control people because, essentially, they have no power. You have power, though you like to deny it.'

'Do I?'

'You did. I can't speak for now. He wanted what you have and when he couldn't get it he tried to get you. But of course you can't "get" a person, or a person's power – real power isn't like that. And when he couldn't get what he wanted he tried to annihilate you.'

'And I let him.'

'You let him try. Your anthropologist man is right. It is, as I said long ago, a kind of spellbinding. I take it Bruno never wrote that book?'

'Not that I've noticed.'

'He never will. Nor any poetry.'

'I never liked his poetry. I should have taken notice of that.'

'It takes a long time to learn to take notice of one's God-given instincts.'

But at this she was finally indignant. 'It was you who insisted we publish his poems, remember?'

'Remember, I was susceptible too, for a while.'

Outside the restaurant a white cat was walking nonchalantly past as if it owned the world, and she remembered her own cat, Arthur, with the odd eyes. Did he die? Or did her father get rid of him when her mother died? She couldn't now remember. Maybe she had never known.

Edwin, watching the cat, said, 'About your poetry, I was thinking what you probably lost over Bruno was your nerve.'

30

When Vi got back to the hotel there was a telephone message from Harry 'breaking the news' of Dan's wedding, which, Harry said, they proposed to arrange once they knew what her 'movements' were. The soul of discretion, he refrained from giving the reason for his brother's sudden decision.

Vi rang her own flat and a girl answered in a mock posh voice, 'Mrs Violet Hetherington's residence.'

'It is she.'

'Who?'

'It's me,' Vi said lamely, feeling foolish.

'Oh, Vi, sorry, we were just kidding about. It's Tanya.'

'Yes, I know. How are you?'

'We're fine. We like your flat.'

'Better enjoy it while you can. I may be back quite soon.'

There was a voice in the background and then Dan was on the phone. 'Mum, how are you doing?'

'Very well, thank you, darling.'

'And how was the Atlantic, apart from being gigantic?'

'It was lots of fun. I learned to dance, well, a bit.'

'But you can dance anyway.'

'No, this was ballroom.'

'Strictly standard?'

'Not quite. So, you are going to be a father?'

'It looks like it.'

'Darling Dan, that is most extremely good news.'

'We've decided she can come to you once a week.'

'She?' asked Vi, leaving the proposed child care arrangement to be tackled another time.

'It's a girl. We've had the scan.'

'But, Dan, how pregnant is Tanya?'

'Oh, quite a bit. Half-way, about. We were going to get married
after Blossom arrived . . .'

'Blossom?'

'You know, after Blossom Dearie, so she could be a brides-
maid, but Tan's dad says he'll pay for a bash if we do it before.
He doesn't want his grandchild to be a bastard and Tan wants
a pretty wedding frock. I'm easy either way. You know marriage,
it's a girl's thing.'

'I see,' Vi said, managing to swallow Blossom without comment. 'So when is this to be?'

'Well, we were kind of waiting for you to come home. When
are you back? I told Hal not to pester you but I expect he will.'

'I'm not sure,' Vi said. 'Can you give me twenty-four hours?'

'Course. Enjoy New York. Go dancing.'

Vi put down the phone and at once it rang. 'Call for you.'

'Ma?'

'Harry, darling.'

'Are you all right?'

'I'm very well, thanks.'

'And the voyage, was that all right?'

'Very enjoyable.'

'Nice people?'

'Entertaining anyway.'

'Good.' There was a pause.

'It's OK, darling. Dan's explained.'

'About the wedding?'

'About the baby. I'm thrilled.'

'I'm bloody furious with him, Ma. He should have told us. She's over twenty weeks.' When her elder son lost his habitual control she loved him especially.

'But it doesn't really matter, does it?'

'It's you I mind for,' Harry said, indignant that she should suppose that there was any concern for himself involved.

'Darling Hal, Dan's like that. It's fine. And I've promised to let them know by tomorrow what my plans are.'

'I think it's really Tanya who is keen to get everything organised.'

'Well, it would be, wouldn't it?' Vi said. 'But that's good. Tan and her dad can organise your brother. We've never managed it. How is Marion?'

'Who?'

'Marion. Your girlfriend. Or is she not any more?'

'Oh, Marion. Yes, she's fine.'

The phone rang again and this time it was Edwin. 'I forgot to say, I'm busy tonight and I'm sorry to say also most of tomorrow. But tomorrow night we could have dinner, if that would suit you.'

'Of course it would. Don't be a fathead.'

He laughed and rang off saying, 'See you tomorrow evening, then.'

And then there was only the question of what to do with the rest of her day.

With only herself to please Vi took the subway uptown to the Metropolitan Museum of Art. There she strolled, letting her body wander through the great museum as her mind wandered through her own memory, itself a kind of museum too.

Edwin's revelation had startled but not surprised her. That there had been a tacit complicity between the two friends, she had known before she ever met Bruno. The poems she had disliked had told her that. Over poetry, she and Edwin so rarely disagreed. And it made sense of other conundrums: Edwin's distress at discovering the affair; his move to Oxford; Bruno's brutality when Edwin needed her. But her own part in it all remained still unfathomed.

She was pondering this mystery when, from the corner of her eye, she caught sight of the flat beige form of Miss Foot.

Miss Foot was standing before a Renaissance portrait of a young woman dressed in black. She turned when Vi approached her.

'I had a feeling we might meet here.'

Vi, who was reassured rather than irked, as she might have been, by this pronouncement, nevertheless registered surprise. 'Did you?'

'It's not such wild surmise. After all – ' Miss Foot shrugged to indicate the manifest munificence of their surroundings. 'And chance can be generous.'

'I usually go to galleries when I'm at a loose end,' Vi agreed.

Miss Foot made a gesture with a freckled hand towards the figure in the painting. 'I was struck by the black veil. She must have lost someone young. A husband? A brother? A parent?'

Vi said, 'I lost my mother young. I was not quite ten when she died.'

Miss Foot nodded. 'That leaves a hole in an immature system through which the unwarrantable can enter.'

Vi considered. 'Do you think that is what happened to me?' It did not occur to her that Miss Foot knew nothing concrete of her history.

'It is possible.' Miss Foot's disconcerting green eyes were fixed at a point slightly above Vi's head. 'You have certainly absorbed violence.'

'That is true,' Vi said.

'Perhaps you thought to neutralise your own violence by taking in another's. It can happen.'

'Yes?'

'Oh, indeed.'

Vi looked at the young Renaissance woman whose luminous beauty had been rinsed clear by sorrow all those hundreds of years ago. 'What should I do about that?'

'Find a voice for your own violence and don't harbour the other's. That is what my poor sister has done. She is at the hospital this afternoon, having radiotherapy treatment. I came here to air my mind.'

Miss Foot and Vi meandered back to the café where they both had tea and Miss Foot ate a brownie.

'I do like these,' she said. 'Another praiseworthy feature of America.'

'Did you finish *Moby-Dick*?'

'I did. On the whole I enjoyed it but I still believe it would benefit from editing. I am reading Mark Twain now. *A Connecticut Yankee in King Arthur's Court*. That is much more to the point.'

As they parted Miss Foot said, 'I enjoyed our meeting. Grace and mercy are also intended for the self.'

Vi, back at her hotel, was sorting out her handbag when she found the critic's card.

'I am so glad you rang.' The critic's droll voice sounded genuinely pleased. 'I have a frightful-sounding show which it is my painful duty to review this evening. If you were brave enough to have it inflicted on you I could give you dinner afterwards while we recover.'

The show, an Off-Broadway mime, enacting an unsuccessful political insurrection in an unidentifiable socialist regime, was as bad as he'd threatened. In the interval, the critic bought her a large gin and tonic. He ordered a dry martini for himself and spent some time in negotiation with the barman, getting the mix to his liking. 'The show is, if anything, worse than I imagined. I can only apologise and attempt to make up for it to you with a reasonable dinner.'

In the foyer, as they were leaving, he turned to her, his hazel eyes behind the tortoiseshell spectacles unusually intense. 'Has anyone ever told you . . .' Vi's heart sank to her six-inch heels, in which, forgetting his height, she had towered over him all evening. '. . . that New York is the best city in the world for lobster?'

Over dinner, perhaps because he did not ask, she explained that her immediate plans were undecided. 'My younger son tells me he is having a baby, rather soon in fact, so he's getting married.'

'That seems to be the way round it is generally done these days.'

'A much better way,' Vi said, loyally.

'Are any ways "better" in the end, would you say?'

This, because it was what she herself in truth believed, made her laugh. 'Maybe not. But anyway, thanks to my other son I have a return ticket to New York.'

'I hope you will be sure to look me up when you are back. I shall try to find something superior to tonight's performance. Fortunately that won't be hard.'

They spent the rest of the evening discussing various Shakespeare productions they had seen.

'Did you catch the famous Peter Brook *Dream* at the Roundhouse?'

'You know, I was going to see it with my husband but I never did.'

'First husband or second?'

'The second. Actually, it was going to see the first which made me miss it with the second.'

'That in itself might be grounds for divorce.'

This reminded Vi of something. 'You wouldn't, by chance, know where this comes from, would you? "They say that miracles are past . . ." and then I don't know how it goes on.'

'". . . and we have our philosophical persons, to make modern and familiar, things supernatural and causeless. Hence is it that we make trifles of terrors, ensconcing ourselves into seeming knowledge, when we should submit ourselves to an unknown fear."' He broke off a crust from his roll and blinked, perhaps even a little impressed himself by this display.

Vi was more than impressed. 'Crikey!'

'It is my livelihood,' said the critic, modestly.

'Even so, I'm stunned. Where is it from?'

'*All's Well That Ends Well*, Act Two, Scene Three.'

'Oh yes, one of those tricky problem plays with a forced marriage at the end.'

'The title *is* ironic,' he suggested.

But now it was her turn to quibble. 'Do you think Shakespeare was ever solely ironic?'

He considered this. 'Maybe not.'

Not knowing quite why, she said, 'Miss Foot, whom we were both inclined to mock a little, I think, said to me that the true sin against the Holy Ghost is the refusal of grace and mercy. We were watching the thunderstorm together. I'd hardly spent five minutes with her.'

'Everything important can be said in five minutes.'

'Is that really true?'

The critic took off his glasses. 'I've heard it said that every-thing real between people is established in the first five minutes.'

'I met her today, by chance, again.'

He was busily polishing his glasses with his table napkin. 'Ah, the enigmatic god of chance.'

'She suggested that we should also apply these, grace and mercy, I mean, to ourselves.'

The critic returned his glasses to his nose but not before she had caught a look of an indefinable anguish in his hazel eyes. 'She left me a note on board ship.' He paused and Vi waited to see if there was more but all he said was, 'It was remarkably perceptive. You are quite right. It was wrong to mock. It is my besetting sin.' Looking at his napkin he said, 'Such a pity that they do not bother here with the Elf's Boot.'

'There isn't really an Elf's Boot, is there?'

'I assure you there is. I have the ocular proof. The instruc-tions, which are complicated but precise, are filed away safely at home. If you visit again I promise a personal demonstration. Now, can I persuade you to share a bowl of wild strawberries? They have a dessert wine here that you really should taste.'

He insisted on seeing her to the hotel in a taxi. 'Au revoir. It has been the greatest delight meeting you. Be sure to call me up before you come again. Don't leave it to Miss Foot's terrible god of chance. By the way, my real friends know me as Col.'

SIXTH DAY

Avast: A naval command meaning to stop or cease.

31

Vi slept fitfully, deprived of the clean salt air, the soporific of the rocking waves and the consoling chug of the engines. She woke at first light and lay on her back trying not to absorb the hooting of the New York traffic, already at full pitch, and the more insinuating drone of the hotel air-conditioning. She was thinking about Bruno. Thoughts of Bruno had run like ravening hyenas through the night.

You knew all along, the voice said. You always do.

But she hadn't listened.

Why not? the voice asked. Why do you not listen to us?

So there was more than one of them.

Of course, said the voice. What do you expect? You can't run a republic single-handed.

Perhaps why doesn't matter after all, she suggested.

What matters is that you heed us, said the voice. Pay attention, will you?

She got out of bed to run a bath and lay looking at her legs covered in geranium-scented foam. She had enjoyed using them to dance.

That's the stuff, the voice said. Song and dance, make hay while the sun shines, a little of what you fancy does you good.

You seem to have resorted to cliché, she admonished.

What's wrong with cliché? Clichés are home truths. Least said, soonest mended. Time and tide wait for no man. Fine words butter no parsnips.

Oh shut up!

Wise up, said the voice. Charity begins at home. They shout for joy, they also sing, remember . . . ?

She spent the day drifting contentedly: buying a novel at Three Lives & Co., where the bookseller was approving of her purchase ('So few people read William Maxwell nowadays'), a belt for Harry, a notebook for Dan, a red silk camisole for Annie. Seeing a pair of low-heeled shoes in a window, she went into the shop.

The assistant was a tall young man whose hair flowed in a sleek waterfall well past his shoulder blades. 'Kitten heels are *so* this season. I just *love* these on you.'

'I was thinking I may need some lower heels.'

At the hotel she wrote a note of thanks to the critic, adding boldly, *Do call me when you are next in London*, and included her address.

In the lapse of time before they met again, she and Edwin had grown more comfortable. He complimented her on the shoes.

'I thought today, you've hardly changed. But you dress . . .'

'Better?'

'No, I was thinking more like you.'

'Oh, Ed. What a very hard thing it is to be like one's self.'

'One of the hardest, I would say . . .'

'I'd forgotten,' she said, as they sat down at the table, 'but today is my mother's birthday.'

'Then you must have champagne.'

'I never got to like it. It makes me maudlin.'

'We can't have that!'

'I'd rather have Chablis if it's OK.'

She told him about her evening with the critic.

'He's a tiger in a dinner jacket. Where did he take you for dinner?' And, when she named the restaurant, 'That's rather a special place. I'm impressed.'

'You know something,' Vi said. 'He isn't a tiger at all. Or only for camouflage. He's one of those overly tender-hearted men who cope by appearing fearsome. We got on, get on. I like him.'

'Watch out. That's what they call here a narcissist.'

'I think I'm fairly immune by now to narcissists.'

'Are we ever really immune to our weaknesses?'

'Probably not.'

She thought of telling him about Miss Foot but decided not to. A silence fell, but not an awkward one.

'That's a beautiful ring, Vi. Is that Ted?'

'It is. And it's only just come back to me. I lost it on the ship and then . . .'

She told him about Dino. He listened attentively without interrupting and, as she spoke, she remembered how grateful she had always been for that attention, so free of the dreadful pleasure people will take in finding fault.

When she had finished he said, 'It was very good of you to let him off so lightly. But in character.'

'I didn't really let him off. He was frightened to death, poor boy. And quite at sea as to why I wasn't shopping him.'

'Oh but I disagree with the modern habit of assuming that generous gestures are suspect and only mean ones truths. It was very kind.'

'It was more,' she paused, trying to form the thought for herself, 'it was more that in some way we were *of* a kind. I had a strange sense of affinity with him. I'm afraid it gave him the impression that I'd fallen for his charms.'

'And had you?'

'Only in his capacity as a dancing teacher. But you know,' she paused, reluctant to rake over newly raked ground, 'with what had happened with you and Bruno so much on my mind, so much *in* my mind I should say, it seemed . . .'

She halted again, unwilling to put into words the feeling that there are moments given to us in life when in sparing others we ourselves may be spared.

Grace and mercy. Grace and mercy. Hardly meaning to do so she spoke the words aloud.

'We are much in need of both. I certainly am. Have you forgiven me, Vi?'

'What should I forgive, Ed?'

'Bruno. I could have spared you him. Should have done.'

'If it hadn't been him it would have been someone else. And, you know, I knew all along so . . .'

'So . . . ?'

'So you've made me know what I didn't want to know. Knowing, really knowing what you know, isn't easy.'

'Not at all.'

But *that* is what you came for, the voice said.

After dinner they walked by the slow-moving Hudson. Over on the far bank, jewelled points of light – gold, silver and rose – shone like brilliants set in the buildings against the teal-blue sky. The white face of the moon was as full as it ever gets, which is never quite.

Edwin threaded his arm through hers. 'I walk here when I'm stuck over a poem. There's something in the flow of the river that unjams the words. Or maybe it's only my belief that it will.'

'You know, it's not quite true that I've not written a line since we last met. I wrote a poem on the ship. I think, maybe, the dancing unstuck something.'

Edwin stood a moment, looking towards the river. 'Perhaps you should go back on board.' They walked on and he said no more except to ask, 'What happened to that whippet you were so attached to?'

'Cleopatra? I took her for a run in the park while Annie collected my things from Bruno's flat. I couldn't go back there again. Not ever. But I missed her.'

'She was a pretty dog, but not the brightest.'

'I didn't need bright. It was companionship I needed.'

They reached her hotel and Vi, still holding Edwin's arm, stopped him outside.

'Ed, if there's a seat on the plane I'm going to fly back tomorrow and put my elder son out of his misery. He'll fret himself to death if I don't.'

'I thought it was the younger one you said was marrying.'

'It is. But his brother does the fretting for him. What with me and his brother to fret over, I worry that my Harry may become too forgetful of his own happiness.'

Edwin took her hands and in the light thrown out from the illuminated hotel lobby she made out his odd-coloured eyes.

'So you're going already?'

'I thought I might decide to go. I've written you a note.'

They stood there as a couple pushing a child passed. Vi heard the man say, 'Surely he's asleep by now.'

Edwin took the envelope. 'If you don't mind, I'll read it later.'

'For what it's worth, the poem I wrote on board ship is in there too. It's nothing, a faint whistle in the dark, but it's yours – well, ours maybe.'

'I'm glad you got back your nerve, Vi.'

They embraced. And then there was nothing more to be said.

'You'll come and visit again?'

'I have a return ticket, Ed. You can trust Harry not to let me waste it.'